Marriage, a Journey and a Dog

Brenda H Sedgwick

Matador
9 Priory Business Park,
Wistow Road, Kibworth Beauchamp,
Leicestershire. LE8 0RX
Tel: (+44) 116 279 2299
Fax: (+44) 116 279 2277
Email: books@troubador.co.uk
Web: www.troubador.co.uk/matador

ISBN 978 1784623 692

British Library Cataloguing in Publication Data.
A catalogue record for this book is available from the British Library.

Printed and bound in the UK by TJ International, Padstow, Cornwall.
Typeset in Aldine401 BT Roman by Troubador Publishing Ltd, Leicester, UK

Matador is an imprint of Troubador Publishing Ltd

To my family and friends.
Thank you for your support.

None of the characters in this book are recreations of people I know. If anyone thinks any part of a character is about them, let me assure you, it isn't you.

The year is 2004. Tony Blair is prime minister, Facebook is called The Facebook, and the only way to find directions is by using a map.

This is where it all began.
This is when I realised what my life could be.

Henri Marcel. French Artist 1938-1996

July 2004
South of England

1

Leaving Home

A warm yellow ball drops from the clattering lottery bubble, into the palm of my hand. I call, "Fifty-nine, the Brighton Line."

"Bingo." The lights flash, music plays, and the proud winner, Joan Littleton, smiles with the satisfaction of a child. I start the clapping. It's time to go home.

Gerry's away cycling in France; home is quiet and empty without him. My fit and sexy husband loves his sport.

Harry is sitting in a cubicle at the edge of the stage. He keeps an eye on the evening's proceedings through scratched plastic windows and counts the cash with his skinny fingers. As the money goes into the bank bags the odd note slips into his pocket. The bingo caller gets an annual bonus, but no such luck for him. My bonus this year is a double reward for long service.

A man from head office came from London to present me with the cheque. A reporter from the local *Eastleigh Standard* newspaper, turned up.

"Smile, love," he said, and flashed a camera in my face, ensuring a startled look.

"Natalie. Natalie." Harry holds out the business phone, and smoke from his cigarettes seeps through the open hatch. He smokes them twice, once when he inhales, and again from the fug that surrounds him. He argues that he isn't smoking near people, but like everyone else, he is going to have to change.

I take the receiver, fresh with sweat. "Are you all right, Katy? What about Gramps?"

"Fine, Mum." Katy has the sullenness of a fifteen-year-old. "It's Dad." She pauses, and I imagine Gerry in an ambulance with monitors attached, fighting for his life. Nervous excitement passes easily into my emotional vacuum. "He's in hospital. Bust a leg – fell off his bike. Wants to know if you'll go to France and get him?"

Cycling is Gerry's number one sport. His muscles are toned and feel rock hard. How did such a fit man break a leg? I need details.

I gather my bag, wrap my cardigan around my shoulders, and say goodnight to the contestants. Once outside the hall, I release the clip holding my unruly black hair and shake it free. High-heeled shoes pinch my toes after standing for a couple of hours, but the walk home isn't far. I wear a company red blouse, the colour suits my olive skin. As I walk along the neighbours recognise me as the bingo caller.

When Katy was small, I noticed an advert in the local paper for a job at the bingo hall. The hours were perfect and it was close to home. I've worked there ever since.

My steps gather pace. I want to know how Gerry is. I pass Eastleigh town centre, with the every-town-should-have-one shopping mall. Parts of the old town survive around it. The newsagents and hairdressers haven't been killed off, but the commercial giants are working on it.

I reach the rows of old terraced houses where I live. They were built for the railway workers in years past, but have become fashionable and have increased considerably in value. When new young owners move in net curtains are changed to bamboo blinds and loft conversion windows appear on the roofs.

Clusters of tired litter take refuge against the curb and a few people are wandering about. As I approach 33A Market Street, Katy and a boy move reluctantly from the low brick wall at the front. He pulls up his hood and slouches off. I follow Katy inside, stopping to admire how tall she is, and her slender figure, lucky girl. She takes after her dad's side of the family. Natural blonde hair makes her stand out, it complements her deep-set blue eyes. I look for myself in her, I must be there somewhere, but it isn't obvious.

Spike runs to the hallway and jumps up, demanding a ruffle behind his ears. His white coat with brown patches is thinning with age. When he's out walking, he holds himself up straight to make up for his lack of size.

I quickly make an iced gin and tonic with lemon. It slips down my throat, helping to calm my nerves. I dial Rouen University Hospital in Normandy, France, and wait… *"Bonsoir."*

"Anglais, s'il vous plaît. Orthopaedics? Monsieur Kenning?" I ask.

"I'll put you through to his bedside phone," is the reply in good English.

"Hi, Nat. My leg is bloody painful. You have to come and get me, and what's left of my bike. It isn't difficult. Catch the ferry from Portsmouth to Le Havre. Follow the

3

signs and bring a map." I take a hard swallow of my drink and listen to what happened, before promising Gerry I'll make it to France tomorrow.

He has a nasty break of the tibia and fibula bones of the right leg and the kneecap is fractured. Injections of painkilling drugs are helping. After it's been set, he hopes the leg will mend in six weeks. I want to be with him.

The accident happened during an evening ride. Gerry was speeding downhill and skidded. After an hour in A & E, he is through X-ray and has been allotted a bed for when he returns from the operating theatre. He assures me there's nothing to worry about and doesn't want fussing over.

Between his cycling photos on the sideboard, there are at least ten of the cups he has won as prizes. I run my fingers over a photo of him crossing a finish line, hands raised as he cycles.

Away from his job managing the 'Practice makes Perfect' sports shop, he plays and watches sport. At least it's sport he loves, and not another woman. I should be more grateful. I have a husband who makes other women jealous. I wish he were here more. Loneliness in my marriage is something I don't know how to change.

When Gerry goes cycling, especially to Europe, he's happy. I know I should make more of my own life. My qualifications are limited, I could have done better, but I was never good with words on a page or with which is my left or right.

Dad lives three doors away, where my brother Chester and I were born. He comes to our house whenever he likes. Katy and Dad get on well. They have an, *Us against the world that isn't fair,* bond, and an, *Everything would be so much better if everyone listened to us,* agreement.

Our house is fifteen minutes from Portsmouth Docks, the home of Henry VIII's *Mary Rose* and Nelson's *Victory*; there is so much naval history here. The France/England, cross Channel ferries, leave from Portsmouth for Le Havre and Saint-Malo. It has occurred to me that I might go to France or Spain with Gerry, but I would get in his way. He needs his own space, so he has told me.

I went on the ferry to Normandy when I was at school, just before my French exam. That was twenty-four years ago. I've watched cars embarking from Portsmouth Docks with children squashed between cool boxes and cases in the back seats; tents, chairs and bikes strapped to trailers. People travelling like snails with their houses on their backs, looking forward to their annual French trip.

I can see planes arriving and leaving Southampton Airport from my bedroom window, they reach for the sky over the rooftops. Always a watcher, never a doer, that's me.

Looking after Katy, and Mum, when she suffered with Alzheimer's disease, has encroached on any ideas I might have had of branching out into the wider world. I love Gerry; he loves me, and our life together ticks away. Friends tell me to be careful because life changes at forty, but why should it? It's just another number two weeks away.

I care about my job at bingo and the people who turn up week after week and spend a bit of their pension. They are delighted with a small prize or a cheque on Friday nights. Thursday nights are when the young contestants come. We play hip-hop or house music in the background, and I like the change.

Will the older ones be all right when I'm away? I see them three times a week, and the empty chair of a regular contestant is a worry. I've experienced a few.

"It should take a couple of days, Mum. Go tomorrow morning. Give yourself a night or two in a hotel and wait for Dad to be fit enough to travel. I've booked a cabin for you to relax in. Didn't cost much. Confirm your sailing time for the return trip when you're ready. Enjoy." Katy flicks her fingers over the keyboard and leaves the printer chugging out the ticket.

The large French road atlas is open on the table. Maps have always been a mystery to me. I need to get off the ferry and follow the signs. I'm sure I can manage that. Rouen isn't far from Le Havre, but the journey still scares me.

I look around our home. Going away is a break from routine, and unsettling. The G Plan furniture in the dining area has been there since we were married. The old oak table would benefit from being renovated and doesn't match the G Plan chairs and sideboard, but we've got used to things.

The shabby faux suede chair by the side of the fireplace should have gone to the tip years ago, but Spike loves it, so it's his.

Katy loves our little dog, and she is close to my best friend's daughter, Anita. I feel sad that she didn't have any siblings for company.

Our fire glows red from the light bulb underneath the false coals. It isn't the best, but it provides extra heat when we need it. Other people on our street have reverted to open fires or have smart ones with stones and a remote control. Our house is in a time warp.

Makeover programmes inspired the change of our lounge wall colours from Magnolia to Heavenly Purple and then to Apple White. If I started to change the furniture we would come unstuck on the cash front. With my bonus I'm looking for a new sofa. I fancy white leather but I need to talk to Gerry to find out what he thinks. One thing is certain, Spike won't give up his chair.

My best friend Lisa has a white leather three-piece suite and bright pink walls; the room is finished with black accessories. I admire her bold choices. They go with her nature.

Her mum was a single parent and so is she. At eighteen, Lisa went to Thailand and came home expecting a baby and with a butterfly tattoo on her arm. The baby, Anita, has grown up with stunning looks and Lisa's strong spirit.

Anita is five years older than Katy but the gap doesn't matter to them. They refer to each other as sisters, because neither of them have siblings. It's an important bond.

Lisa shared my dad as the father she missed. When she got pregnant Mum said, '*People were very unkind, and the child never stood a chance.*' I couldn't see that. She looked to me like someone living life twice as fast as anyone else. Lisa still lives around the corner just off our street. Eldred lives with her from time to time, but they aren't married.

At school, I thought Gerry might have gone for her, but Mum said she could see why he didn't. He was looking for someone more stable, and a homemaker. It was obvious to her why he married me. I had been brought up the right way. That was the nearest Mum got to saying anything unkind about Lisa.

Lisa and I have a close friend, Susie. She was adopted. In our teens, we always went shopping together. Short skirts were not for me. The tops of my legs have always been too plump, but there wasn't any harm trying them on. Lisa was too big all round, but it didn't stop her wearing anything she liked. With Susie, short skirts and skinny tops fitted just right. We each had something the other two wanted and our close friendship has lasted twenty-four years after finishing school.

"Mum." Katy calls my attention to the printed ticket. "Ten o'clock ferry, Portsmouth to Le Havre. Then follow…"

"Your dad told me. I'll take the map anyway. Probably won't need it. Thanks."

I don't have a natural interest in maps and rely on having Gerry around to work out directions. I go on holiday to Cornwall with Dad and Katy every year but we travel by train. They were happy days, when Mum came too. For the last two years of her life she went into respite care when we went away. It wasn't the same without her.

"I've never driven on the right… left… no it's right, of course." I think I'm dyslexic but it's too late to bother about it now. I'm probably not very clever; although my mum used to say I had a brilliant memory, and an artistic streak in me.

"For heaven's sake, Mum, sort it out," Katy remarks with a degree of desperation. I wonder if Katy's life will be one of more opportunities. She is good with books and aware of what it's possible to achieve.

"Time you finished your homework and went to bed. Who was that scruff sitting on the front wall?"

"You mean Matt?"

"Matt who?"

"He's my new boyfriend."

"If he was an animal you'd leave it outside," I say, trying to influence her.

"I like him." Katy stands her ground.

"How come his hand was on the top of your leg and you were standing in the street?"

"Because he's my boyfriend, like I said."

"Bed."

"I'm not a child." Katy goes upstairs, a magazine in one hand and hot chocolate in the other.

The light has lasted well into the evening. Early July is my favourite time of year when summer has come with all its promises.

At night I dream of stalling on the ship's ramp, trying to reach the car deck. I can't follow the attendant's instructions as he beckons me forward. Waking is a relief.

Sun falls through the dull green taffeta curtains and reaches across the faded patterned bedroom carpet. Looking down to the street below, our turquoise Fiat Cinquecento nestles between larger vehicles. In spite of its age, it never lets us down.

Gerry's side of our bed lies undisturbed. When he's at home, his presence is comforting. He reads the paper, the sports pages, of course. He watches football on the telly, and spends hours with his bike in the shed. Conversation between us is limited; we have entered a comfort zone that can be boring at times.

In magazine surveys, having sex twice a month is not unusual in the category of *Married eighteen years and about to turn forty*. *Five times a week* is in a different category. Been there, done that. Lisa says they didn't ask her or the average would have gone up, but it might be higher for the not married.

Rather than renew our sex life, I want to renew a few things in the house. This journey to France is going to cost quite a bit, and so is Katy's school trip to Japan.

The first educational trip to France for Katy was when she was ten. In the following years, she has travelled around

Europe and will now be going to Asia on the second part of an exchange. Business Link is subsidising twenty high-achieving children from her school, and she has been picked to go.

Dad will be coming soon to see if there are things he can do to help and to see me off.

I put out his mug and wait for the kettle to boil. Dad is a man of his era; he has travelled little and spent his working life at the Eastleigh train sheds, latterly taking redundant engines apart. His roots were in steam, he never became attached to the generation of diesel engines.

He worked ending the life of mighty engines and watched their parts pile up leaving empty shells behind them. Lord Beeching, the so called Railway Axeman, said steam should change to diesel and run to a third fewer destinations. Privatisation changed where repairs were carried out. Dad thought he was lucky working on station maintenance until his retirement. Jobs had gone on the scrapheap along with the engines and carriages.

As a child I sat on his knee and listened to his stories; I could hear the rhythm of the train on the tracks... close my eyes and travel with him to London, Brighton or Torquay. He should have written a book about the life and death of engines. When I asked him, he talked for ages about the *Bournemouth Belle*, the *Brighton Belle*, and the *Flying Scotsman*.

He has given Katy some money towards going to Japan. I waited for the war to come up. "Going to Japan after Pearl Harbour," he muttered, as if he had been there instead of watching the film. I think he knows Katy has done her history and needs to enjoy the good things about the modern world.

Resigned to my journey, I rush upstairs to our wardrobe

and check from hanger to hanger. Thank goodness Katy has never sent the TV makeover team to sort out my clothes. It's the sort of thing she would do. The team would have delighted in filling rubbish bags under the eye of the camera. Not only would my clothes have been thrown away, but the wardrobe would have been chucked out as well.

My red case with wheels is open on the floor. It was a present from Mum. It's ten years old and looks like new. Jeans are in. I need a jumper, two T-shirts and a smart blue blouse in case something interesting happens. Toiletries in, click, click, and I've packed.

We can use the roof rack for the bike. It will need to be mangled down to size but, by the account Gerry has given, that isn't a problem. His leg will be plastered to above the knee, somehow he has to be able to stretch out in the car. When there are no alternatives, you go with what you've got.

The hospital says he'll have to stay until he's well enough to travel. I can book in the cheap, but adequate, hotel close by and visit for as long as necessary.

With all the excitement and expectation, I start getting hiccups. I'm not sure why they have come now. I've no plans to enjoy myself. I must go and hope I don't do anything too stupid. Gerry must be suffering, poor love. I've packed his favourite chocolate, clean underwear and new pyjamas.

Katy reminds me that Gerry will be grumpy without his bike. She's right. He needs sport; he needs to be good at something. It's a big part of his male identity and compensation for things in his past. It belongs to a space in his being that is not replaceable with anything I've been able

11

to say or do. We would both lose something if he couldn't ride his bike.

Dad's key turns in the front door lock. He enters the living room holding a large bottle of water. "Don't drink the French stuff, it hasn't been cleaned like ours." The bottle hits the oak table with a thump.

We were warned French toilets were smelly and dirty when I went to Brittany before my French exam. Then I went to the toilets on Brighton beachfront and had to hold my nose and pull my knickers down at the same time. I could only imagine that that was what the French ones were like, but they were worse. Men and women shared so you spent ages with your legs crossed, hoping you would never need to go.

"Where did you get the idea about the water, Dad?" I make his coffee and he takes it with a smile and goes to sit on the sofa.

"Your granddad, when he returned from the war. He said if the Germans don't get you the dysentery will."

Am I going to fight a war? Has the EU passed Dad by? He's slipping into the past like older people do.

I make myself some sandwiches in my oh-too-small kitchen, and then take my bags and bundle things into the Fiat.

Dad is leaving again.

"Don't worry about Katy, she'll be fine with me. I'll carry the water out for you. Take care of yourself. Gerry will be riding his bike again in no time."

Dad leans over more these days, but he is still strong. He has gained his share of moles and warts, which add to his rugged looks. He keeps himself busy and manages to stay happy most of the time.

A vision of Gerry trying to ride a mangled bike lightens my spirit, and then I remember his broken leg and correct myself. A final check I have everything, and wonder, did I turn off the gas, and pull out the iron?

Katy's gone to school and I'm out of my routine. I sit in the car and watch in the wing mirror, as Dad disappears into his house. I turn on the ignition, and take one last look at our house to notice Spike at the window. The net curtain is resting on his shoulders, his nose is pressing against the glass, and his tail rushes backwards and forwards.

If Katy's out, Spike comes everywhere with me, but not today. Dad loves him, but has a habit of tripping over if he gets under his feet, so I try to keep them apart.

Spike bounces and barks against the window.

"This is it, Spike." We stare at each other. I move the car forward slightly. He stops bouncing and his paws scratch wildly on the glass. His tail stops wagging and a look of bewilderment enters his eyes.

Our love affair has reached a crescendo; I can't leave without him. He will fit in the large shopping basket that's on the hall peg. The blanket from his chair will be a comfort for him in strange surroundings. I'm not sure how it will work out, but he's coming with me.

I write a hurried note;

Dear Katy and Dad,

Spike is with me. Don't worry. See you in a day or two.

Halfway down the motorway, I remember that Spike needs a vaccination record, microchip and passport. Rationalisation is needed. He is fine and healthy and I'm not going for long. No sooner there, than back – in fact, hardly there at all.

We went to the Costa del Sol four years ago. Gerry

thought I needed a holiday after Mum died. I thought that going to the Costas was fantastic. Lisa and Susie explained it was a starting destination and that it would be the beginning of discovering the world, but family deaths don't happen that often, so the opportunity hasn't come again.

When Dad dies will that warrant a long-haul trip to India? If an aunt dies will that equal a trip to Blackpool? What sort of trip would my own death equal for Gerry?

On the Costa del Sol I loved the entertainers with keyboards. They cheered up the streets at night singing Chris de Burgh's *'Lady in Red'*. The flamenco dancers were magical. Gerry said the singing was awful and the dancers were on the old side. I thought, the dancing was exciting, and best of all we were on holiday together.

When I got home, I joined a flamenco dancing class. Lisa had been going to belly dancing classes. Now she's good at it. She has belly button studs and loads of jewellery that rattles as she shakes her body.

I bought a pair of black patent dancing shoes, but it became too expensive to buy a selection of the right dresses as well, so it was no longer for me. I wouldn't have made a good dancer, anyway.

Katy was eleven when we were on the Costa del Sol. She loved the sun and the swimming pool. We went shopping for T-shirts and shorts before we went. Shorts I keep for holidays, where no one I know sees me. Gerry says I should lighten up; he thinks I look great in anything, but rarely appears to notice what I wear.

The lorries on the M27 trundle past as we make headway towards the ferry. My butterfly brain flits all over the place. The idea that Katy and Gerry have trumped this whole thing up so that I will find my house transformed or my wardrobe dragged out and held up for ridicule, bothers me. I look round in case a camera is secretly filming me. Maybe the viewing public wants to see me naked on a billboard outside Portsmouth Dockyard or on the Spinnaker Tower. When I'm nervous my worst fears take an unreasonable hold.

The Portsmouth channel ferry dock sign is clear. I join the queue at the dock entrance and wait until a man points to the ticket barrier and drive up. Yup, it's easy, just as Gerry and Katy said.

The check-in booths are elevated; they are made of clear glass, and clean. Harry needs a smart new cubicle made like these, but he prefers things the way they are. I wonder if he will miss me, and will he die of lung cancer? He has always been skinny, but now he has lost most of his hair and some of his brown teeth.

It's ten years until he retires; surely, the bingo hall will be refurbished before then. Would that *60 Minute Makeover* programme fancy doing a bingo hall? The dirty cream paint, basic tables and red plastic chairs, could be replaced with pink walls, wooden coffee tables and comfy sofa seats. I decide that my house, wardrobe and body are safe and that the bingo hall is getting a surprise upgrade.

"Passport, please. Ticket?" The woman's piercing eyes are searching my car. Spike is tucked away. I hand my papers up to her as she sits in her elevated position. "Put this on your central mirror. Lane 4." She hands my papers back. All is well.

Lane 4 is for those without pets and lane 5 for those with. A boxer dog hangs its head out of a car window. Slobber drips from its mouth and is caught by the wind and drops on to the car behind. An officer walking between the

15

cars, checks pet papers and pets. Spike doesn't move under his blanket.

An inspector knocks the window – my heart misses a beat. The embarkation label is not clearly displayed. "Oh," I say. I turn it around. Everything is ready. Car after car, we drive into the bowels of the ship.

I must remember how to return to the correct car deck. Gerry would automatically have figured it out. Spike is tucked in his basket ready to come with me. The sign *ALL DOGS MUST BE LEFT IN CARS* means big ones only – I'm sure.

My feet clang against the metal stairway heading for the upper decks. Families drag themselves up with heavy hand luggage and spare jumpers and coats, even cushions for extra comfort.

I muddle my way through the passengers buzzing around Reception and join the queue for cabins.

"*Bonjour,*"… "*Excusez moi,*"… "Oops, sorry,"… "Bugger off." Children run around playing hide-and-seek and chasing, screeching in both languages. Now we are half French, half English, and belong to the special culture of the ship.

As I move towards the desk, a man invades my personal space. He's so close I can smell his garlic breath. The large man rests his flabby abdomen against the brass desk rail next to me, and shoves his fat fists in his pockets.

I hand over my ticket. Blankness rests in the receptionist's eyes as she twists her mouth a little. Maybe I'm not going to France.

"You have the wrong booking, Madame." She stares at her screen then at me. "You're booked into a lorry drivers' cabin with three men." Her mouth twists a little more.

I wait. She waits. The garlic breath man smiles a ready smile. Is he anticipating my company? I don't want to fail so early in the day. I would forego the cabin, but I have Spike.

"It's all right. I have a single cabin." She smiles professionally, placing a key on the desk. Success.

"Ah, Monsieur Jacques." The once seen, never forgotten lorry driver is flattered by the receptionist's recognition.

I slide the key into my hand. Spike shuffles and sneezes in the basket. Monsieur Jacques's stomach grumbles loudly, he gives a satisfying belch, filling the air with a fine spray of spit and garlic. We're saved.

I sit on the cabin bed, absorbing the vibrations of the engines starting up, and listening to the sea churning as the propellers burst into life. I stroke Spike's head and whisper, "We are sailing."

2

Paris

Le Havre shouldn't look like this, modern and concrete. Dad said the war did much to destroy the old parts of this once-beautiful town. If I could stop, I would find better places, like the baroque cathedral – and a few old houses that, I'm told, survived destruction.

Rather than sort out which is the right way I follow the car in front, and grip tightly on to the steering wheel. I figure this system will take me part of the journey and help me stay on the right side of the road. Signposts will do the rest.

The first one reads: *EO5, Quai Colbert, ROUEN/A131/PARIS (partial toll)*

Muscles in my neck and across my shoulders ping loose, the hands of a phantom masseur are at work. Rouen will have its challenges, but disembarking and getting on the road has been straightforward. Bananarama and Adam Ant are on the old stereo, and twenty years fall away. I sing along – with the sun warming me through the windows – and I want the journey to go on and on. Emotive music by Vangelis from *Chariots of Fire* hits an eighties note. I leave the town for open countryside, where there are traditional Normandy houses made with wooden beams in a rural setting, scattered in the fields.

Gerry was my boyfriend at school, and my only

boyfriend; it felt natural that we should marry. I'm walking down the aisle again in billows of white, and Gerry is waiting for me.

Mum made us a three-tiered wedding cake with a mirror for a pond with glass swans – a bird that mates for life. We went to the Isle of Wight for our honeymoon. Katy was born a year later and we shared the second tier of the cake to celebrate. One tier was left for a future event; I kept it so long I had to throw it away.

Beads of sticky sweat run from my hairline, and Spike is panting. I try to open the window more but the handle sticks. I cross the long bridge over the River Seine, follow the Rouen/Paris road and drive. A turning off to Rouen is nowhere to be seen and the afternoon is passing. Signs are for Paris, Paris and Paris. I dip in and out between the lorries on a toll road and I'm grateful for the euros from the ferry. The line with the green arrow and yellow *t* looks like the right lane, but I'm on the wrong side of the car and have to get out to retrieve a ticket.

After twenty minutes on the motorway, I stop at the toilet and picnic area. Spike needs a drink and I need a break. The toilets are the squat-down type that shower your ankles before you can get out – an awkward manoeuvre when holding a dog. With wet feet, I'm on the road again. Gerry will be waiting and beginning to worry. Normandy? Rouen?

I think about phoning him, but I want to do this on my own. I want to be capable.

Katy assured me it would take about an hour to get to Rouen Hospital from the ferry. She also assured me she had booked a great cabin.

"Sleeps four but you have it to yourself," she told me.

Gerry says I'm a slow driver and, with maps being deceiving, I'm sure I'll get there soon. Paris, Paris, Paris. If I turn off will I find the sign for Rouen? Maybe the French show Paris first and it comes before the Rouen sign. It's time to leave the motorway and to relieve the building tension. I drive towards Paris in the early evening and the lights of the Eiffel Tower loom. I take a deep breath and, as my breath takes flight, I shout, "I'm in Paris."

The huge roundabout ahead houses a large arch – and before long I'm in the merry-go-round of traffic and pulling the car close to the inside, where I feel safer. Round and round I go, not daring to come off. Will this be my life, stuck by the Arc de Triomphe?

"Bloody Napoleon," I grumble and thump the wheel.

Fear turns to tears. I think of stopping right here and getting out. I want to shout at all those beeping vehicles,

"Don't you know I'm English and I've never done this before?" Spike can't help me – and dogs, like children, know when to ask for an impossible toilet break.

On what must be my sixth time round this bumper-car-at-the-fair roundabout, a vehicle horn vibrates above me, then again. I'm ready to beep my squeak of a horn in anger when I catch the eye of Monsieur Jacques. He looks bulky and right, sitting behind the wheel of a heavy goods vehicle. He is way above me, and banging his windscreen, and then he pulls his HGV across in front of me. I follow him round again. In slow motion, he pulls across the lanes, stopping the traffic and causing a moment of chaos.

My tiny car is about the height of his wheels. As I drive past, he's swishing me on with his hand, "Come on. Come on." I assume he's saying.

With a feeling of importance, I hold my head high. I'm

on my way along the Champs-Elysées. I pick a bridge across the River Seine and head for what I find is the Left Bank and Latin Quarter.

Driving along the rue Saint-Jacques, a vision of Monsieur Jacques crosses my inner mind. He is sitting in his lorry with a halo. The angels are singing, 'Hallelujah'.

"Thank you. Thank you, Monsieur smelly Jacques," I hear my voice say.

From a long-stay car park, I go to look for a hotel. The prices are outrageous, but a euro is less than a pound and that makes it sound more expensive than it is. Gerry isn't coming out of hospital tonight; I can stay in Paris until tomorrow. The streets are lighting up and a spectrum of electric emotion releases itself, buzzing up and down my spine and on to my fingers and toes.

The first two hotels say, "*Non,*" then at the third… "*Oui, une petite chambre pour une petite madame,*" says the man behind the desk. Across in the hotel restaurant, the early diners are preparing to order. Under the colourful voluminous skirt of a large lady, the nose of a little dog peaks out, confirmation that Spike and I will be all right here. We can eat in the restaurant, without risking venturing out and getting lost in the swelling crowds.

The room in the attic of Hôtel le Select is small but comfortable. It suits us fine. I open the small window and look out on to the Place de la Sorbonne. There are people looking into the restaurants in the street below and my insides warm. The start-up smells of the kitchens waft their way up. I'm between the street and the sky. I'm not afraid of the evening on my own and desperately want to touch Paris.

In the bottom of my bag, among the dead sweets,

hairbrush and half-empty water bottle, I find my phone, and fiddle with it until I've fixed my new SIM.

"Gerry. How's the leg? Sorry I'm not there yet, but I will be tomorrow."

His voice is odd; my being in Paris has surprised him. I can see and feel everything is all right, but in hospital, he can't quite get it. He wants to get out of bed and be in control of his life and mine. It will be another day or two before he's walking with a stick. I will be in France longer than planned.

"Come to Rouen tomorrow. Leave Paris before rush hour. Make sure you know the route. Study the map." Gerry is raising his voice.

"Say goodbye to Daddy, Spike."

"Spike? What the hell's Spike doing there?"

"Didn't Katy or Dad tell you he's with me? See you tomorrow, Gerry. Take care." I phone home.

"Hi, Dad. How's Katy?"

"They're upstairs, playing quietly."

"Who do you mean by they?"

"Young Matthew. You met him just before you went away."

In the past twenty-four hours, I have been so involved with my own world that for the first time I have taken my focus away from Katy. Matt, the scruff from outside the house, is alone with her. Anything could happen.

"What are they doing upstairs, Dad?"

"Katy… Matthew…" he calls. "What are you doing up there?"

"Snakes and Ladders." That's Katy.

"Ludo." I presume that's Matt. I should never have left them.

"They're fine, Natalie. Don't worry. You know it's Bastille Day tomorrow. Our men are out there. You should stay an extra day and enjoy Paris."

Bastille Day? How was I to know? One big party is brewing in the streets, firemen are the big attraction and firecrackers are popping on the pavements.

Stay in? Why? Perhaps I'll get lost. What about Spike? He can stay on his own for a while. I can walk a short distance and take in the sights while listening to the evening.

No one in Eastleigh would grab a woman and insist she dances with them. It gives me the giggles when I find myself twirled around and giddy.

"*Merci, Madame. Merci. Très bon.*" I shift to avoid a hand on my bum. That's enough for now.

I brush past the receptionist's desk and he holds out a ticket. "*Non. Non, merci.*" I say.

"*Non? Non?* It's the best boat trip in Paris."

Gerry wants me at the hospital, but he doesn't need me when he's resting. One whole day in Paris, what harm is there in that?

"Well… yes, then. Uh… *Oui. Merci, Monsieur.*"

"*Très bien.*" He smiles.

I creep round the narrow, crooked staircase to my room, to be greeted by Spike's wagging tail and lots of tickling licks. He needs fresh water in his bowl and some biscuits.

I'm ready for bed early, anticipating the drive tomorrow. My head rests on fresh, clean pillowcases and I fall asleep with a little dog cuddling up close.

The early morning light catches on the window, calling me to look down on to Place de la Sorbonne awakening. I shower and dress then, with Spike for company, I brave a cafe and manage to order a croissant and hot chocolate. I

23

dip the croissant into the frothy top and watch other customers sipping coffee and reading papers.

I take the crumbs from my fingers and napkin, sprinkling them on the floor for Spike, then head for the *Jardin du Luxembourg*, over the other side of the main road. We wander about and watch vendors setting up stalls. French flags are for sale, and there are wooden sailboats for children to rent and float on the ponds. The French have set fountains and statues in a large open space, leading the eye to a palatial building. A day in Paris… and I feel happy. My eyes rest on the children's carousel as horses and unicorns are polished. Parents and children will be so lucky to be here.

Gerry is stuck in a hospital bed and I wonder if he feels lonely. I wish he were with me. We do little together as it would interfere with his training schedule, and if his body is with me, his mind usually is not. I'm used to it. Even without him, it feels good to be doing something different.

After visiting the gardens, we return to the hotel. From the foyer Spike needs carrying to our room, he's ready for a rest. I settle him on his blanket and make tracks into Paris alone. On a pocket street map, I draw every twist and turn in the hope that I can retrace my steps.

A market stall is selling sun hats, some covered in flowers, others more plain and stylish. I try them on, perching each one at different angles and studying my reflection in the shop window behind me. I choose a white one with a large floppy brim and deep crown, without any flowers. It will keep off the sun and is soft enough to roll up in a travel bag. Here I am in my jeans, T-shirt and sun hat, gazing at my reflection in a shop selling high-class Parisian fashions; dresses and suits for smart people and the dress-conscious – a part of the world that has passed me by.

In my old railway town, I don't go looking for high fashion, and it doesn't come looking for me. If this shop wasn't shut for the holiday, I would venture through the doors. I want to touch the fabrics and try on clothes, something I definitely couldn't do with Gerry. He has a habit of whispering, "Not for you, Nat," and guiding me in a different direction.

I think he is scared of what we have not become, and the picky comments made by his mum circle in his mind. She was ambitious for her only son, and I wasn't the person she would have chosen as his wife. Enid and I get along, but we don't meet up much. Gerry's mum and dad had a house in Eastleigh, before they sold up and bought an apartment in Spain. We are invited to visit but I don't think the invitation is sincere.

They decided that buying the Spanish apartment was bettering themselves and, to be fair, Enid wanted a more interesting life. Originally they came from Hull and their town in Spain is nicknamed Little Hull because so many people from that area have sold up and bought into a dream. I don't blame her. I watch my feet as they pad the pavement and my brain chunters away.

A bell chiming calls me back to Paris. My guidebook is full of exciting places to go and things to do. Can I make it to Montmartre and the white Basilica of the Sacré-Cœur? I want to take a photo of the windmill sails of the Moulin Rouge. So much to do, and too little time.

Crowds have filled the Champs-Elysées for the parades. I find it impossible to see over other people's heads. I would only be able to hear the Bastille Day bands. It's better to head for higher ground.

I loved *Moulin Rouge*. Lisa, Susie and I went to see the

25

film together. That night, after the cinema, we went to Lisa's house and shared secrets. Lisa told Susie and me all about the new man in her life, Eldred. His name was Nigel. He was a bricklayer, and when he became a property developer he changed his name. He stayed at her house on and off but she said she couldn't stand anyone around all the time. Typical Lisa.

I wanted to know why she never married. Lisa said she'd never met anyone who was right for her and Anita, and pointed out I was lucky to have Gerry. She was right, life without him would be unimaginable. We love each other, I know, but we only say it on cards.

I wish my friends could be here and share this day with me. It's my turn to board the funicular up to Sacré-Cœur. As I step out at the top, a roar hits from the sky and everyone cowers. Heading for central Paris the Red Arrows fly across, leaving trails of red, white and blue smoke. Is this what Dad meant by 'our men in Paris'? French people nudge me so hard I feel unstable, pointing to the planes while making grunting noises of appreciation. Wow… there they go again, zooming across and forming a shape, hovering, ready to do their Starburst formation. President Chirac has invited the Brits to take part in the celebrations of the storming of the Bastille, and Natalie Kenning from Eastleigh is joining in!

From hesitating at the top of the steps, I move to join a small crowd and rest against the balustrade, taking in the view of the buildings of Paris. I check my watch before turning to walk towards the array of artists wanting to draw pastel portraits of tourists. Eventually I succumb to persuasion. My artist is about fifty, with a goatee beard and a ponytail. He sits sideways on his stool, poised with his easel and pastels. He knows how to flirt and flatter, and how to make money from my pocket, while blowing smoke from his cheroot in the air. With a gush, he hands me the finished picture. I'm in the centre of a line-up of can-can dancers, with red frilled skirts, and skinny legs that will never be mine.

The cafe bar on the corner offers the opportunity to battle for a drink. With everyone partying loudly, I'm self-conscious at the bar on my own, and height matters here.

I lift my *jus d'orange* with ice, and turn to look at the sepia photos and faded newspaper cuttings on the walls. There are pictures of musicians and dancers who made this part of Paris their home. Prints of paintings by Henri de Toulouse-Lautrec adorn shop windows. Picasso lived in Paris, and I will find his original art sometime, somewhere. Most of his paintings and sculptures I read about are tidied away into a gallery near-by.

Sitting in a corner is my artist. Through a haze of cigarette smoke, he raises his glass of cloudy pastis to me. Over the loud babbling of French voices he mouths something I don't understand. I smile shyly before sliding discreetly towards the door, where I watch with the pigeons as *Vive la France* choruses round the square. My guidebook has a Bastille Day supplement, and information about the Terror that followed the revolution. The guillotine beheaded anyone and everyone around the time of the execution of Louis XVI, but let them have their *fête*.

It's time to retrace my way to the hotel and Spike. I walk down the steps, watching the jugglers and stilt walkers around me. Walking on past the buildings, drinking in the midday sun, I look up at the decorative street lamps as I go.

The nearer to the centre of Paris the busier the streets are, and I'm glad to turn off in the direction of the hotel.

I climb the final twisting flight of stairs of Le Select to hear Spike snuffling under the door. He looks curiously at my floppy sun hat. I toss it on the end of the bed, where he quickly jumps up and makes a bed of it.

I shed my shoes, wriggling my toes free. We top ourselves up with water, while drips spill on the purple bed cover. My thoughts travel back to Eastleigh and I feel a thousand miles away. I imagine that when I'm home Paris will, conversely, feel unreal. My pleasure has been rising like a spring and tumbling into a brook.

I need to talk to Gerry again, to hear his voice. I want to share my adventure, and return to my life of home, family and bingo.

"Hi, Gerry. I'll leave about ten tomorrow and I'll be there some time in the afternoon. Paris has been great. Can't wait to tell you about it."

"I'm pleased you've enjoyed yourself, but remember I've been there to watch the Tour de France. Check your map, Nat. Check your map. It isn't going to be easy getting out of Paris. Get someone at the hotel to go over it with you. Don't go out tonight. You don't want to be bothered by French men."

My mind leaps to the artist in Montmartre. We are romping around on the bed together. A cough mixed with laughter rises, and I blurt the sound down the phone.

"Have you been drinking, Nat? Concentrate. Get out of the mess you've got yourself into. See you tomorrow. Take care, won't you?"

"Of course. Of course." I collapse on the bed and doze to pass an hour and to revive my aching legs.

28

I wear my special blue blouse for the evening. As we pass the receptionist he nods a knowing smile. *"Bonsoir, Madame. Amusez-vous bien,"* he says.

The glass-covered boat waits on the River Seine. The people in the queue stand patiently, looking in at the tables with white starched tablecloths and candles flickering in glass lanterns. I hand over my ticket as I board and I'm grateful for Spike's company. The waiter shows me to a table for one at the far side. He pulls out the chair and – as gracefully as I can – I manage to sit, and place Spike at my feet. I have the best view of the river, and it's still light.

The waiters hold themselves straight and tall. Dressed in black and white uniforms, they work as a well-drilled team. Langoustines on a bed of salad are served for starters. I struggle to keep my fingers clean while removing first their heads and then the pink flesh from the crusty tail. My chin is getting messy. A waiter places my serviette around my neck and points to the finger bowl.

The main course is breast of duck with orange sauce, and a selection of vegetables with butter dripping through them. I appreciate the serviette tucked under my chin.

The ropes are released and we pull away from the quay as the plates are cleared. Crêpes Suzette are brought to the tables and covered in citrus sauce. Using a long taper, each waiter lights hot brandy in a spoon and spills it over the crêpes. Fire rises from every table simultaneously. The flame-lit boat floats along the River Seine and my pleasure is in full flood.

An awkward thought encroaches when I don't want it to. Am I spending too much of my bonus? It's worth it right now, but I hope the day of reckoning doesn't come soon. There are always needs at home, usually someone else's.

The thought is enough to give me a guilt crisis until I get it under control and stop it spoiling my evening.

Drips of orange sauce have sprayed on to the tablecloth. I poke at them with my fork, spreading the stains. I've had duck cooked this way once before, and that was at Lisa's house when she had a dinner party. Unfortunately, the duck was tough, and the sauce too sweet and thick. Lisa didn't have fireworks, or a small band playing with a French female singer trilling away for our entertainment, either.

The captain gives us a guide to the river in French, Spanish and English. He said it flows through Paris and on to the docks in Rouen, before reaching Le Havre and the English Channel... I knew I wasn't far away from Gerry.

Spike stays at my feet as we see Notre-Dame Cathedral. Illuminated from the ground up, the two towers and the circular glass window make a dramatic picture against the navy-blue sky. The captain proudly announces that 200 years ago the coronation of Napoleon and his wife Josephine took place here.

A shudder hits me as I remember the Arc de Triomphe, where I would still be if it weren't for Monsieur Jacques. The captain proudly talks of a writer called Victor Hugo, and *The Hunchback of Notre-Dame,* then carries on at length about Proust and the great literary figures of Paris. It's interesting, but my brain is getting in a jumble with too much information. I'm grateful when he apologises for being quiet and takes refreshments.

I try to take photos with my old but reliable film camera. It has a decent lens, but I doubt the light and distance settings will do justice to this view in the evening dusk. I never go anywhere where I would need a camera, apart from the streets around home and Cornwall. I've taken more photos than people know. Eastleigh is a rich source of characters, with their lives printed on their faces, and the craggy Cornish coastline is inspirational in all weathers.

In the romantic air of Paris, I want Gerry with me, but it's not the kind of thing he would enjoy. His mind would be with sport. He isn't good at sitting still or being entertained; God knows what hospital is doing for him.

The fireworks over the Eiffel Tower are like an exploding Christmas tree. Spike buries his head as far as he can into my lap, and covers his ears with his paws. Stroking him firmly doesn't stop his shaking. Together we sail back to Pont Neuf to disembark.

The waiter steadies my arm and jokes he will let me fall in the river, making me clasp his hand tightly. "*Bonsoir, Madame. Bonsoir.*"

The streets are full of shouting and music. We dodge tipsy men to find our way to the Place de la Sorbonne and our hotel.

Climbing the stairs to our hideaway at the top, I think of tomorrow and driving towards Gerry and home.

"Goodnight Spike," I say, before turning in. Sleep is good, deep and heavy.

Refreshed, I gather my things and pack. The freebie shampoo, shower hat and mending kit will help me remember I really did make it to Paris on my own (except for Spike). As I cross the room, the floorboards creak under my feet. The small window is open and a light drizzle falls. With a spider's web in front of my nose, I watch the big clear-up from the night before.

I struggle down to checkout. No one is around to take my bags.

"Do you want to leave yet?" I hear a voice from nowhere

say. Temptation is growing. I have always enjoyed anything to do with art and painting. I love learning about artists on rare visits to art galleries. Charity shops are a source of fantastic books on art. In Paris I can go to the *Musée du Louvre* and see the paintings for real.

Why not? I'm deep in thought, and tapping my fingers against each other, when the receptionist reminds me that I'm supposed to be paying the bill.

I pack the bags in the car, plonk my sun hat on my head, come rain, come shine, and with Spike on his lead we walk towards the Place de La Concorde. The glass pyramid of the Musée du Louvre beckons. Only a few people make up the queue, the visitors must be getting over the revelry of last night. There will be time for what I really want to see – the *Mona Lisa* and *Venus de Milo*. With my hat in front of me, and Spike tucked well behind it, we enter the tall space of the glass and aluminium pyramid.

I need to get back soon and on my way, so we race to where the *Mona Lisa* hangs; slowing down as we get closer. I look at her looking at me. For a good ten minutes, we have a silent conversation. She is full of feminine mystique. Her charisma outweighs her beauty, and I wonder if I could be like her.

"Leonardo da Vinci painted that, Spike," I whisper. I look at her smile and the rich tones of Nat King Cole's '*Mona Lisa*', play in my mind. The tune travels to my lips and I quietly sing. I peel back the hat just enough for Spike to glimpse the painting.

Crowds start to file into the room behind me. I must keep moving, and hurry to find the *Venus de Milo*. I haven't been this excited for years. I fly past great works of art, as if I were passing hanging jewels. Tempting signs point in different directions, but I must stay focused.

With only a few other people in this marbled room, I move slowly towards her. She is standing before my disbelieving eyes… the Goddess of Love. So beautiful that men have died fighting over her. I forget everything in her presence, she has been broken, but has a strange serenity. She has the power to tell me what it is to be a woman. I want to stand and absorb her spirit.

I let Spike pop out his nose. "So what do you think of that, Spike?" He yaps with appreciation at being uncovered, then wriggles from the hat and falls to the floor. He slides around trying to fix his feet and I place my hat near to him, hoping he will jump on.

The warden's eyes catch mine as she leaves her seat. She sticks out her buxom chest and heads in my direction. Male wardens gather behind her. It's time to go.

With the help of other tourists, I gather Spike up. My feet trip along towards the exit and into the park. I dance my way in the direction of the Left Bank, and my car. Parisians in their smart clothes, and well-behaved children with their nannies are staring. I don't care, they will never see us again, and they can share in my mad happiness.

I head towards the shops where the Parisians are going about their daily business of shopping, chatting and looking smart. I steady myself down and wind my way more sedately through the streets, stopping at the crêpe stall.

A lady is spreading thin batter over the flat stove from where miniature streaks of steam rise. She hands me the crêpe in a serviette that is tissue-thin, and the rich dark chocolate spills over the edges. It's dripping down, feeling soft and warm on my hand and threatening to spill on to the pavement. I catch the chocolate and relish the licking of my fingers.

In the rue Saint-Jacques, an English-speaking group stands by a wall plaque that marks *The Way*, going to Santiago de Compostela. I stop to listen as their leader talks about St James and the mysterious light seen in a field in Spain by a shepherd. A blessing is pronounced and I'm offered a leaflet mapping their journey ahead and explaining The Way.

"We are going to be in Santiago de Compostela for St James's Day to visit where his bones are buried. It's a special year because 25 July falls on a Sunday. You might like to walk it sometime," the leader explains. Everyone is passionate and friendly.

I want to join them and go to Spain, but that kind of freedom isn't for me, unless St James wants to shed his light on my world. I don't want my home life to change; I want friends and family to stay the same, so that I can always dip into their fun and affection, but I want to do more with my life. This experience has been great, but too brief.

As I pass the newspaper stand, I glance along at the front pages; the papers near the edge are still damp from the earlier rain. Pictures of the Grenadier Guards parading along the Champs Elysées make me smile. Their tall bearskin hats and red jackets look out of place away from London. Where's the Queen? Where's Buckingham Palace?

I buy a paper to take home, and half expect to find an article about me and Spike with a picture. I stupidly pose towards the shop window as if for a photo. I've made it to Paris on Bastille Day, but the rest of the world doesn't care.

Dad will love to see pictures of the Red Arrows flying in formation over Paris. More urgent than the paper, is buying a map of France on one large sheet. Maps are all the same to me – confusing, misleading outlines, but a single sheet might help.

The parking ticket cost for two days is enormous. I hadn't thought about it in advance, but I won't confess to Gerry. I make sure I hold the keys tightly before fixing them in the ignition; a lost key would spell disaster. I open the map, balancing it on the Fiat bonnet; first straight up, then sideways then upside down. I don't know how to relate to the direction from Paris to Rouen. I run my finger along the possible route then decide to leave and hope for the best.

I call Gerry and let him know I'm on my way. I tell him more about Paris and he tells me more about his bike. The back wheel is bent and so is the frame. We must take it back to England for the insurance company to inspect. A new bike is a priority. First, we must buy one, then reclaim what we can. He's decided the sooner he is cycling again the better it will be for his leg. Guilt and shame at what I've been spending are here again.

"Hitting a tree stump near the edge of the road was unavoidable," he tells me. "I'm lucky to have got away with just a broken leg. I just missed being run over by a car coming in the opposite direction, due to my quick thinking, and rolling sideways."

"Thank goodness you only have a broken leg." I feel a sense of relief as I reply.

"What a daft thing to say," he states.

He says the nurses are not pretty or attractive. I'm pleased. In fact, he has a male nurse looking after him most of the time. Boredom is setting in and he wants to be home. Home or with me? It's a question I can't ask, because he has never given me cause to doubt him. We don't have fireworks, but it isn't entirely his fault. I recognise that hopes of a close friendship within a thrilling marriage have disappeared. If he was home more he might appreciate my company. I wonder if his broken leg will provide us with opportunities to be together.

Dad and Katy are doing fine, and Dad has started to teach Matt to play chess. He loves the game and can never find anyone to play with. Matt isn't showing signs of being good at it, but there's time for improvement. Dad thinks Matt is not a bad kid but doesn't like the ring in his bottom lip.

"Go north," Gerry said. "North, towards the English Channel." Gerry is right, there will be signs. Turn left or right, would have been more helpful.

How the hell am I to know north or south, stuck in a car park with an upside-down map? I live in the south of England. Maybe I need to go north. Eastleigh is in the south of England and Rouen is in the north of France. What clue does that give me?

"Get a grip, Natalie," I say out loud as I turn on the ignition.

It's time to leave the security of the car park. I follow the black Citroën estate in front, which helps me get on the road out of Paris. The more out of town I am the less sure my sense of direction is. I hit the *Périphérique* and drive.

So many places; so many choices. Should I try somewhere? Yes, I will. Normandy doesn't crop up but Bordeaux does. I have heard of Bordeaux lots, but mainly to do with wine, and the signs do look important. I will follow one of them rather than keep looking for a slip road off to Normandy. The right sign must turn up sooner or later. In less than two hours, I will be with Gerry.

The Fiat is so small between the weighty lorries. They spray up water from the earlier rain, spreading traces of mud all over the windscreen. It's the sports model Fiat, but too old for that to make any improvement to its speed. There's hardly a vehicle that can't overtake; no wonder Gerry hates it.

No one has been lost on the roads forever. I need to keep driving and everything will be all right. A smile creeps over my face and a sense of unfounded security sets in. Making no decisions is not an option and a few hours are left in the day.

Text from Gerry: *Let me know when u r on the right road and where u r. Waiting to hear. xx*

3

French Wine and Brandy

After three hours it's clear something is wrong with the direction I've chosen. Spike needs a comfort stop and so do I. The poor little chap is miserable without food, drink and a pee. I take the next exit off the motorway. Minutes later I'm driving through the countryside, with distant horizons and vineyards. This is France, how I imagined it would be.

My feelings are divided between enjoying myself and thinking I should be somewhere else. Gerry isn't ready to leave hospital yet, so there's time to correct my mistakes.

Raised on the hillside are the fairy-tale turrets of a chateau. The sign says *DEGUSTATION – VENTE/OPEN FOR FREE WINE TASTING*. I drive up a sweeping, fir tree-lined avenue towards the chateau and park on the gravel frontage. Someone may be able to help with directions.

Spike jumps out and pees over the Fiat wheel. I wish I could do the same. The warm alcoholic aroma of wine from inside the barn catches me. With Spike under my arm, we follow the arrows inside and join in the tasting session. I look around, hoping for a toilet, but don't see a sign. I consume all the olives and little cheese biscuits I can, dropping some on the floor for Spike.

"Over there, Madame," says a kind man, pointing to an old wooden door. Thank goodness, it's a proper toilet, although it doesn't have a lid.

Feeling better, we return to the eager gathering of wine tasters.

"You like this one, Madame? Try this one." The man talks so fast that his English doesn't make a lot of sense, but a glass of wine is a glass of wine whichever language you use.

I try them all. The sickly sweet dessert wine… the dry sharp one that makes my eyes smart as I swallow – and the easier-on-the-palate light fruity one, which I like. Different tastes brush my lips and tickle my tongue, others hit the back of my throat and change as the aroma lingers in my nose.

Mainly it's a totally pleasant experience until I'm offered a red wine that tastes like the inside of a rabbit hutch and interferes with my ability to swallow. A group of connoisseurs in suits mull over the rabbit-hutch one and sip at it before projecting wine into a tin bucket. They slide their bare hands across their lips, pausing for a moment… then they order crate-loads of the stuff while guffawing with pleasure.

Gerry says I need to be educated about wine and that the cheapest from the local supermarket isn't any good. Perhaps this disgusting red is what he's talking about. If this is the education he's referring to I'll stick to the supermarket's special offer. Lisa and Eldred drink good wine, or so they say. Eldred reads books on it and orders boxes online. When Gerry and Eldred get together Gerry talks about the wines he would love to drink and can't afford.

I reflect on Gerry's mother's comments and ask myself if she was right. Did he marry the wrong person? "Someone who would hold him back and not help him reach his full potential," is what she said about me at the time.

I try to learn from the salesman giving his performance. I would like to make something of myself that Gerry and his mother could be proud of. At forty it's probably too late.

Glasses are collected and our orders are taken. Before leaving, I must get directions, although nothing matters much in my light head. A middle-aged couple, walk across the car park ahead of me. Madame is on the round and short side in a pink floral frock, and Monsieur is wearing a traditional French beret.

"*Bonjour Monsieur, Madame. Pouvez-vous m'aider? Je voudrais allez à Normandie.*" Is alcohol improving my French?

"*Ah… Oui, Madame. Vous allez à Paris, puis à Normandie.*"

"*Ah non, j'ai déjà été à Paris, et Normandie n'est pas là.*"

"*Nous avons une carte.*" Monsieur digs into his bag.

Oh no. Not a map. He unfolds it with precision and holds it up for me to look over his shoulder at the squiggles, lines and letters sprawled across the page. He jabbers away in French, so it's no better than trying to understand my own map. Probably, worse.

"Bordeaux? Normandy?" I enquire, studying his face for a sign of any direction I might understand.

"*Paris est très bon, mais je ne voulais pas répéter l'expérience.*" Do they understand I'm trying to say I've already been to Paris and there's no point going there again? I must find another way.

We stare at each other for several seconds until Madame pulls at his arm. I walk away, feeling alone. Spike walks behind me with one ear inside out. I can feel his trust and lack of concern. I wish it were well-founded.

It's late afternoon already, and after all that wine there's nothing to do but curl up and sleep on the front seat of the car. With hard seats numbing my bum and the gearstick digging in my leg, I doze.

"*Madame. Allez-y.*" A fist bangs on the window. "*Madame. Vous partez.*"

No one is left in the car park, and the heat of the day has passed. We slowly make our way back down the tree-lined avenue to the exit. The man scratches his head as he stares at my car. Adjusting his cap, he walks away.

I've driven along the road to the left to get here, so I'll turn right. No point going back on myself. I come across a bed and breakfast place with red geraniums in every available pot and hanging basket. Gerry will have to wait, there is little more travelling to be done today.

The French couple from the wine tasting are ahead of me at Reception, but they don't notice me.

"So strange how you meet French people, and when you think your French is OK communication breaks down. That's odd, now, isn't it?" the lady says, and sucks on her finger.

"Lost, if you ask me. Doesn't know her own country. Too much to drink," her husband replies, with distinct Welsh tones.

He was right; I had had too much to drink. For someone who has the occasional glass of wine at the weekend and a small gin and tonic after work, a more measured approach would have been better. Spitting good wine into a tin bucket is against my nature, but putting such a mixture in my stomach has made me feel sick.

At the chateau, I bought ten bottles of white and ten of red. Rather than go by taste I went by price and paid more than usual, but not too much. They are for my fortieth birthday party and I hope Gerry will approve… better still, be pleased.

The thing to do is avoid the couple at the desk to save making a bigger fool of myself. They don't know where Normandy is any more than I do, and they thought I was French. With a door key in my hand, I escape down the opposite corridor.

After a wash in cool water my mind and body are refreshed enough to venture downstairs to the dining room. The red check plastic tablecloths would not be my personal choice, but they probably come from the local market. On every table is a complimentary carafe of wine, and a friendly young lady hovers around to help look after the guests. The smell of stale smoke pervades and the windows are shut to keep the evening mass of insects at bay.

I choose a quiet corner, away from the view of the French/Welsh couple or anyone else. With Spike in my room, I'm more aware of being on my own, it's something I've never had to experience. Now I'm the one in the corner reading my book.

Music from the sixties crackles its way through the speakers. Thoughts of my young childhood begin to surface. Whatever my parents may have done before we were born, they didn't own up to Chester and me. Chester was born four months after they married and that sort of thing was talked about back then. Two years later, I came along. In spite of raised eyebrows from people who liked to gossip, they loved and supported each other for forty-five years.

I dreamt of being married, from my early teens, with a home, children and a dog. When Gerry and I drifted into marriage, I was ecstatic.

I was cocooned in a life that didn't change a lot in place or outlook. I enjoyed the untroubled security of my childhood; what more could my parents have given me? Marrying Gerry, a local boy, felt like a natural progression.

The ease and comfort of my life has meant I've never burnt with desire to see the rest of the world. Right now I want to be a child again, at home, playing with Sindy dolls on the carpet in front of the fire. I think of the Wombles – Orinoco and Tobermory, they were my favourite characters – collecting litter on Wimbledon Common. There was that snug feeling in front of the TV, on days when it rained or I wasn't feeling well. Crumpets with butter and jam always made me feel better, and I still have Marmite sandwiches to cheer up a dull day.

Mum taught me about art and literature. She was a slow reader like me, and she showed me how to learn through pictures and from listening to radio.

I didn't expect to be homesick; it must be because I don't know exactly where I am, or where I'm going. I remind myself I'm nearly forty, and expect the feeling to go away. There's space to hide in my corner and speak to Dad.

"How are you?" my voice croaks, and I swallow hard.

"I'm fine, thanks," Dad says. His voice is cheerful, thank goodness.

"I'm not drinking tap water. Neither is Spike," I assure him. He tells me all is well at home without me. How can that be? I try not to quiver in my voice as I say, "Goodbye."

Gerry has phoned me twice, wanting to know where I am – and I've played for time. I guess I should speak to him.

"Gerry, I'll be there tomorrow. I hope you don't mind but I got lost, and it's taking longer than I thought." He sounds more resigned than cross. He has to stay at the hospital until he can walk easily with crutches. His allotted nurse has changed from Stephan to pretty Agatha, who is brightening his mood.

Steak and *frites,* without the wine, goes down well. I chop what's left of the steak and wrap it in my serviette for Spike's treat.

"Tomorrow is another day," I sigh, as I clean my teeth in the little pink sink next to the faded chintz curtains.

The mattress is a bit lumpy, but I manage to sleep for most of the night. Spike stays curled up on the end of the bed, breathing rhythmically. In a single bed, I don't miss Gerry so much.

Breakfast is continental, which is a way of saying French bread and jam. I don't feel like hanging around afterwards so I pay and, with Spike sitting-up watching, drive away from the B & B with too many red geraniums.

I wish there was a way of controlling my emotional raggedness. I desperately want to find the right direction, and working myself up doesn't help, it only makes things worse.

The man on Reception said, "*A la gauche*" and "*A la droite*" so many times I had to butt in with "*Merci*" and "*Au revoir.*"

I turn left then right, and drive past fields and vineyards stretching for miles. The big horizon lifts my thinking. It's a good direction, if not the right one. A carefree spirit has returned.

My focus emerges through drifting thoughts to a French man riding his old bike, with two chickens tied by their feet and slung over his shoulder. His backside spills over the edges of the seat and he's wearing a squat French cap that looks like he's had it for fifty years. The chickens are plump, white, and hanging completely still. The chickens (or maybe the drinking of pastis) are making him wobble in a fascinating pattern. The road is narrow and he's happy riding down the middle.

Beep… beep. He must be deaf. He holds his position, riding a path of personal ownership.

"Shit." The Fiat swerves in time but there's a second's delay as I remind myself which side of the road we're both supposed to be on. I didn't knock in to him; I think it was the fright of discovering me so close that made him lose control and hit the verge. It's not too hard a fall, and I wind down the window to check if he's OK. The man looks bad-tempered as he sits on the ground with squawking chickens attempting a three-legged race and his back wheel spinning in the air.

"Bastard *Anglaise*," he shouts raising his fist. "*Toujours la même.*"

"Don't worry, Spike. He's used to it. Even the best cyclists fall off sometimes. Look at Gerry."

Spike delights in the breeze on his face as it whips through the open window. My sympathy and thoughts for the French man soon pass.

We sail along on the open road. It's a clear day and Normandy can't be far away. At lunchtime, we take a turning off into the nearest town. I reach a bridge that's wide and welcoming. We drive over to park by a wall close to the river. This busy town should be easily identifiable. A weird-looking black mould clings to the walls of the buildings. I feel relaxed here; there are lots of people out and about on their own like me.

We find a table in a shady square across from a small bar. Spike and I share a cheese and pickle baguette and I have a small beer before heading for a seat by the river. It's time to take out my map and find out where this is. It doesn't mean a lot, and it's a good time to ring Gerry. "Gerry, I don't know where I am."

"Where do you think you are? Describe something to me."

"A big building opposite says *Hennessy*. A signpost said Cogg Nak."

"Tell me you're not in Cognac?"

"That's it, Gerry. That's it. Am I close?" I want Gerry to be pleased but I get a moment of silence, followed by resignation.

"No. No… but you can stay there a couple of days. I can't leave yet. I stood up to help Nurse Agatha with some bed linen and fell, damaging my wrist. It needs an X-ray. Nurse Agatha told me off for getting out of my chair unassisted."

I shouldn't think like this, but he's making mistakes too. I'm not the only one. Does anyone get things right all the time?

"I'll ring Chester and see if he has any ideas on how to find you and lead you back, then he can pick me up. His car is more comfortable than the Fiat." Gerry pauses before adding, "Buy some cognac while you're there."

"I don't need Chester; I *will* pick you up soon," I state. "Bye Gerry. I love you."

"Hmm," is his reply.

Gerry thinks I'm OK as long as he is in charge, and now Chester feels responsible for his younger sister.

I may not be experienced when it comes to travel but the sun has appeared from behind a tall house, making me find my sunglasses. I want to explore this town and its river. I'm not stupid, and I *will* sort out my sense of direction. It's only a matter of time.

The Hennessy building opposite looks interesting, so I decide to walk back across the bridge and look around. Spike holds himself tall beside me, sniffing the air.

Once inside the entrance, the smell of cognac pervades. I take a tasting glass from the tray and swallow hard. It reminds me of Christmas and wedding cake. A bit harsh, but I can see why people like it. There are barrels of cognac, and bottles in small, large, and extra-large sizes. I buy a litre bottle as instructed by Gerry. It's packaged in a shiny maroon box with gold writing, and looks as expensive as it is. I return to sit close to the car, and try to decide what to do next.

A seat by the river is perfect for basking in the sun for a while. The grass is full of daisies beneath my feet, and tended gardens with roses over pergolas are attractive on the far bank. I will find a place to stay later.

A smallish man, sitting on a bench close to the bridge, absorbs my attention. He has his guitar beside him and a bag that might contain his life's possessions. He must be a Brit with his Liverpool Football Club badge on his old denim jacket.

He rolls a cigarette and lights up. Smoke rises from his lips as he rests his elbows on his knees. He's accompanied by his thoughts, unconcerned by what I perceive is an aura of loneliness.

A cold-water spray hits the side of my face. Drops trickle down to the front of my blouse and the residue makes my nose twitch.

"Oops… sorry."

A woman shaking a pair of wet trainers and oozing fun and enthusiasm approaches until she is close to my seat. Her hair is light ginger and curly. She's a bit on the dumpy side like me, with a free and easy manner not like me – but like I used to be.

Wearing shorts doesn't bother her and gingery freckles suit her chubby arms and face.

"Sorry, again. Alan, my brother-in-law." She points with a wet trainer in the direction of a lanky figure on a hire boat. "His turn to clean the deck… water everywhere. He couldn't be bothered to move my shoes so now I have to dry them. I didn't mean to splash… Can I sit here?"

"Of course." I'm pleased to hear an English voice and meet someone about my age.

"Pete's my husband. He said we had to bring Alan." She nods at the man busy on deck. "Two men are a bit of a trial. Pete is the intelligent good-looking brother, thank goodness. Not like Alan." My new companion gives her wet shoes a hard shake away from me, and then rests them on the grass to dry.

The boat is moored by the steps and has two bikes strapped on the top. Alan is still slopping a mop in and out of a bucket full of river water – the slightly smelly stuff that hit my face.

"Pete's in town buying supplies. Then we're off upriver. What brings you here? Are you on your own?" She looks around, expecting someone else to turn up.

"A Fiat and hopeless map reading. I'm on my own here, but not on my own in France."

"This your dog? He's so cute."

Spike turns over and over, enjoying the fuss. "Left my dog at home. The vaccinations were too much trouble, for a short trip. I miss him. By the way, I'm Sarah."

"I'm Natalie, and this is Spike. I'm looking for somewhere to stay in Cognac for a couple of days and then

I have to find my way to Normandy. I'm not used to driving long distances on my own, nor am I used to France."

We chat and get along well, making easy conversation. Sarah tells me she lives near London and I tell her about Bastille Day and Gerry.

"How about a couple of days on board? We're going to Saintes and back again. I'd love female company, and we'd all love Spike."

What else is there to do? Spike has taken to jumping up and down and yapping with excitement. Sarah gives me a warm friendly smile. That's it; decision made. I need to return to the car and collect our things.

Spike sits on the front driving seat so I stand and take a closer look at the maroon box with gold writing. The tips of my fingers glide over the shiny exterior before I open it to inspect the bottle inside. The bottle changes colour when I hold it up to catch the sunlight.

Living in the car for four days has resulted in a mixture of bags, bits of food and drink and Spike's travelling baggage, all making a mess. I must put the bottle away and tidy up before going to the boat. Spike isn't helping. At the moment of returning the bottle to its packaging and deciding to keep the plastic bag for collecting litter, Spike jumps up, trying to scrabble past me through the open door. As I grapple to hold on to Spike, the cognac slips from my hands. I'm fixed in a moment of time. It crashes to the ground by my feet, with a sickening thud, shattering into thousands of tiny clear brown glass shards.

The amber liquid drains uncontrollably away, and the last drops trickle between the shattered glass. I'm mesmerised as the dry rain gully laps it up. The smelling and sipping, the warming-in-my-hands experience and the extra euros for the darker colour are all finding their way down to the river and out to sea. I'm left with an empty box.

I turn from my disaster to look at the wall. My eyes pass over a sign for the meeting of pilgrims, and directions to Spain and Santiago de Compostela. I wonder if the group from Paris will come this way.

"Damn it. Never mind. We'll find Gerry something else. Come on, Spike." I gather up a couple of bags and Spike's dishes and food before heading down the bank towards the boat. It has a friendly bobbing motion and I forget about the rest of my life. That sense of freedom experienced outside the *Musée du Louvre* is here again. I want to skip and dance when my phone rings.

I drop my baggage to the ground. "Hello," I answer.

"Hi, Sis. How you doin'?" Chester didn't have to adopt an American accent as well as an American wife. "Gerry tells me you've got yourself in a bit of a muddle and he's asked me to come and get you. Now tell me… where are you?"

Chester and I haven't spoken for eighteen months. He divorced Tracey and married Stacey and I made a mistake on my Christmas card. It was a mistake but they said it was deliberate. They said I preferred Nicholas, his son, to Blake, the now stepson, and I shouldn't make it so obvious that I would prefer he was still married to Tracey.

I thought Tracey was better off without him but I regretted the divorce. When he became an IT executive, he outgrew his roots and his wife. At a conference in Los Angeles, he met Stacey, a bit-part actress working as a part-time waitress at his hotel. It hasn't done Tracey any harm – she has built a better life – but ignoring Nicholas is a selfish thing to do and Nicholas is suffering for it. I haven't lost touch with Tracey and Nicholas but we could have been closer if the divorce hadn't happened.

Chester lives an hour away and makes little effort to come and see us. Dad goes on the train to see him, so I have little need for contact, and here he is, trying to sort my life out.

"How's Tracey? Sorry… Stacey."

"Now come on, Sis. Stop being silly. I will be in Cognac in two days' time. I might bring Stacey and Blake along for the ride. All you have to do is follow me home. Do you think you can manage that?" His words rise in tone. I can feel his patronising smile.

"No. No I don't. I'll find my own way." I turn off my phone, pick up my things, and light foot it down to the boat.

"Welcome aboard." Alan is leaning on his mop, and I wonder if I can persuade him to wash my brandy-stained trainers. I introduce him to Spike. He pretends to be scared and I laugh out loud. It's a release after the tension I've felt. I last fell around laughing when Susie and I talked about Lisa and Eldred.

"Hello. We got company?" A pleasant medium-all-round man is on the edge of the boarding plank. He wears checked shorts, showing his hairy legs. Why is that the privilege of men? If evolution were true we'd have hair only where we wanted it by now.

"Let me help." Sarah takes bags of food from Pete and we head for the galley. "This is Natalie. She's going to join us to Saintes and back."

"Sounds good to me. I hear this is Spike." Pete shakes Spike's paw. "Let's get to know you over a drink and then we'll cast off."

"We're from the south side of London. What about you?" Pete enquires.

"Eastleigh."

"Where?" Three people are looking at me as if I had said, "Outer space."

"It's not that far away from the coast in the south of England."

"So it's easy for you to come to France," Sarah comments.

"I guess it is, but I don't. I have to ring Katy, my daughter. We both need to know we are all right. Won't take a minute." The back of the sun deck is the ideal place to sit and talk.

"Katy?"

"Hi, Mum. Where are you?"

"Cognac."

"What are you doing in Cognac? It's completely the wrong direction. You lost?"

"I'm not lost… I can't find the right direction. Don't worry. I'm OK."

"That's unreal. I'm on the school radio tomorrow. Can you ring in? I'll announce you as the lost mother and you can talk to the whole school and anyone else who listens in. Is Spike OK?"

"Spike's fine. How's Gramps?"

"He's teaching Matt chess. Says he's worried about you being like Grandma. She kept getting lost before they realised it was Alzheimer's. One day the police brought her home, and he wonders if that will happen to you."

A sigh of sadness escapes my lips – the sadness of losing Mum and the shadow it has cast, and that my family can't see me perfectly happy.

This is the first time I have faced losing Mum on my own. Dad, Katy and Gerry hadn't wanted me to be unhappy so we braved it out and went around cheering each other up. I need to look for a quiet place and to tell Mum I miss her. In reality, I know she can't hear me, but it would make me feel better; a token of closure.

I promise Katy I'll talk to her on the school radio, and it's encouraging I'm not viewed as a boring mum for a change. Pete shows me to the little bedroom at the end of the galley and Spike takes up the position of lookout on the prow.

"We're going down river. That suit you, Natalie?"

I look at Pete and try to explain. "Up? Down?" I cross my hands and point both ways across my chest. "It's all the same to me. Is there a word for people who have no sense of direction?"

"Yeah. A woman." Alan tidies away the mop and bucket, listening to our conversation between his own clattering. I try to make up my mind if I like him or not, but for two days I'm sure we can keep the peace.

Pete has taken control at the helm.

"Cast off," he calls. We all help coil the ropes on deck. Pete turns the boat around and motors gently away from Cognac. Behind us the bridge and my turquoise car slowly disappear.

We pass Cognac, with the office for booking daytrips and holidays. Boats bob around on the wash, waiting for customers to board. I go to the bow to sit with Spike, watching as we glide through the water and the river disappears under us. Ducks swim out of our way and I love them, but I'm waiting for the flash of blue of my first River Charente kingfisher. The river guide says they're common here but we need to get away from the town to stand a chance of seeing them.

The banks are a big mix of green foliage and white flowers with thriving insects. Plantations of tall alder trees with fluttering leaves add to that distinctive French look. I rest my arm on Spike while smelling the freshness from the banks and catching the breeze. I close my eyes to dream when Pete yells, "Lock, everyone."

"Good… another pair of hands. Do you know what to do?" Alan hunches his shoulders and looks sideways at me.

"Point me in the right direction. I'll give it a go."

"Great. The gates are in our favour. That'll save time," Pete says, and takes the boat towards the lock entrance. "Don't tie the boat or we'll end up stranded in the air when the level drops. Go with Sarah to the back gates." We climb on to the quay.

Alan jogs to the front gates. "Right. Now turn the handles and keep going until your end is shut. Close the paddles then I'll open them this end," he calls.

As we turn the handles to make the gates close, they labour and crank into motion. Not a spot of rust can be seen on the lime green-painted wheels that turn, nor on the heavy chains that are covered in thick grease. The French care for their locks, and they pay them back in tourist money.

We run to the front gates to help Alan. The paddles open and the boat drops until it's level with the river. The putt-putt of the exhaust echoes against the wet walls. Soon it's safe to open the gates. Two boys arrive, speeding along on their bikes, hoping to help and to pick up a euro. Pete slips the boat from the lock and throws coins to the boys, who have done little to help apart from holding the boat at the pontoon. They wait for us to board; in two minutes we are on the boat again, coiling wet ropes on the deck.

"Do you… um… mind if I take a shower?" Without waiting for a reply, I grab my toilet bag, rush to the tiny shower room and lock the door. I look in the little mirror. Tears are flowing down my face and dripping into the stained plastic sink. I turn on the shower in case they should hear me crying. In a few minutes it's over, my make-up is on, and I'm back joining in the small talk.

Am I missing Gerry? I ask myself. Well, not that much. Mum, perhaps? Well, no. I have missed her, but I take pleasure at having had her as my mum. Susie said that sadness can come to an end. She had felt upset about a mother she never knew. She loved her adopted mum but there was still a sense of loss. It came at the time when she was making a decision whether or not to find her biological parents. She decided if they wanted to find her they would, but it might open up things she didn't want to face. After losing my mum, sharing with Susie helped.

Puzzled by my crying, I ignore it for now. It probably won't happen again. I stuff spare tissues up my sleeve, announce I suffer from hay fever and not to worry.

"All hands on deck." Pete steers the boat alongside the bank. Alan reaches for the fishing rods while Sarah and I get ready with the ropes and the boathook. We tie the bow rope to the trunk of a small tree and the men hammer in a metal pole to fix the stern. I don't know what to do, but I follow the others and hope not to make mistakes. A system that has not been good on the roads works in this situation.

The men are soon fishing, sitting on the picnic chairs. Sarah and I make salads and prepare a small barbecue – hoping, like the men, that we are going to have fresh fish.

When the fish come, they are on the small side, but who cares? We have plenty to eat. Pete bought goat's cheese and white wine from the market in Cognac. Anything would taste good in this setting, as long as we ignore the flies and bees that stop by.

I lie on my stomach with my heels in the air, running my fingers through the wild mint... then crushing a few leaves between my fingers and holding them in front of my face to sense the full aroma.

"Good. I'm fine," I reassure myself. I pick another handful to sprinkle on the potatoes, and I enjoy the rural art of gathering food.

The effect of the wine and the light changing, renders us into a subdued mood. Pete picks up his guitar and quietly sings,

'*Are you lonesome, tonight?*' His singing isn't bad, but he's nothing like Elvis.

"Are you married or with a partner, Alan?" I ask.

"Nope. Lost my wife." He looks distracted and uncomfortable, picking at his chipped fingernails.

"I'm sorry. What was wrong?" Why didn't I see what was coming?

"She didn't die. I lost her... you know, like you... only we found you."

"How did you lose her?"

"We were returning from our holiday early so I could watch the match at the pub – you know, the Man U v Millwall big one. I stopped to fill up, got in the car and started off down the road. After fifteen minutes I realised she wasn't there. It was too late to go back or I'd miss the match. I went on, watched the match, only had one beer, then went straight back to the garage."

"Don't tell me? She'd gone." Unwittingly, I feel sorry for him.

"Correct. I looked everywhere – in the toilets and the shop – but that was it. That's the last time I heard from her, apart from a lawyer's letter. She'd taken all her stuff from the flat."

"His story has been in the local papers and even reached Radio 1. All he could say was, 'It was the FA Cup'," Sarah says, studying him with a look between disdain and incredulity. Gerry's obsession with sport isn't looking too bad.

"Here's a photo of me the day I lost her." Alan shows me a much-handled picture of himself with the Millwall blue and white paint on his face. Gerry is certainly reasonable about football compared to this.

"He's been a Millwall fan since Dad bought us the kit. I was five and he was three. I got over it; he didn't." Pete gives Alan an affectionate grin.

Alan hands me another photo. He's a small boy holding his dad's hand surrounded by football fans, and they're off to a match. I hold the photo for a moment before handing it back.

The weather changes and rain falls softly. We sit a while longer until the rain becomes heavy. A flash of lightning and a rumble of thunder sends us scurrying for the shelter of the boat. Pete pulls on his anorak and heads for the deck.

"Where are you going?" Sarah calls through the sound of the rain and wind.

"We don't want to risk drifting downstream. We need to check we're firmly moored, the river can swell after a storm."

"I'm with ya." Alan legs his way close behind Pete. The

brothers work together in the rain until they're happy the ropes are firmly fixed.

We all go off to our rooms early, to read or to dream. I feel safe in the boat, but if the river swells it could be dangerous.

I find my pen and paper and start to write words… any words. I do that sometimes.

Chester, me, dolls, schoolteachers, the smell of Vick… no, that isn't what I want in my words. I need to be more up to date.

Gerry, wedding, bridesmaids, happy day, Katy… no, that isn't the line I'm looking for. I need to be in touch with something else.

Tears, me, person, boy… yes, this is more like it. Learning, reaching, living. That's why I cried. I was facing something deep inside myself. I will face it, but not now. These thoughts are way off, but coming closer.

The picture of Alan as a boy, and his dad, is swirling around in my head like cognac in a glass, warming in my hands.

The rain splashes on the river and drums on the roof. I'm aware of Spike breathing easily, snuggled against my side. With the pages of my writing pad still open, I fall asleep.

4

Messing About on the River

We're up and about early. Alan is in the galley making bacon sarnies for breakfast. The frying pan spits fat and it excites Spike.

I open the small kitchen window and, through a layer of mist resting on the water, throw scraps of bread to the waiting ducks.

"Shut it. It's cold." Alan raises his voice. He insists on putting his thin shorts on first thing to save changing later. "You girls washing up, I hope. I'm not doin' everything."

"Girls? Who are they?" Sarah retorts.

"Must be underway by 9.00 or we won't reach Saintes today," Pete says. He takes a sandwich and crunches on crispy bacon wrapped in soft bread. Alan does make the best breakfasts.

"Pete, can I have a go at the helm? You'll have to keep an eye on me. It looks fun."

"I'll help you, Nat." Alan passes round the coffee pot for refills while reminding us we need to get organised and ready to leave without the luxury of being able to sit around.

Wiping his half-washed hand on his T-shirt, Alan continues standing up to eat. We all have dripping butter, but only one of us cleans their plate with his finger and licks it.

Sarah goes to work on the dishes and Pete casts off. I'm

a bit nervous at the helm but this could be a bonding experience with Alan, and we need one to keep the team ethos.

"Stay right, Nat. Pull the throttle to go faster and push to go slower. That's it. Any idiot can do it. Follow the river guide." Alan opens the guide at the right page and props it up by the wheel.

It has to be easier than following a road map. There's only one direction to go and that's straight ahead.

"Thanks, Alan." He sits behind me reading a fitness magazine. Clearly, he only reads it but doesn't put anything into practice – he manages to be skinny and lazy at the same time – but I'm judging him on holiday and that might not be fair. I think about describing Gerry's fitness, but decide not to.

There is no phone reception here. I swing between worrying about Gerry and forgetting altogether that I'm supposed to be at the hospital. His new pyjamas are still in my car, but Nurse Stephan went shopping for him yesterday so I expect he's OK for now. His wrist was only a sprain so that's good news. Gerry's French is limited, like mine. Conversation isn't easy for him unless someone speaks English. I will be there to take him home soon. Anyway, apart from visiting, what could I do?

There's a peace to rhythmically motoring along, passing the odd fisherman and watching the banks changing from greenery and trees to the occasional vineyard and picnic area. The morning progresses and we see locals going about their business in a small town. I'm happy behind the wheel. We pass French men playing boules by the river, but mainly they walk around with their hands in their pockets muttering. They remind me of the man who fell off his bike and I wonder if I should have stopped to help. Too late now. Why did he blame me for his own mistakes? It wasn't entirely my fault, but at the time, I felt it was.

Does Gerry blame me because he hasn't made more of his life? His mother does, I know. Will he be more disgruntled at times if he can't ride a bike? Do I want him at home more? On different terms is what I really want, but how do I change him?

The markets have been open for a while; women are hurrying along the path with their baskets full. They will have searched for the best vegetables and fruits, and bought their cheeses and meats.

"Lock," Alan shouts in my ear. "You gonna navigate through this or shall I?" He takes the helm and I prepare to throw the ropes.

Wheels are turned, river levels change, water drips... and we're through. The boat continues in Alan's hands with its gentle rhythmic sound until it's time for lunch. We find a perfect place, with the breeze rustling through trees close by. Pete's happy with our progress and ready to relax.

So much stuff has to be transferred to the grassy area: chairs, suntan lotion, food, the bottle of wine... where does it end?

"Salt... where's the salt?" Pete asks, rummaging through the food bags.

Alan holds tight to the bottle opener, for fear it might get lost. I jump back on board and, after much opening and shutting of doors, I return victorious with the salt and a bottle of mayonnaise.

The meal is simple: French cheeses, sparkling white wine, langoustines and salad. Alan bashes away at two tins of rice pudding with a bent tin opener. He manages to slop most of the contents into a saucepan before warming it on the mini stove, and offers an option of fresh raspberries or both.

Most boats we wave to as they pass – it's bad manners to ignore other river users – but we stand and stare at a boat three times the size of ours approaching from astern. It slows as it passes and the crew wave.

"Can we join you?" is a familiar rich and sexy voice. It belongs to someone I know well but who doesn't know me. It's Gary Blain, my favourite celebrity chef. I'm overcome with excitement, which makes me feel silly, but I manage to stop short of acting out the dance happening in my head.

"We're filming on the canals and are interested in what people are eating." Gary Blain is speaking to us! From the corner of my eye I see Alan slide the empty rice tins into the garbage bag.

The rice pudding is ready for serving and Alan makes a flourish with the raspberries on top. Gary and his film crew have reached the bank and are transferring from their boat.

"Try some?" Alan offers.

Gary gives an indifferent nod to several of his team to try the offering, clearly not keen on it himself – and anyway, he's busy supervising the setting up of his improvised kitchen. The guy in charge of the filming equipment whispers in my ear,

"Where're the tins?" I try to cover schoolgirl blushes and we both know Alan has no future in cooking

"Alex," he says, introducing himself. He puts his filming equipment down and holds my hand in a warm handshake. I'm oddly aware of his male touch and he relaxes into easy conversation. Setting up takes time and there's nothing for him to do right now, so he's grateful for company.

I blink, taking stock of his physique. Not too fit – but kind eyes… lots of hair, even though he is at an age when it could have been going thin. If I look hard, he does have the odd grey hair mixed in. An edge of dark curls cover his ears, they help add up to his free-spirit appearance. We have cut-off jeans in common. Damn. He is going to see my knees.

He looks at my feet and works up, resting his eyes at breast level before resting on my face. He grins and nods. My eyes are tempted to flirt, but before they can I launch into conversation.

"Do you mind explaining how the sound and the filming work together?" Phew.

"Of course not. If you give me your email I'll send you more information and where to find out about filming, if you like."

"It's Natalie, and here's my .co.uk address." I nervously hand it over.

"Put yourself on The Facebook and I'll be your friend." He smiles, lightly curling his lip and reminding me of a country and western singer.

Katy was on about The Facebook, saying I can easily keep in touch with her in Japan or wherever else she might go. She can upload photos for us to see.

There are free computer courses at Eastleigh's community hall that I should think about joining. The forms were put through the letterbox just before I came away. I hope they haven't been thrown in the bin, but tidiness is not part of Katy's young personality.

Alex and I chat undisturbed for an hour, while Gary and the rest of the team prepare to cook fish and wild herbs. I take a lot of photos and Alex gives me advice. He thinks my old camera has something going for it but I'd be better off with a new one as well. Digital is essential.

He tells me about his work and the travelling he does. I discover he likes art and – of course – photography, even when he's not at work. Alan is sleeping on the grass; Sarah and Pete are sitting in the chairs, quietly engrossed in their reading.

Gary Blain is about to cook and Alex needs to start working. An exciting musky smell hits me before he moves away. I watch too long and too closely as he films. When Gary finishes he gives us a taste of his cooking, and the camera rolls on us. The food is so good. I could fall in love with Gary's deep voice and ready smile, as so many other women have done. It all helps distract me from the odd fancy for Alex – who looks intriguing and in control, with the filming equipment slung over his shoulders.

Don't make a fool of yourself, Nat, I think – and turn my attention to Sarah and Pete who have moved to sit at the water's edge, and are dangling their feet.

Spike is in on the act, chasing Gary's dog Whitey. Neither is very sprightly because they're both getting on in dog years. If they stay still long enough, this will be a photo opportunity not to be missed.

I look at Gary Blain and conjure up a picture of Gerry in an apron making an exciting dish with aromatic spices, in our small kitchen. It would be great if he learned to cook. An easy recipe would do – but I can dream.

The filming is finished. The excitement has died down and everything is packed away on the floating studio. We wave goodbye and I flash one last smile at Alex.

"Well, that was fun." I turn and make myself overly busy collecting things.

We throw what remains of the messy white gunge of

rice pudding in the river, to the delight of the fish that bubble on the surface. I wonder why fishermen spend all day trying to catch them when all they need is rice pudding and a net. Now we must repack and get on board.

Pete has a plan for the afternoon, but the rest of us don't care and are happy to lounge around. He announces we will carry on to Saintes and spend the evening there, sleep overnight and return to Cognac tomorrow.

Return to Cognac… I haven't been thinking about that. Will Chester be there, waiting to take over my life? As he doesn't know exactly where I am, this is only imagination. It extends itself to seeing Stacey and Blake with him, and a cold shudder releases itself. What if they spot my car?

Where was Chester when Mum was ill? He visited twice in three months then went off to America. He said that since I wasn't working he was sure I was better without him getting in the way. I pointed out that I worked at the bingo hall and looked after Katy. He said he was talking about real work like his and, when Mum was gone, I should take the opportunity to look for a proper job; I should retrain for something.

I will ring home and Gerry from Saintes and let them know all is well. At least Gerry is the faithful type, not like Chester. We do go to the cinema occasionally, and he buys my favourite flowers, lilies, once a month on payday.

I take another turn at the helm and manoeuvre us safely past the leisure area we share with canoeists and water skiers. They rush around, shooting up a spout from behind their skis. There are no problems, and I feel encouraged. Alan doesn't look up from his reading. That could be because he's half asleep. He tells me he's a night owl but I've yet to see it.

I'm left alone for the next hour.

"Well done, Nat," Pete says, and offers to take a turn. I'm pleased to take a break and sit with my legs hanging over the edge, enjoying cuddles from the sun and splashes from the river.

I have two pairs of jeans with me and I locate some scissors. After rummaging around for the pair I'm not wearing, I'm happy to chop them off at the knees. I'm showing my knees and I don't care who sees them. Why should I?

We pull alongside to stop for drinks and ice creams, and discover a brocante drawing a small crowd in the small square nearby. Before the men can say "No" we're off to join the French customers scrutinising the goods for sale. The men stay on board and relax with a beer while we rummage through old china, broken clocks, odd tools and textiles. We return to the boat with a felt cushion shaped like a pink rose that I liked and a white plate with a blue Breton lady in costume for Sarah's mum. The men are not interested in our purchases and are pleased to be motoring off to Saintes.

Tidying my room is a necessity in such a limited space, as there isn't room to spread things out. I listen as the boat pushes its way through the water, and the rose felt cushion emits its smell of wood smoke and of someone else's house.

Before long, the engine slows. I pop up on deck to watch Pete turn the boat around in the centre of the river before pulling alongside, close to the bridge that crosses into the town.

No sooner are we moored than Alan is transferring the bikes on to the towpath.

"Come on, Nat," he encourages, sitting astride, ready to ride along the path.

"I can't ride a bike," I call from the boat.

"Really? How dumb is that. I'll hold the saddle and run. You'll get the hang of it." Alan throws his bike to the ground and stands waiting.

Me, ride a bike? Where we grew up there was no safe place outside the house. A scooter was all I was allowed to ride. Aged thirty-nine years, eleven months and twenty-three days, am I going to learn to ride a bike? Will my bum look big on this?

Alan complains he's not finding room to hold the saddle. I try to ride but it's hard to avoid the grass verge or stay upright. Half an hour later, with a bruised knee, I can turn the pedals two or three times before laughing my way to the ground. Tomorrow will see an improvement.

"Practice makes perfect," I quote. What will Gerry think of me learning to ride a bike?

"I don't like to say this, Nat, but if you slimmed down it would be easier to keep the bike upright." Alan wheezes with exertion.

"You should spend more time keeping fit and less time reading about it," I shoot back. I can see why Sarah finds him difficult. It's time to pack away the bikes; we've had enough for now.

On the boat, we drink tea and dunk ginger biscuits, looking at the cathedral, elevated on the far side and the Roman ruins on this side. It's an impressive place to be.

The French are enjoying the early evening and, no doubt, thinking about their meal tonight. They look somewhere between Parisian and rural and I like their easy friendliness.

Our minds turn to supper, "I fancy a vindaloo; hot stuff, and loads of beer. I'm fed up with French food. If I see another steak and *frites* followed by crème brûlée or île flottante, I'll go mad," Alan announces.

"Never thought I'd say I can't face eating any more prawns," Pete adds. "I think I smell like one."

"There's not much by way of Indian restaurants. A Chinese is recommended in the guide. Why don't we give that a go?" Sarah passes the book for us to choose. The Indian is furthest away. A long walk could be an issue; so is the thought of Alan full of vindaloo and loads of beer.

"My vote is Chinese," I say, with my fingers crossed.

Time for Spike to have his wash; if he's coming out with us he has got to look his best. After a shampoo and hose-off he smells of fresh doggy soap and his coat is extra fluffy. He's never keen on washing but loves the toweling-down. I'm sure he understands when everyone admires how good he looks.

Outside our mini shower we create a queue. After our showers the men fix the hose to the outside tap to fill the tank, complaining at how quickly it empties with two women on board. We are told to be more careful, as taps for refilling can be far apart. The boat is rocking as we all move around getting dressed.

"Damn. No jeans with full legs…"

"Borrow my maxi skirt if you like, Nat, but you look good. Chill. You're on holiday."

How odd it feels that I'm not in Cornwall for my holiday with Dad and Katy, or at home with the family. I'm not sure how much they're worried about me but I imagine they don't trust my judgement. I'm not in the habit of showing this degree of independence. Why aren't I crying for help? The family must be undecided whether to panic or ignore me, and they expect me to be back soon. Anyway, what can they do? Best to ring in.

I try Gerry, and a French voice says something I don't understand. I try again… same thing, and a third time. I can't reach him, so there's nothing more that can be done for now.

I ring Dad's house, and his voice is a little cagey. I hear someone offering him tea. It's a woman's voice.

"Who's that?" I ask.

"Just a friend. No one you know. Katy's late home… she's on the school radio. She wants you to call in most evenings if you can. I'll tell her you've rung." The call is unusually brief.

I try Gerry once more, there's no answer. He can ring me if he's bothered.

The inevitable nit picking from living in such a small space is forgotten as we walk across the plank to terra firma. Extra-clean Spike walks tall, and we hope they will accommodate him at the restaurant.

In the half-light, I stop and lean on the bridge, watching the river run underneath. It's so peaceful. Alan comes to join me. His aftershave wafts around, aggravating my nose and throat. The chances are we will stay outside long enough for it to wear off. Cheap stuff doesn't usually hang around.

"Look, Nat," Alan whispers, moving closer, "how about you and me… you know? I've lost my wife; you're lost… we could find each other." He stops to wipe spit off his lips.

"No, no, and definitely no," I state with a smile.

"I've got five weeks. Don't miss the opportunity."

"Five weeks?"

"Yea, before the footy season. Since my wife left I've made it a rule not to give promises to women I can't keep. In future there will be no women during the season, unless they happen to be a Millwall fan."

"Tempting offer, Alan… but still no."

"That's a shame."

"I'm sure a Millwall fan is waiting for you somewhere."

Pete and Sarah have gone ahead, enjoying time without Alan and me. I catch up before they reach the town.

"Do you think Alan fancies Nat?" Pete is asking. I fall back a pace.

"Of course he does, Pete. He fancies almost anyone, but not a hope."

"My brother's not that bad, is he?"

"Yes, he is. Come on. Let's get to the Chinese."

We go for the buffet meals; help yourself to anything you like and pay a set amount. Two hours later – with bloated stomachs full of fried rice, sweet and sour pork and banana fritters all washed down with mediocre French beer – we leave, clutching our fortune cookies wrapped in crinkly silver and gold paper. Spike was happy to be quiet under the table and to avoid the large dog in the opposite corner.

The walk back is slow. We stop with a small crowd gathered on the bridge, they are watching a family of otters playing on the mudbank below. The half-lit cathedral is magical; streetlights and the moon are casting subdued shadows around.

We sit by the boat on the grass, quietened by the beauty of our surroundings. The muffled sound of party revellers upriver can just be heard. The rustling of foil paper begins before we crunch into our fortune cookies and read the messages inside.

"*Blue is your colour,*" Pete reads, unexcited.

"Blue for a boy," Sarah points out, then reads her own, "*This is your lucky year.*" I think she pats her abdomen. "Come on, Nat. What's yours?"

"*This is your year for travel*. Alan, you're next." I pass the verbal baton.

There's a glint I've seen before is in his eye when he looks at me. "*Tonight's the night*," he reads out.

"Not with me it's not." My voice rises with nerves. I leave their company to phone Gerry again, and get ready to turn in.

Sarah picks up Alan's screwed-up fortune and reads aloud, "*Slay your dragons*."

"Ah, well. I tried. There are plenty more babes out there just waiting for me. I'll leave you two lovebirds. I fancy a walk."

When Alan is out of range the two of them talk. "Does your brother have redeeming features?" Sarah asks.

"Yes. He's honest; no pretence."

"What happens if our child turns out like Al and not you?"

"We'd all love it. That's life. Time to turn in. Do you really think Al fancies Nat?"

"Of course he does, but she's happily married," Sarah replies.

I'm reassured that Sarah has understood, but wonder if I should really be listening.

"But?" Pete sounds hopeful.

"But nothing. Come on. Let's go back on board," Sarah replies.

"We'll leave the plank across for Al. Underneath his bravado he's lonely." Pete has a caring tone.

I find my magazine and prop myself up with pillows to read, aware that Sarah and Pete have gone quiet. It isn't difficult to enjoy the moment and not contemplate what might lie ahead. Hints of lavender emerge from my cushion and I find the scent relaxing. It must have had a rural existence. What will it smell of after being in 33A Market Street, Eastleigh?

I must remember to ring Katy tomorrow when she's on air. All this media stuff might give her false hopes of what her career might be, but I don't know what else to suggest. I can hardly recommend she becomes a bingo caller like me, or manages a sports shop like her dad. Most young employees working for Gerry have degrees and are hoping for something better to come along. Journalism is not likely to be the job she imagines, but she's young enough to dream.

Alan has got under my skin. Not the person he is but the little boy he was, going to the football match with his dad. There it is again, the welling-up of tears. I hold Spike close, burying my nose in his clean-smelling coat as he catches my tears.

I had a little boy. He was born three years after Katy. Three weeks after his birth he was gone. We didn't talk about it – just locked it up and pulled together, making life work in a superficial way. We could never forget, but talking wouldn't bring him back. Even worse, we knew there wouldn't be any more children. When death came again with Mum we were frightened of revisiting the loss of our child and were determined to stay focused on the present.

Dad wanted a grandson, Gerry wanted a son – and although I knew it wasn't my fault, I felt I had let them down. *No right to let myself go and enjoy life* is a thought that has stayed with me. Illogical, but I've never been able to shake the feeling off.

I couldn't console Gerry; he couldn't console me. With our needs unfulfilled we went for emotional burial. The only photograph of my baby is tucked away in my purse. Rarely do I look at it, but I always know it's there. The need to hold the photo is explosive. I clamber over the bed, kneel by the little window, and look across the river at the cathedral. I hold the photo close. Only three weeks… but he had still been mine. My crying has brought with it a release of emotion.

I will sleep better tonight than I have slept for years. I've made a resolution to talk about my son whenever I want to. Other people will have to deal with their own discomforts.

Katy was hurt, too. She was just three when he was born and couldn't understand where the baby had gone. In time, she forgot, and I didn't want her burdened by the thoughts and emotions of grown-ups. Maybe that's why I'm not happy about her having boyfriends. Is it the threat of loss again?

One day, not so far away, Katy will spread her wings and go. The trip to Japan has shown me that. When she came home with her letter from school, I wanted to say "No". Then I realised I was wrong; she needed to be allowed to grow up.

I think of Alan, a small boy holding his dad's hand and going to a football match. I want to hold Gerry and make him feel better, but I can't.

I have tried to talk to him but he looks confused and cuts me out. There are compensations, my job for instance; all the people who come to play bingo. Hidden under the cards, under their clothes, in bags and beyond empty chairs is loss and sadness. The bright lights, the familiarity, the friendships formed all make their lives a little happier. Caring for people is part of being a bingo caller that's difficult to explain. Targets and tick boxes ignore this side of life. The other week we were sent a big bundle of forms asking contestants to fill in their views and opinions, and to rate the staff. For now, they're on a shelf in Harry's cubicle, gathering dust.

I wonder how Joan Littleton and Harry are. What about Frank since his wife died, and how is Mary's arthritis and her diabetic eye problem? I hope the bingo caller, who's doing my shifts while I'm away, looks after them. They need their usual chairs in the same place and a fuss made of them when they win.

Harry fixes broken light bulbs and does the odd spot of painting to keep the place cheerful. Our group of regular contestants would be a burden to the state if it wasn't for bingo. The clatter of churning coloured ping-pong balls should go on forever.

Profit is what it's really about. That's why we had a meeting and came up with the idea of a young ones' night. At first we wondered if they would come. When they did come they treated it as a joke in front of their friends, but then became regulars and brought along others. It was the same system at a younger level, except their needs aren't hidden. If they are upset they cry in front of you; if they are happy they laugh out loud. The girls chase the boys and the boys chat up the girls, and money goes into the owner's bank account.

They wanted to change another night to bring the under twenty-fives and the older contestants together but were persuaded by the staff not to, with the reasoning that older people liked a bit of space and young people liked to be packed in like sardines. There are afternoons for mums and babies – but that is not my shift – and I don't want it, anyway. The good thing about the mums-and-babies afternoon, and the under twenty-fives night, is that they will be the bingo contestants for the future.

When Theresa died, aged eighty-six, she wanted her ashes buried inside the bingo hall. We couldn't organise that, so we planted a cherry tree on the small patch of grass outside and buried her ashes underneath. A plaque reads:

In memory of Theresa Southwick, who played bingo in this hall for seventeen years.

The water is rippling and playing with the reflections of the lights. Before going to sleep we have agreed to meet on deck and share a brandy – theirs, of course. *Money down the drain*, I recall. I relive the rich smell of cognac flowing down the rain gully and on to the river. The air is heavily perfumed with oleanders and feels warm. The odd dog walker passes by and can see us in our pyjamas raising our glass to whoever cares to notice.

Alan returns from his walk in a melancholic mood. He drinks three brandies quickly and that makes him worse. I suspect the loss of his wife goes deeper than he wants to let on; it was only a couple of months ago.

Jealousy rises in me as he uses Spike as a comfort blanket. I wait a few moments before saying I'm tired and taking my lovable dog off to bed.

Spike is nine and I want him to live for a long time yet: *Please, God, don't let him catch rabies or any other nasty dog thing. Keep him safe.* God didn't keep my son safe, so why should he look after a dog? But the whole God thing was never logical to me.

I throw a bunch of wilted wild flowers out of my window and watch as they drift down stream. The wind is picking up, cooling the bedroom. It's time to slide the window across.

My chopped-off jeans are drying on a hanger suspended from the door hook. Washing takes up valuable space and there are no launderettes within easy walking distance.

I'm not keen on returning to Cognac and finding my way to Normandy and Rouen. It's not only about directions but it's also about one-way streets and roundabouts, all on the wrong side of the road.

I've missed a call from Gerry. I quickly call back. "Hi. Sorry I… "

"Where the hell have you been? You're behaving like some irresponsible child. All you have to do is ring me or answer the phone."

I think of my flowers drifting down river and wonder, *where will they end up?*

5

Return to Cognac

I dream of being chased, then I spread my wings and fly away. A call for breakfast is a welcome break from the mixed-up blankets caused by the turmoil in my brain.

Sarah busies herself in the galley, where steam rises from bowls of hot chocolate – and the smell of sticky French pastries is a comforting pleasure. I'm still in my dressing gown, forgetting that in France you get going early and rest after lunch.

I grab my jeans to iron, using towels on the draining area. A small ironing board is tucked away under the bed where Alan sleeps, and I don't want to venture in there.

Spike and I add to the chaos in the galley. We collect our breakfast and find room on the seats at the helm. I can't sip my frothy chocolate without first wrapping my hands around the drinking bowl for warmth and smelling the milkiness. Flakes from my pastry fall on the floor for Spike to lick up. Alan comes my way, swearing because his *pain aux raisin* has broken off in his chocolate. He hates drinking from a bowl like the French, and how the hell does he know if he's meant to be eating or drinking?

I throw more crispy crumbs for Spike.

"I'll catch those." Alan reaches his hand out in the direction of my breasts; he is too close for comfort. I knock him away, threatening him with a green plastic fly swat.

"Coming to market, Nat?" Sarah is ready, with her traditional round French basket. "Leave Spike. He'll be happy with the men and he won't get jostled in the queues."

Alan takes charge of Spike. I know he'll be all right because whatever else Alan is he's a dog-loving person at heart, and that's a big redeeming feature.

Sarah and I join the brigade of French women going uphill to the market. At the stalls we taste cheeses and buy baguettes and lots of salad and fresh fish. The fish counter has specimens we don't recognise, including large fish with their open mouths, resting whole on the slab, ready to be chopped up. Crabs are still alive and no doubt confused; eels slither around each other.

The fishmonger raises his chopper and removes an eel's head before popping the wriggling body in a plastic bag for a happy customer. We buy melon and fresh ginger from the fruit stall and, finally, large red tomatoes that smell freshly picked. I'm tempted by bags of walnuts, cured meats and honey, but there's only so much room on board and a limit to what we can eat. What will Spike think of French dog food? I'm sure it's much the same as home, and he has to eat more than just our scraps.

We plan to enjoy the cafe culture. The *pharmacie* offers one-hour photo developing so I leave my film as we pass. We're spoilt for choice of where to have a coffee, and decide on a small café with a bar and an awning that was once bright red and flaps above the tables on the pavement.

Everyone introduces themselves and is kissed, including us. I marvel at their ease of greeting. We find a table inside.

"*Deux cafés, s'il vous plaît.*" Sarah sighs as she releases the basket to the floor.

"*Café au lait? Un express?*" asks the bar man.

"*Deux cafés au lait, s'il vous plait.*" On goes the ritual of ordering coffee. We've adjusted ourselves between the shopping and chairs when the ritual starts again.

"*Bonjour, Mesdames,*" … kiss, kiss. At this rate our coffee will be cold before we get to it.

Those sitting inside are regarded as locals and outside you manage to avoid most of the kissing. We bundle our shopping out to a pavement table, giving us more chance to chat and watch the market even if we are in full sun.

"I've never done anything like this before. I've been waiting for Gerry to want to come with me on holidays to Europe, but he's always too busy with his cycling and work," I say.

"I'd have said you were happily married."

"Oh, I am. I am… but I'd like us to do things together sometimes. I go to Cornwall with Dad and Katy; Gerry goes away cycling with his mates. There's no time or money left for another holiday. I hope we can manage a few days away before his leg is completely better. We went to the Isle of Wight for our honeymoon and then to the Costa del Sol four years ago, but nowhere else."

"How many years have you been married? Sorry, not my business. Pete is great, but his brother…" Sarah sips the last of her coffee. "We should be getting back."

A text from Alex arrives.

Hi. How you doing? When I gave him my email I inadvertently added my mobile number.

Fine, thanks, is my simple reply.

Just checking.

It's time to collect my photos and a new film from the *pharmacie*. I'm handed an envelope with twenty-four shiny photos. Digital isn't the same. Putting them in my bag for later gives me a pang of excitement. I've taken twenty-two photos on this trip already.

I fiddle around fixing a film in the camera before leaving the shop. I walk past the shiny new cameras in the window, but decide to think about cash flow before buying one. It's time to dash to the boat and help get underway before the men start complaining.

There's little available space in the galley to store our lunch and supper, but we cram it in. Alan reaches across and grabs a beer. Sarah takes it back, making sure he waits until lunch. She's right to monitor drinking on board. Spike joins in. He thinks they're fighting, and nips Alan's ankle.

"Hope you've had that thing vaccinated against rabies," he says, nudging him away with his foot.

Thing? Admittedly, he's angry at having his ankle nipped (not bitten). How dare he call Spike *Thing?*

Pete casts off on his own, showing a demeanor designed to shed guilt. Spike is banished to the bedroom while Sarah washes and dresses Alan's small wound.

"Anyone want to see my photos? Maybe I should check them first." I quickly flick through them; there are three of kingfishers, and several of us, mainly being idiots. There are two of Gary Blain and one of his dog Whitey. One is of Alex (back view) filming. Two are from home; Dad and Katy by the front door, plus one of Gerry with his arm around Lisa and me in the back garden. The rest are of Paris and odd shots from the boat at Saintes. I like the ones I've taken of French people going about their daily business.

Studies of everyday events and people that catch my eye fill my photo albums, but they only interest me. I love taking pictures that make me think about the subjects and who they are.

"Hey, they're good," Pete calls from above us. "You bring something special out in your subjects."

"They'd be better if she had a decent camera. Why haven't you gone digital? Only morons use film these days." Alan rubs his wet nose with the back of his hand.

"We've got one, but Gerry's taken it cycling. Can't afford another one."

"Course you can. Plastic." Alan takes a handful of credit cards from his back pocket and waves them in the air.

"No credit cards. Never wanted one. What isn't in the account doesn't get spent," I say firmly.

"Boring. Everyone that comes into our shop uses one. How would people buy TVs, CD players and all that stuff? I'd be out of a job if they were all like you."

"So you can help me choose a camera, then? I've been thinking of doing a photography course. Art is always interesting, and I can paint reasonably well. Photos... they're something else. I buy books from charity shops with old photos of film stars or famous photographers' best collections... I've got books and books of pictures."

Alan gives a minor yawn but I plough on, listening to my own voice.

"I used them for ideas for art. Then I started asking myself, *Why don't I try and take excellent photos?*" Sarah and Pete are still listening. "I can take good pictures with my camera. It has a reasonable lens, but digital would help a lot."

"I'll help you sort something out." We are on common ground until his next remark.

"You can take photos of me. I look my best naked. That reminds me... need a leak."

"Not there," Sarah shouts.

"Too late." An arc of steaming wee goes over the bow.

"Nature's nature." Alan pulls up his zip as if he's with a bunch of blokes. "Ha, ha… That your mobile?" He points towards my hand then takes a closer look. "Haven't seen one like this in years."

"He doesn't mean to be offensive. It's his way," Pete says, raising an eyebrow.

"Don't worry, Pete. He doesn't bother me." It's only two days together, I don't think he'll upset me. I'm enjoying myself too much to take much notice of what he says.

It's time for some personal space at the back of the boat. The sunbed tempts me and Sarah wants to apologise for Alan. She brings me a glass of cool white wine and a glossy magazine to read.

Two seconds later Alan's head pops round the galley door, "How come she can have a drink and I can't?"

"Go away," Sarah orders.

The not-so-cool ringtone comes from my bag, where I hid it from Alan and his sarcastic remarks.

"Ringtone?" Alan gives a slight sneer. "You need a better sound. Here, I'll fix it."

"Later, thanks." My phone rings again.

"Hi, Nat." It's good to hear Gerry's voice.

"How are you?" I ask.

"I've got a wee infection. Drinking buckets of water. Stephan's in charge. I can't leave yet. Could you come and get my bike? Take it home and get the insurers to look at it. You must be bored by now. Chester will come and help you if you're worried about getting back, and then he'll get me if you come for the bike."

The cool sparkling wine refreshes me. A single black cow moos loudly from the water's edge, where she is trampling her hooves.

"We agree, then. The answer is no to Gerry and no to Chester." I raise my glass to the cow.

"Stop mumbling, Nat. I can't hear you."

"I'll be in Cognac tonight and leave for Normandy tomorrow, and I hope the roads are easy to follow. A day's driving. I'll be there late afternoon. Drink lots. Love you. Bye."

"Nat, your turn. We boys are chillin'." Alan sits in a deckchair, firmly holding a beer, and I adjust myself at the helm.

It's easy to navigate and stay right as instructed. No other boats are on the river, but there are lots of birds and a myriad of tiny flies to watch. Butterflies are out drinking from the riverbank foliage and warming themselves, perched on the wild flowers and grasses.

It's twenty minutes before a boat like ours approaches from the opposite direction. Someone is sitting on a deckchair on their roof space – the space where our bikes are stored.

Pete and Sarah's muffled voices are coming from the back of the boat. By the wheel is the river guide. It shows twists and turns, how close to the bank you can go and where the official mooring places are. Icons for locks and water taps are easy to recognise.

I'm ready to wave at another holiday boat approaching from the opposite side when a day-tripper large enough for thirty passengers, appears round the far bend. All is well, but I know to be careful.

Silt by the banks is marked in the guide and with red and white buoys on the water. Willow trees dip their branches, and I watch as the other holiday boat goes dangerously close to the edge.

Relaxing in a deckchair on the top deck, an elderly lady reads her book. Her grey hair pops out from under her sun hat. Her book is absorbing her every thought.

There isn't a way of communicating a warning across twenty-five metres of water. The boat brushes under the willow's tentacles, and the lady with her book – deckchair and all – are gathered in its clutches. The boat carries on unaware.

With the throttle out, I turn the wheel hard. The engine drags itself up to the most knots possible and we cut across. By this time, my heart is trying to get out of my chest. The day-tripper is catching up. They have timetables to keep to so they blast their horn, ignoring the unfolding drama.

Pete is first at the helm.

"Nat, what the bloody hell are you doing?" He tries to grab the wheel. I hold on tighter and yell in the direction of the tree and the disappearing holiday boat.

We have escaped injury and are on the other side of the river. The day-tripper goes by and no one is waving. Ladies clutch their handbags and the men look hard down on me. Anything I try to say is lost in a rush of wind and the sound of the wash. We are uncomfortably close.

Sarah looks as if I have let her and all of womanhood down. Alan hates having his alcohol-induced nap disturbed. The right words won't come out and I can't see her anywhere. I point and point at the floating white hat sinking under the weight of wet false flowers.

"She nearly killed us for a hat. I thought you were more intelligent than that, Nat." Safety is Pete's priority.

"Sarah, there was an old lady," I shout.

"Where?"

"In that tree." I'm pointing at the ripples in the water and the deckchair hanging under the branches.

"In you go," Sarah, says, pushing at Alan and Pete. They both look at me for a get-out clause, but instead I help to push them over the edge of the boat. They are not sure of my sanity.

The men have kicked off their sandals and abandoned them on the deck. The water is cold on their previously warm bodies, making them shudder; they're probably exaggerating. Two skinny black snakes were swimming in a lock earlier today. I scour the water, not knowing what I'd do if I saw water snakes close to them. The spindly old lady is rescued, covered in willow twigs and leaves. She looks bemused.

The men push and Sarah pulls the dripping individual on board. I fill a bucket with warm water for her feet and find a big towel to wrap her in. The boat is drifting until Pete takes the helm.

I help take off her wet attire and note the German labels. We have no German language between us and I suspect she has no English.

Soaking wet, Alan stands back and pulls at the debris on his T-shirt.

"So… now what do we do with her?" He holds up his arms, flailing them around.

Her boat has carried on at a reasonable speed, leaving us to mull over the options as we watch her tucking in to tea and cake but saying nothing.

"We should take her to Cognac and drop her off at the boat company. That's a fair suggestion. If we try to catch up we could be going in the wrong direction all day, and who knows when they will discover she's missing?" Pete is eager to shower, change and get underway.

"How about the lost property office in Cognac?" I suggest.

"That's miles from here. I vote we take her back by that tree and leave her there. Take her with us, and it's like stealing someone." Alan adds he has better things to do with his time than look after *her*.

"What if they don't come back right away, Alan?" Sarah asks.

"Let's vote." Alan is planning abandonment.

"Al, she's with us. We'll decide what to do when we get to Cognac," Sarah says, and takes the helm. Pete hands around another plate of buttered toast and yet more tea. Our new guest manages to take a large handful.

"Where's mine? Should have left her." Alan screws up the empty loaf bag and kicks it at the bin.

"Let's get off to Cognac. Chill and enjoy the rest of the day." Pete goes to the shower and Sarah takes the boat upstream. I boil the kettle for more tea and plan a pleasant evening. The warmth on our skin is heaven for Brits. The dull insect hum and the rhythm of the engine relaxes our minds and we watch herons fishing, unbothered by the fuss. Now there are five of us boating on to Cognac.

A ringtone I don't recognise plays a couple of times.

"Yours," Alan points out.

"Katy, how are you?" I ask.

"What do I do with a white potted chrysanthemum? Joan Littleton came round. They collected for you at bingo. She didn't know if you were dead or just sick, and chrysanthemums do nicely for either. She needs new slippers, the ones she's wearing have tatty flowers on and they're frayed."

"Your dad is getting over a wee infection and has to practise walking, so there's no rush as long as you and Gramps are OK."

"Dad's bored. He wants you to be there, so why don't you go?"

"I need more map-reading time. I'll be in Rouen tomorrow. Spike is having a great time and we have a funny little old German lady with us. She was lost overboard."

I look at the vulnerable human being sitting opposite, and my heart reaches out to her beyond language. I give her a hug and hold her head to my chest.

"You're another lost soul. How many more lost women are there in the world?" I say to her. Her body is thin and bony. She looks at me with her big blue eyes but I can't pick up what she's feeling.

"Mum, you're getting faint."

"Sorry, darling. I'll ring again from Cognac. Very happy with your success on the school radio. Well done."

Alan stares at me with my arm around our newly adopted guest.

"Oh, God," he mutters and continues with his daily routine of mopping the deck. "Mind the shoes out of my way. No point moaning at me when they get wet."

"We'll reach Cognac and moor within the hour," Pete announces.

We approach the shelter of the bridge and throw the ropes ashore. I'm sad my trip has ended.

"Nat, your car needs moving." Pete is staring at my Fiat parked near the wall of a tall building. It's at an angle, slightly sticking out towards the narrow road. With a small diversion, even larger vehicles can get past. It's been that way for a couple of days so there's no need to move it now.

The car and Spike are my contacts with home and I don't take to any critical mention of them. Emotions regarding family are never far away.

Sarah wants to go to town and look for a restaurant in the square at the top of the hill.

Alan jabs his finger at our adopted lady, "What we gonna do with Brunhilda there?"

Pete jumps ashore to secure the ropes. Sarah finds a warm cardigan for our guest.

"You're going to carry her, Al. She's only bird weight. She'd be too slow walking," Pete states.

"Where's lost property?" Alan scours the area.

"Shut up," we say in unison.

While we all get changed, Sarah assists the old lady to the indoor seating area where she'll be safe. Her hand slips out and she fills it with biscuits as she passes the worktop.

With five of us – and a dog – the galley area, which doubles as a corridor, becomes extra busy. The result of washing and changing has rendered us presentable. Even Alan has made an effort, but the blue and white theme of Millwall is never far away.

My trainers constantly stick to the floor as yet more brandy seeps out from the soles. A wash hasn't solved the problem, but at least I can't smell the hum of alcohol. Gerry will be disappointed when I tell him how I watched the liquid trickle away.

Sarah's yellow cardy is wrapped around our old lady and she makes no effort to stand. Alan crosses the plank, deliberately looking into the distance. We file off and *she* remains stubbornly on board. We shuffle in silence and look at Alan. Finally, he gives in and whips her up in his arms. She grips his neck and we stride up the bank to cross the bridge.

Stopping to watch the river flow is irresistible. I lean on the bridge and drift in thought. Lots of little streams have fed this river for thousands of years. Ghosts of times past are walking the banks and a rusty pram rests on the bottom, growing river weed. I'm hungry, and think of the thousands of people who have picnicked here with their wine and cheeses.

The boat belonging to the German crew interrupts my thoughts. It pulls alongside the quay, and they throw their ropes ashore.

"No one cares about my aching arms," Alan complains. He's right, I was taking no notice of him waiting and carrying another person. He follows my line of vision, "That's her boat." I point.

Alan finds a rare burst of high energy. "Ahoy there… ahoy there," Alan shouts, gesticulating while balancing the old lady on the wall next to me. He grabs her up and is away, starting at a slow trot that develops into a jog as he descends the bank. He's bouncing his load all over the place and is in danger of slipping.

An angry middle-aged woman wearing shorts and an apron, is on her way towards him, threatening him with her mop. Spike growls, so I put him on his lead; at least he feels he belongs with Alan. The mop and abuse change direction towards her husband. Alan is about a hundred metres away from the boat when the old lady shouts, "Halt… halt." He's unable to stop quickly. She sticks her nails hard into his neck and he drops her. Undeterred she jumps up, shakes Sarah's cardigan off and runs into the arms of her daughter.

Alan hurries back up the bank.

"There's gratitude for you. I told you we should have left her. No one listens to me." He refuses to see the funny side. With suppressed laughter, we walk up the cobbled street to look for an outside table at a restaurant where we can enjoy the balmy evening atmosphere.

"Here, have this back." Alan throws Sarah her cardigan. "I'm havin' no more lost people on our way to Angoulême. I'm done with 'em. D'ya hear me?" I receive a hard stare as he rubs at the scratches inflicted on his neck.

"Where's it to be, then?" Pete says, standing back. We survey the restaurants lining the pavement. The one on the corner has smart white tablecloths and leather menu holders. The clean, cream sun umbrellas are about to be taken down for the evening. Alan and Pete rattle the coins in their pockets and look around for cheaper options.

"What do you say if I pay for drinks? A thank-you for the last couple of days. It's been brilliant; it really has."

The decision is made. We're ushered to our seats and I drift my hand over the starched white cloth before sitting down. The waiter flicks his lighter and ignites our candle. We study the wine list and menu in quiet appreciation.

"May I take your order?" He certainly can. "Wine? Red or white?"

"A bottle of each, please. We'll take your house wine." I hear a new confidence in my own voice. Spike spreads himself across my feet, waiting for what food might come his way.

Tonight I must find a bed and breakfast place, close to where my car is parked, and prepare for tomorrow. I look around to reassure myself that Chester is not going to turn up and spoil things. He is nowhere, of course. I take a long cool swallow of white wine.

A man of small stature is leaning against the barrier that divides us from the restaurant next door. I recognise his denim jacket with the Liverpool badge. Encouraged by my staring, he picks up his guitar and sidles across towards our table.

He plays and sings, '*I thank the stars that sent you from heaven. You make my night bright, and I love you… yes, I love you.*' I receive a special smile.

We clap our serenading busker as supper arrives. I remember this man, he was by the riverside when I first arrived in Cognac. He has been singing his way around town for the last couple of days.

"Where are you from?" Pete makes small talk.

"Liverpool," is the reply.

"He's not joining us," mutters Alan.

Sarah and I give the man a few coins. I think his wrinkles disguise his once good looks. He drifts off to find another audience.

"Sad." Sarah picks out a large prawn from her starter, catching the garlic butter sauce on her serviette.

"What is?" Pete asks.

"He's a drifter," Sarah explains.

Our fillet steaks and side salad with French fries are brought to the table. Our fish knives are exchanged for steak knives and our first mouthfuls of succulent steak taken. We help ourselves to crisp French bread and start on the red wine.

When Alan has eaten enough to stop for a second he points his knife in my direction.

"She's a drifter. Not a sad case yet, but probably will be. I can see you as a bag lady."

The wine is making me bold… or stupid. It's a glorious moment. Alan's fork is a centimetre away from his plate when I whisk the remains of his steak away.

"Spike, attack. Eat." Spike pounces on his supper as it hits the ground.

"Give it back," Alan orders.

"Willingly." I steal it back from Spike and return it to Alan's plate, covered in grit. "You have it," I say.

"No, you have it," ensues from Alan.

The waiter is heading in our direction. With the shame of naughty schoolchildren, we sit on our hands. Pete and Sarah are not amused.

"*Un problème?*" the waiter politely asks. He picks up Alan's plate and shortly returns with a clean one and a freshly-charred, small steak. We behave ourselves until the end of the meal and I slow down on the wine.

Time is ticking and there are things to be sorted out. The waiter recommends a place I can stay; it's a small B & B belonging to his friend not far from where my car is parked. There's a time to go, and this is it.

"See you at home, maybe? I hope you can come to my party. I'd like that… here are the details. Loved the boat trip." I leave them to their after-supper cognac and pay my share of the bill. I turn several times as I walk away and raise my hand. With Spike on the lead I cross the bridge, glancing at the lights and the river.

Behind an old wooden door I find solace in a smart but small B & B. My ringtone sounds; it's Big Ben chiming. How many more options are there?

"You haven't been kidnapped, then?" Dad says. I should have checked in more often and I'm not making enough effort to be on the right road home. He could be right.

"Matt is getting the hang of chess." I imagine Dad has fixed Matt to a chair explaining kings, queens and knights. At least he's keeping him away from upstairs and Katy.

"Is Katy doing her homework?"

"She's looking up Japan on the computer. We're fine. Just worry about yourself. I'll book up Cornwall. You'll need a holiday when you get back. Your mother was always getting lost towards the end. The last time she drove a car two policemen brought her home."

Katy takes the phone, "Mum, your story's going down a bomb. Ring when we're on air again. The whole school is staying late tomorrow, when I set up another phone-in with the lost mother. I didn't tell them it was my mum. Hope they don't work it out."

"Thanks, Katy. Look after yourself and Gramps. Love you. Bye."

I miss the boat, but not the tiny shower, awkward toilet and small bed. It's great standing under hot water and using lots of sweet-smelling soap without worrying about how much water I'm using. I climb into a double bed with clean white sheets and enjoy the after-effects of a good meal and French wine. Spike is at my feet and I try to figure out if he's enjoying himself. I decide he's OK as long as I'm looking after him and, in return, he gives me his loyalty and love.

Sarah phones to check if the bed and breakfast place is comfortable. "I forgot to ask... what was Alex texting about?"

"Just saying 'Hello'. I'm not interested, and he's out of my league."

"What does that mean?"

"I'm married and I'm not looking to change. He's better educated than me and he has an exciting life. Goodnight, and thanks again."

What do I know about Alex? Next to nothing, nor does he know anything about me. Because I'm away from Gerry, it doesn't mean I'm available.

The boat trip was fun, and so was talking to Alex.

6

John Goes to Lourdes

The café with a small bar, at the edge of the square, serves milky coffee and fluffy croissants. I sit under the trees outside, having breakfast at a badly marked and slightly wonky wooden table. The French are buying papers, having coffee and heading for work, all at a slow pace. The sun is up and a warm day is coming. I can go to the water's edge with Spike to observe the boats and buildings one last time before leaving.

My new friends have gone on to Angoulême. I feel bereft and alone again. I must focus on my own life and get things in order. It's important to ring Katy later and contribute to her radio programme.

The boat hired by the Germans has been vacated; workers are preparing it for the next crew of holidaymakers. My baggage is packed in the car and I stop to clear up any remaining shards of broken glass from the road and gully. The smell of cognac hangs around. It's the atmosphere of this place, as well as the dregs of my litre bottle.

I take a collection of rubbish over to the bin to find myself face to face with the busker from Liverpool.

"Hello," I blurt out. I'm not sure what to say or if he will remember me. "How's your day?"

"Oh… I'm off somewhere, as usual. How about you?"

"I need to get to Rouen Hospital to pick up my

husband. He may be there a couple more days but he'll be relieved to see me."

We part company and, faced with a wretched map, my brain leaps into turmoil. I arrived over the bridge so I will go back that way.

Just try and relax, I think, breathing deeply, as if that will help. There's still time to discover the right direction.

The Fiat has acquired a nasty scratch on the passenger side while I've been away. It will make Gerry angry, he's sensitive to carelessness. I need to stop worrying, as it doesn't oil any direction cogs in my brain. The truth is, I've enjoyed being lost so far, and it's only at times like this that I feel scared, and panic. A large bug is zooming around inside the car, bumping into the back window then bashing around in the front; everywhere but out of the half-open window. It catches in my hair before flying outside of its own accord and I'm hugely relieved.

I drive across the bridge and up the hill. In the distance, the busker is thumbing a lift. He seems harmless enough, and maybe I could help him on his way. What if he can read maps? It takes a couple of seconds from me pulling up beside the curb to him jumping in.

He straightens his guitar and bag on the back seat and sits in front. "Thanks," is all he says. I can smell cigarette smoke on him like on Harry.

"Can you read maps?" I ask.

"I was a pizza delivery man once and had to find my way around Liverpool. I always have a rough idea of where I am without a map." *Typical man,* I think.

"I'm not sure how much Liverpool counts, but my rough idea of where I am is usually where I'm not." While talking, I concentrate on the traffic. "I'm Natalie. Where are you going?" I console myself with the thought that so far I've not caused any major accidents.

The busker glances up at a large poster of Mother Mary and baby Jesus on the roundabout.

"How about Lourdes? But I'll go where you're going."

"Lourdes. Is that far?" I ask.

"Don't think so, but I've never been. What about you?"

His lack of concern is infectious. One day extra and I can make Rouen by the time Gerry needs me. France doesn't look too tricky on my new European map. I'm never that far away from Normandy – and Normandy is just across the channel from Portsmouth, Eastleigh and home. As long as I keep this picture in my head then I will make it to Rouen in a day or two. I feel good.

"What's your name?"

"John Lennon."

"Why Lourdes?" The John Lennon thing irks me and I question his state of mind, but he has a pleasant disposition.

"The sign." He points up to Mother Mary. He's a bit odd, but clean. My mother had gone on about Lourdes and going there to get healed. Dad had sniffed at the idea and then, along with most things, she forgot.

You have to be adventurous and give some things a go, my heart voice is saying. I drive towards Lourdes, wondering if we will end up there or somewhere else. For a man who says he is John Lennon, or for me, it really doesn't matter that much today.

"What direction do you think we are going in? Do you know?"

"South. Look where the sun is at this time of day."

I'm impressed. He settles down behind his old trilby hat and leaves me to it. The sign for Bordeaux comes along

– and that must be OK as that was where I thought I was going when I ended up in Cognac. Not too sure where to go from there, but with the sun in the right place and no clouds it will be all right as long as my companion stays awake.

Gerry won't want me to turn up with a busker, so plans are needed for dropping him off. Lourdes will be a good place to part company, and he can give me directions according to the planets.

Bordeaux is a mix-up of roads with loads of traffic, even Gerry couldn't find his way around here with ease. I wake John and, trying not to look as if I'm pleading, as I hand him the map and point at many confusing signs along the road. Spike is quietly curled up on the back seat behind John's guitar. He's comfortable with our companion, and I believe he would detect it and tell me if anything was wrong.

A black limousine – part of a cavalcade, with escort cars and motorcycles – drives past. A Union Jack flies from the front of the sizeable car bonnet and I'm fascinated.

"Follow that," John breathes, pointing close to the windscreen.

I manage to jump the car into a gap between motorcycles and cars. Now we can rush along as part of the entourage. "We must be pilgrims," I say, thinking of Lourdes. Mum taught me about Chaucer's *The Canterbury Tales* and the pilgrims. When the book was read on the radio, we laughed together at the bawdy characters, but I don't know much about modern-day pilgrims.

"Who do you think a pilgrim is, John?"

"They think a lot, say prayers and go to places like Lourdes, looking for something to keep their lives on track.

I drift around Europe and I sing songs. I meditate a lot, but I've not caught up with praying. I'm not sure if any of that counts."

"If you know any hymns or have a direct line to God, now might be a good time to ask if we're going the right way."

John starts to sing, "*Love makes the world a happy place. Love unites the whole human race. Let's get together and celebrate… Celebrate a world of love*"

"That's not a hymn."

"It is to me. '*Celebrate a world of love. Love makes the world a happy place*,'" he continues.

"You're right. It does sound like a hymn." I join in, "'*Celebrate a world of love. Love makes the world a happy place. Love unites the whole human race*.'"

The Fiat rocks with our animation but the motorcycle police are tired of us. We do as directed and fall back, still with no idea who might be in the limousine with blacked-out windows.

We drive up gradients into mountainous terrain and find a roadside cafe to buy baguettes. John is vegetarian and enjoys his with salad and cheese. For me, I have cold chicken and coleslaw washed down with a bottle of *pamplemousse* juice. We stand to eat, as there are no chairs. It's difficult getting my teeth into the crusty French bread without dropping the filling out, but I struggle on.

In the bottom of my bag is the mint chocolate I kept from last night's supper. It's enough sugary taste to finish my meal. Spike has his biscuits and I give him a drink. There's no time or the desire to hang around for long. Doubts about what I'm doing enter my head – but so does excitement, in equal measure.

The wheels are turning again and soon we are behind the cavalcade with the UK flag.

Now and again we strike up a song, '*Mary mine. Life of love. Warmth of cloves, and sweet tamarind. Mary mine…* '

Signs with religious symbols have become more frequent. The cavalcade turns ahead of us and is escorted to the far side of the parking area. We find our own space and check the surroundings.

This is a strange place when seeing it for the first time. Carers are pushing sick people in wheelchairs and on stretchers with trollies. Hundreds of tourists and pilgrims are walking about. On that basis, there must be some good reason for being here.

John and I go our separate ways and arrange to meet up before we leave on our own personal journeys starting tomorrow.

"Bye then, John. See you around. If you can explain how to find directions from the sun and the moon it could prove useful to me."

I know that a long time ago ships sailed around the world guided by the planets, but back then navigation was a man thing. As far as I'm concerned it still is, but I'm learning and will learn. My school took us to the Royal Observatory, Greenwich, and they must have thought it would make navigation clearer to us. We had lessons on longitude, which is still a meaningless word to me. I was bored and confused, and looked forward to the boat trip on the River Thames afterwards. Perhaps if I'd listened more I would be better at reading maps.

Gerry had been on the same trip to Greenwich two years before. He understood so much more than I did, and I've always looked up to him for his ability to absorb that kind of knowledge.

"Stars as well, if you like," John's voice calls to me as he walks away, "But that's only useful on a cloudless night. Thanks for the lift. Quite a place, this."

John's an interesting person and I wish I had had more time to get to know why he became a busker. He has a quiet efficiency at finding his way around or not worrying where he is. He's an amiable, capable man who chooses to live with no fixed address. I'm sorry our brief encounter is ending.

I stop to read about Saint Bernadette outside the grotto and walk past crutches hanging on walls. They're supposed to signify the healing of pilgrims who arrived using crutches, and left cured and walking unaided. Outside the cave entrance, where St Bernadette's vision of the Virgin Mary is said to have taken place, clusters of people are singing hymns and saying prayers. There are opportunities to splash yourself with spring water from taps or bathe with assistance. I just observe.

I look across to see John chatting to a priest under a Liverpool banner. This group of pilgrims is singing with gusto and devotion, *'Amazing Grace, how sweet the sound in a believer's ear. I once was lost but now I'm found…'* John catches sight of me and comes across. I cast a light-hearted remark. "Well, John, have you found yourself? Has your pilgrimage been worthwhile?"

"Yea, a bit. Father said I should stop calling myself John Lennon and use my real name."

Singing drowns our conversation so we move back to find space away from the main throng, where we can hear each other speak.

"My dad's name was Bush and my Christian name is George. No one had heard of President George Bush when I was born."

I try not to laugh – it could hurt him – but sometimes laughter just won't go away.

"Now you know why I call myself John Lennon."

"Come on. I'll treat you to supper." John is proving to be good company and I hope he will save me from eating alone.

"I'll sing for my supper. That's who I am and what I do. Thanks, anyway."

We drift apart again and I have the sense of being an extra in a film scene. The sick people don't look real. Their carers are dressed in white, all working hard to push them around for blessings and prayers. I want to find a quiet place where I can ring home, but the priest from Liverpool has spotted me. He reaches out his hand.

"Do you need help?"

"I'm lost and I want to stay that way for now. Thanks, anyway."

This isn't the place to find solitude and phone home, so I return to the car park and collect our things. Spike is ready to sleep and the local hotel where we will stay tonight will be better for him. If we don't mind sleeping in a basic room under a cross of Christ it will do.

Spike turns round and round on the end of the bed, trying to get comfortable; the room is spooking him. Finally, he sleeps with one ear raised, listening for any small sound.

My bags and clothes were security-checked at Reception. My passport was also checked and numerous questions were asked to satisfy them as to why I'm here.

"Are you alone?"

'No, I'm with John Lennon,' I wanted to say, but decide that remark wouldn't help. It might result in me getting registered in the psychiatric section.

I've promised to ring Katy on the radio. She's popping back to school especially to keep the lines open. Her enthusiasm is touching.

"We have our very own lost mother talking to us from somewhere in France. So where are you now? Have you any idea?"

"I'm in Lourdes."

"Lourdes… that's miles away from where you're supposed to be. Perhaps you'd like to tell our listeners what it's like there. While you're doing that I'll tot up how much this trip is costing."

How do you describe Lourdes to a load of school kids? I mull it over before clumsily starting.

"It's a very large churchy place of pilgrimage, with lots of tourists and sick people and sad people mingling. When it comes to religious souvenirs, you can buy almost anything made from plastic. There's a church in a big open square. It's like being on a film set, with lots of uniforms around for the helpers. I might go on the candlelit procession tonight; hundreds of people do." I don't think I've described it very well.

"Thank you for that interesting insight. Are you missing your family, and have you remembered that the rest of the money for your daughter's school trip to Japan is due? I have a message from your daughter, father and husband, 'They are struggling without you and wish you would learn how to read a map'. Goodbye for now, and thank you for being a part of our North End radio phone-in." Katy gives an emotional sniff in her tissues as she unplugs the radio for the night. Now we can have our own catch-up chat.

Katy tells me she's impressed with the feedback from

her on-air time, talking to me. Before broadcasting tonight, a keen reporter from the *Eastleigh Standard* had been to interview her. She imagined he was going to be dynamic and was disappointed to find he was overweight with nicotine-stained fingers. He leant too far forward on his chair when he asked questions.

"Do you think your mother is becoming a celebrity, or more of a joke?" He sniggered, and smiled at the same time. His reporter's nose had discovered the family connection.

"Sorry, Katy, but girls can't read maps. Now give me the story." He talked into a recording machine and made some notes, then took a photo of her at the radio station desk. I think he made Katy question whether journalism might be a dead end job.

I've begun to worry what kind of following the *Eastleigh Standard* is creating. It can only be a limited piece of column space on the back page and some publicity for the school radio.

Alone in my room I get into the God thing, it goes with the surroundings.

"Well, God, am I stupid? Guess you're not going to tell me. I get the feeling you think I'm not that bad." Speaking out loud leads into quiet meditation… wishing Gerry and I could have conversations that were more meaningful. We emotionally dance around each other, holding on to the pretence that our lives are too full to give us time to truly connect.

Supper is on my mind – and no way is Spike going to stay in this room on his own, so we go out to look for a takeaway together. We don't find John; presumably he has sung for his supper. I'm not sure if we will meet again.

What do people eat and drink on a pilgrimage and in a

holy place? Bread and cheese, with a glass of water, sounds right. I find a takeaway Margherita pizza, and it has to do. I watch as queues of people file in for a service in the basilica. However, it's not for me.

This is the time for choosing souvenirs and drifting in and out of the shops for tourists. The faces of people in this strange place – and their body language – are fascinating. I want to take photos, but I'm aware I might cause an intrusion into the pilgrims' private space and the reasons they have come here.

There are cameras for sale. It's time to buy a digital one and take photos of the buildings and crowded areas. Taking photos of sick people doesn't feel polite.

It's incredible what a digital camera can do, but I don't want to abandon my old film camera completely. Experimenting shows me how to take mini videos. Alan gave me good advice; I'm grateful to him for that.

It's a little thing, but I went ahead and bought the camera without referring to Gerry. I think it will surprise him, but not in a good way. He likes to be in control of income and outgoings.

The shiny red camera fits neatly in my hand. It has better technology than the one we bought for Gerry two years ago. There's still time to book for the winter term photography course. I hope I will know enough not to look dumb in class. Gerry will be happy as long as I keep some money coming in, and run the home.

It isn't like the flamenco dancing classes, where buying the dresses would have been frivolous as there was no future in it. I like to get a good shot, and I can learn how to use the computer to improve my images. I am missing my books of old photographs and photo albums. I look at them often. If I learn photography properly, in my dreams it could become a future job.

Katy is encouraging about the camera. She says I should find a cybercafé, download some photos and email them to her. I know how to email but that's it. The word download sends my brain spinning, like map reading. Note to self, 'Must learn more about computing'.

I've added a litre bottle to fill with Lourdes water to my purchases. It's pale blue and in the shape of the Madonna. When I turn the top against the base it plays 'Ave Maria'. This time I will take more care, but if I drop it, it won't break. Plastic is big in the place of miracles.

There are people buying bottles for water, like they bought wine at the chateau – by the crate-load. They are convinced that anyone at home who is sick will be grateful. There are no degrees of potency to the water, just differently shaped and decorated bottles. It's prayer and faith added that gives it a mystical ingredient.

Time to go to the hotel and read for a while, Spike's looking tired; it's been a long day for both of us. I can pick up a drink and biscuits there and order a continental breakfast for the morning. I wonder if there will be any other English pilgrims at breakfast. It could be interesting to talk to other people and find out who they are, and why they are here.

Before settling down, I look out on the candlelit procession weaving its way uphill, and marvel at the number of people carrying flickering candles, creating an intoxicating atmosphere. I don't join in as the day has been long enough, and Spike doesn't want to be left alone.

Spike twitches with his dreams most of the night – and mine are about chasing and chasing something, but I'm not sure what. I'm pleased to be up and rid of the night.

In the sparsely decorated dining hall, a mixture of nationalities meets. We take our bread and jam and hot chocolate. Dipping French bread in a bowl of hot chocolate is the nearest experience to heaven I've found here. My stomach is chocolate-heavy. A few last sips from the bottom of the bowl and breakfast is done. I thought there would be conversation, but instead it has been whispers spaced with silences.

As I clamber over the bench to get out, the waiter's voice comes from behind me,

"Your Tony Blair and Cherie are here." He has disturbed me as I'm in silent mode. "Lots of security. They're outside the basilica at 11.00. Your Cherie... very pretty woman."

I gather my few belongings from the foyer and cross the gardens to my car, stopping to take a photo of the parked and guarded black limousine with a Union Jack. I recognise the entourage but they don't recognise me or my turquoise Fiat. We were travelling companions for a few miles but I wasn't clocked as any kind of threat, and ranked as unmemorable. The visit of our prime minister and his wife will be worth seeing so I return to join the crowds. I'm not sure if they are waiting for a glimpse of Mr. Blair or God. Whoever it is, a sense of reverence pervades.

Leaving Spike in the car isn't an option, he doesn't like the crowds, but has no complaints as long as I hold him.

The breeze wafts the smell of pine trees around as I wander about the paved area. Gold carpet has been laid by the basilica doors. French police are milling among the crowd, and plain-clothes security people are staring hard at everyone and everything. Even Spike comes under scrutiny. Hanging about and people watching is the only thing to do for now, and try to find a decent spot to see the P.M.

I glance up and note that John is sitting in front of the basilica, on the steps. He's with a gathering of about twenty people. He's playing his guitar and they're singing, '*The world needs love (clap clap). The world needs peace (clap clap). The world needs war-free days (draw a world in the air and end with palms up).*' The mantra is infectious and others in the vicinity are joining in. The group with John light candles, and hold up an Iraq war protest banner, before sitting cross-legged, blocking the approach path allotted for the arrival of Tony Blair and Cherie.

Security is soon there and one by one they are removing the protestors. John stands up clutching his guitar, and has to steady himself. It's eleven o'clock exactly. He stumbles backwards and slips from the hands of security men before trying to stand and straighten himself.

Tony and Cherie arrive at the top of the steps. She is wearing a grey dress and a white fascinator. The priest walks towards them with his hand held out in a welcoming gesture, then waits as they turn to the crowd and raise their hands in a regal wave. John is uncomfortably close to the unfolding scene, but about to step aside after raising his guitar in one last defiant gesture.

Expectant quiet creeps over the crowd when a zip thud sound happens. John falls to the ground and I think he has tripped again. Writhing on the ground, he looks like he's having a fit. Tony and Cherie are pushed back behind a door. That's when the crowd at the front starts screaming. I can't see what's going on.

There are plenty of ambulances around and they

converge to where John has fallen. I think he's been lifted inside one. Nothing is very clear from where Spike and I are standing, and the jostling crowds give us no way to go forward. We move to the edge of the throng and I ease my way around to find where the ambulance has gone. A sense of fear and chaos has replaced orderly reverence.

The damp air that caused the pines to smell has turned to drizzle and runs with my tears down my face. I'm sad and disturbed by the unfamiliar as I take the path across to the hospital. Spike is clinging closely to me, and I can feel him shivering under my cardigan. There's a small room where John has been taken. I ask a young nurse, "Can I go in?" I'm security-checked by the lady gendarme and asked if I knew the victim, and had we travelled here together? In the absence of anyone else to help, they are interested in who I am and not at all friendly.

I didn't bring John to Lourdes to lose his life but he has taken a bullet straight through the side of his brain and, in doing so, has saved the French government a lot of embarrassment.

His body is on a cold slab: I touch his forehead and it's still warm. The room is clean and smells of sawdust and disinfectant. The ever-present statue of Mary and the Christ child is on the otherwise bare walls. I stand in disbelief, holding on to Spike, waiting for something else to happen, but I don't know what. The tap in the corner is useful, where I wash a smudge of John's blood from my hands and dry them with the rough paper towels. Spike is not keen on being put down to floor level, not even for a moment.

The priest from Liverpool arrives and saves me from my confusion. Together we walk outside and find a spot where the sun is causing the wet earth to steam. Oleanders are swaying gently and birds are singing; the beauty of nature makes me feel stronger. My legs – and especially my knees – won't stop shaking at the thought of the hole in the side of John's head where the bullet entered. I think this image will stay uppermost in my mind forever, recurring endlessly.

Two forensic photographers dressed in black went in as we came out. If Tony or Cherie had died there would have been chaos at Lourdes. Very little attention is paid to John. I have the impression that the sooner this blip in events is dealt with the better. The mass has continued, but inside.

I've only seen members of my family dead. Mum's death was expected, and she had left us some time before. When the hospital asked if I wanted to see her I said yes, because I wanted to see that her struggle and confusion were over.

With our child, Gerry and I sat in the hospital and held him, then we buried him and I went back into hospital for the operation which meant that I would never have any more babies. We thought about other avenues like adopting, and then decided Katy was beautiful and enough for us.

"Did he have any relatives?" A man in a white coat comes to us and asks.

"Not that I know of," I answer.

The priest hands me a small bag and a guitar.

"Can you stay a while and help me with a service for him later tomorrow?"

"Yes. Yes, of course. Here's my number. You can find me at this hotel. I'll stay an extra night." Secretly I want to leave, run away, but there's no one else and I'm holding John's guitar and bag. The music has stopped.

Walking towards the hotel with Spike beside me, I ring Gerry. "Try not to scratch," I advise him. Gerry has always had sensitive skin, which makes wearing Lycra for cycling difficult unless he shakes powder on to the tops of his legs. It must be horrible with a plaster when you can't reach inside. The night nurse lends him a knitting needle if he's desperate, but she won't let him have a deep poke around or keep it handy.

"I was getting better until this rash; it's driving me insane. The wee infection has gone and I'm drinking most things – but nothing that dehydrates or doesn't work with antibiotics, like alcohol. Only a few more days of this, thank God."

"Sorry… I can't make it back today. My friend is dead and I have to be here for a service. Please understand."

"I'm going mad in here. Agatha is back but she still insists I drink litres of water."

"Is it bottled?"

"Pardon?"

"The water. Never mind. See you soon, and do take care. Celebrate love."

"Why are you behaving so oddly, Nat? I'm worried about you and I don't need it."

"It's losing my friend."

"Be rational, Nat. You don't make friends that quickly. Let's call him an acquaintance. What on earth were you doing with him, anyway? Your real friends are at home. See you as soon as you can make it. Make sure you keep in touch and let me know exactly where you are and what you're doing."

In my room I try to select something suitable to wear for the service in the chapel. There's only a pair of cut-off jeans and my blue blouse. I find a needle and thread and make my jeans look neater. Sarah gave me a midi skirt, which will be better. My clothes are on the plain wooden chair, ready for tomorrow.

The night passes at an unhurried pace, especially the early hours of the morning. I'm up at 5 a.m. and creep downstairs to try to go outside, but the door is locked. The doorkeeper has detected my movements and rises from his bed. We say nothing to each other before returning to our rooms. A cup of tea is brought to me, and I'm grateful. I open my book of words and write: *Love. Peace. Music.* I think about the words and discover I've gone to sleep sitting up on the bed.

Breakfast can be skipped because I don't want to be with other people. In the garden, I pick purple daisy-like flowers and carry them to throw on the cheap coffin provided by the hospital. Spike's collar will be a suitable place for a few wild flowers.

Spike is washed in the sink in my room. All this water around and yet it's difficult to find a place to bathe a dog. He has his smart black collar and lead on, with purple and white flowers ready to tuck in. A few more hours must pass in a place I find emotionally cold. A gap is present inside me, I want a loving friend; I want a husband to hold me. Phoning Gerry will remind me of what I don't have, but wish I did. He is sort of loving and sort of a friend, but it isn't enough. When I need him he isn't with me, not even in spirit.

At three o'clock, as arranged, we enter the small chapel and stand with the priest at the side of the coffin. It's all basic stuff, there isn't money to pay for anything else. His body will be returned to Liverpool when the French have finished their investigations. There are no relatives we know of as yet.

I place his guitar on the coffin and scatter purple daisies. Spike twists around in my arms, observing a situation he doesn't understand. The priest starts up on his portable keyboard.

"*Amazing Grace, how sweet the sound in a believer's ear... I once was lost but now I'm found...*"

The priest says a short prayer committing him into the arms of Jesus. I don't think he was a religious man but the prayer sounds nice and it helps sanitise the horrid affair. I think he had Catholic connections. Maybe the authorities can use that to see if they can discover any relatives, but who will want to know? The only thing a relative might receive is a very large bill for the repatriation of his body.

When John's body is flown back to Liverpool the priest is going to arrange for the council to have him cremated. He's on his own now, and what little that could be done has been done.

"And now for our final hymn."

"*From the place where you are born...*" The priest rocks wildly; he is himself a leftover from the seventies. It's difficult to do anything but shuffle a bit with Spike in my arms. "*You will walk a pathway, a pathway leading to the end. We all walk a pathway, a walk where we value a friend.*"

A pause for silence.

"Good luck on your journey, John George Lennon Bush." The priest rests his hand on the coffin in a form of blessing.

"Good luck," I repeat and touch the coffin. Spike is sitting upright and on his best behaviour. I thank the priest; the service reflected what little I knew of John.

In the visitors' book at the back of the chapel I pick up the pen and write:

> 20 July 2004
> IN MEMORY OF JOHN GEORGE
> *To Tony Blair:*
> > *This man died because of your Iraq.*
> > *He was a soldier for peace.*
>
> *Goodbye. I'm sorry you're gone.*
> *RIP*
> *Natalie Kenning, Eastleigh, England, UK.*

I leave the book open and hope that other people will come by and read it and add thoughts of their own. The priest shakes my hand and once again gives me John's guitar. "You might as well take this. There's no one else."

"Thanks. I'll keep it and remember him, even if I am the only one."

Another night passes and I'm awake early enough to take a short stroll in the gardens before joining the people in the refectory. The gardens are quiet and scented with lavender and pines. I watch the butterflies waking up and listen to the birds chorusing. Too soon, it's time to get on with the day. First, I have to visit the security office and answer again any questions I can about what I saw.

After a breakfast of French bread with apricot jam and a bowl of white coffee, it's time to be on my way. I've studied the map and it's on the back seat; what isn't in my head now, isn't likely to reach my understanding. Gerry said to keep in touch and I will.

Before leaving, I check the newspaper stand to see if

there's mention of the death of John. I find a reference to someone being arrested by the wonderful French police and how they miraculously averted an assassination attempt on Tony Blair. That's it.

The road out of Lourdes finds me with feelings of emptiness. I have lost a lot and faced a lot. Who am I? Where am I going? Home?

A Madonna magnet was free with the litre bottle for water from the taps. It's fixed on the dashboard next to a miniature Eiffel Tower. Perhaps the Madonna can keep me on the right road. I drive to a junction. Left is the way back to Gerry, but right is calling. I look left and there's no response from inside me. I look right and hear the gentle sound of bells chiming.

I pull slowly to the right and glance at the Madonna. She winks. I've witnessed a miracle.

7

Travelling Over Mountains

I'm searching for something deep inside myself. The majestic mountains and solitude might help me find answers. It's too early to leave what is now my personal pilgrimage.

It's strange to be away from Katy and Dad. I miss the love and fun with Katy as I watch her go about her day. Dad is always around, doing much the same things. He likes to collect a daily paper and a few necessities from the newsagent, and has his meals routine. There's something about routines that make everyone around feel life has stability. He's going to miss the newsagents if it shuts down. It won't be the same for him, shopping at the supermarket where no one will know who he is.

When Gerry goes away it's only for a week at a time. It has been ten days since I have smelt his loving scent, touched his clothes or known his presence. I take comfort from thoughts of him. He is the place I rest my mind, but is it a game of pretend and wishful thinking?

Katy enjoys our phone chats and I've stopped worrying so much about her. I reflect on Gerry and me, playing with her in the parks when she was just three years old. That was a special time together, protecting and loving our small daughter.

Katy said Gramps has been out looking at flats, which

has surprised me because I can't imagine him living anywhere but close to us in the house of my childhood. He is managing well, but if he feels he wants to move there's room with us.

Gerry has been remarkably controlled. As long as I tell him exactly where I am, he won't interfere. We have a deal.

I think about him in the hospital – good-looking and strong, yet on crutches with his leg in plaster. I wonder if his rash is getting better. He says he's taking some pills and the itch is subsiding. The physiotherapist is helping with exercises to assist his recovery, now and for when he gets home. He's in the best place and doesn't need me at present or for a few more days. He's more in need of his spare pyjamas that are still in the car boot, and complains the hospital ones don't fit and make him look like a convict. He wants me to buy him a tracksuit with roomy legs for travelling home. The thought makes me nervous as I'm not sure exactly what he wants, and he's extremely fussy about having the right clothes to suit a situation.

I confess that on the pyjama front I feel guilty. The nurses must find me a strange wife. He has no one organised to do his shopping and washing for him. Nurse Stephan tried shopping but the pyjamas he bought were baggy and the material flimsy.

The Fiat flies along the road. The sky ahead is a clear blue backdrop to the mountain ridges. Large birds of prey soar, and lift my spirit with them. After many short stops to look, take photos of a river running along in a valley or of snow-capped mountains, I notice a small town in the distance that beckons me for lunch.

Oh, yes… I should ring Gerry and tell him where I am. He knows the road I describe to him and says to keep in touch and tell him when I've arrived at the next town or village.

Spike needs a drink and a handful of his biscuits to keep him going. He's looking miserable. He must be fed up with spending so much time in the car.

I stop again on my way down the road and reflect about being on my own. What am I doing here? Is it a form of madness or a pleasant holiday break? Am I finding myself? Should I have turned left from Lourdes instead of right? Nerves have kicked in again.

Watching travel programmes on TV isn't the same as experiencing places. Driving along the high mountain roads, I smell a chill in the air and feel the touch of the sun at the same time. I can stop and run my fingers over the grass... hear the gentle wind as it whispers to me. The sensations of sitting on a verge overlooking a mountainside envelop me. Purple alpine plants struggle for life in the mountain crevasses. Tiny blue and yellow flowers are scattered in patches like rugs.

Niggling away is the thought, *Will I be safe on my own in the town?* I hesitate to absorb the clarity of the view and the air for one last time before sitting in the car. I leave a message on Gerry's phone, struggling to sound confident on where I am and about my plans.

At the roadside a sign for English-speaking tourists reads: Pyrenean Mountain Village 4 km. This is for me.

It must be busy at certain times, but in the middle of the day in July it looks empty. With my sun hat on I read my book sitting on a wall and potter about on the cobblestones taking in the quiet atmosphere. Houses made mainly of wood are newly painted in white, pink or yellow, and huddle around the square. Brightly planted hanging baskets and pot plants have been placed on verandas and by front doors. Cars no bigger than mine occasionally roar over the cobbles. Speeding around the narrow streets between the houses, their noise destroys something of the fairy tale image. Everywhere is tidy. The odd leaf in a corner is too lazy to blow around. Any sound echoes.

People who live here must know their town, their neighbours and the mountains intimately. No one is walking around, but I think I can be seen and observed.

I sit with Spike at a round metal table that just fits on the pavement outside a shop that serves as post office, bakery and grocery store. A rotund man turns up and I order a coffee and two delicious-looking chocolates in little paper cases.

From the pointing at the pictures on the walls by the proud proprietor, I gather that the chocolates are made here by his family and, of course, sold in the shop. Chocolate making has been his family's tradition. With more pointing and pictures, he tells me he exports them to Belgium. The smell of chocolate escapes from the shop door and irresistibly pervades my desires.

"Thank you. I'll take two more," I request, assisted by more sign language. He adjusts the parasol to give me shade, and places a bowl of water on the ground for Spike.

I'm drawn from my chocolate ecstasy towards music echoing along the street from the old stone arch and through into the square. Whistle pipes and small tin drums create a cacophony that heralds a bustling wedding party.

I leave my table to take photos. I wonder if the bride and groom have lived here all their lives, like I live in Eastleigh. Male dancers perform a type of ballet, dressed in white jumpsuits. The bride has a full white dress, her long black hair contrasting under a white veil.

I've been married eighteen years. I think I'm happy. When people said that life changes at forty, I didn't think it would happen to me. The fact is… Katy is growing up and Dad is getting older. Gerry hasn't changed a lot, but what difference will the broken leg make? Irksome is the right word to describe my home life, thoughts of which are going round and round in my head.

The proprietor delivers his bill and takes his chocolate-stained white apron off. He pats his chubby hands together and indicates he's going to join the party at the church. It's time to shut shop and take his trays of pastries and cakes with him.

Underneath the village clock at the *mairie* is a wooden seat in the shade of the wall. I make myself comfortable here with Spike and faithfully ring Gerry. He's interested and listens as I explain how pretty this village is. He's particularly kind and suggests I stay the night in the main hotel in the square. He assures me I will get back tomorrow if I follow his instructions.

I need someone to have faith in me and I have faith in myself. Finally, we are communicating on the same level. Is it possible to enter a better phase of our life together? If so, my journey will have been worth it.

I'd like to stay longer, but this is the right time for me to return. I plan to enjoy this last day of my pilgrimage and resolve to come back next time with Gerry, even if he has his bike. The trouble is… the bikes are transported in the club van and we don't have a big enough car. On club trips I'm superfluous to his requirements.

I click the phone off, and this is when Katy rings. She's so excited it's difficult to calm her down; her voice is slightly distorted and I'm not sure I'm making sense of what she's saying.

"Dad's read it. He got an English paper. Listen: *Mother lost in France. Child's school trip money disappears.* It says you've been seen at service stations on CCTV and the police know where you've been taking out money. There's a map here of the English Channel showing your crossing and pinpointing where Dad is and where you are. The line goes on for miles past where you're supposed to be. You've done some cool stuff."

"I'm in the Pyrenees. Spain isn't far away."

"Costa del Sol?"

"No, the mountains. You should see this place."

"If you say so. I know you haven't really spent my trip money, but it's good for the journalism course I want to do. I have to make up stories or at least stretch the truth. Gramps says Dad's been drinking the French water and it's making him sick. Dad wants to know when you're picking up his bike. It's with the gendarmes and they want to get rid of it."

"What's that banging noise?"

"It's Gramps. He's lost his chess set. Don't know how he's done that, he has it out every time Matt comes round."

"Have you seen my chess set, Katy? I'm sure I put it in this cupboard," Dad calls.

"Gotta go. Gramps is in a state. He says it's your age giving you trouble and you need to start taking vitamins. There was an article in the paper about the importance of vitamins on the brain. It was next to the story of the lost mother."

I think of Dad settling down for a whisky on the rocks, it's his treat once a day. I hope Katy isn't getting too much for him and that he will soon discover where he put his chess set.

The hotel in the square looks like the best available option for accommodation and I've agreed with Gerry that I'll stay there. The receptionist welcomes us with an air of suspicion.

"Where are you from? Where are you going?" I can't really answer the last question so I say "Lourdes," as it will make sense.

"There was an attempt to assassinate your Tony Blair there just the other day. It wasn't a problem; the gunman was a useless shot. He hit a silly man who got in the way. You might hear about it."

"He's not my Tony Blair, and John Lennon didn't deserve to die. And the dead man wasn't silly." I judge that this statement is, fortunately, beyond her comprehension even if she speaks reasonable English.

I unpack my case and Spike's things, in a room that is comfortable and not too small. It's trimmed with white linen and lace, all freshly laundered. The sun's a little cooler and I ask for a late lunch.

The restaurant smells of firewood ash. Candles flicker, lighting up the dark corners. It has small windows and low beams. The diners are one couple finishing their coffees and me. I choose my table in a corner as single people do and find a magazine to look at. The waiter goes off with my order for their traditional leek and potato soup.

The soup comes, and more people are arriving in Reception for late lunch or drinks. English/American voices cheer me, even though I can't hear them clearly. The new guests enter the restaurant and I continue to mind my own business.

"Aunty Natalie." The voice is clear and shrill. The extra

people fill the spaces between the tables as they head in my direction. "Can we join you or do you want to join us?"

"Chester. How nice."

I indicate to the spare chairs and make space for Chester, Stacey and Blake.

I want to say "Hello," but all that comes out is "Uuh."

"Have you lost Spike?"

"No, Chester, I haven't. He's resting in my room." I swallow hard.

"That's good, then. Why don't we all take lunch together... go for a little walk around this pretty village? At supper we can prepare our route back for the morning. We are all going to have a good time and return to a very relieved Gerry."

I scrape up the last of my soup before resting the spoon against the table. My misshapen features stare at me as I twist it round and round. Stacey leans across and rests her hand on mine.

"You don't look as bad as Gerry said you would. You don't look lost and confused." She is studying my face, searching for signs. If she searches long enough she will come up with all sorts of theories as to the state of my mental health. *Please don't tell me I need a therapist*, I think, as it just might make me angrier than I already am.

"Blake, would you like to see the goats? We can leave your mum and Chester to chat on their own for a while." Blake is seven but not too grown up to take my hand.

"Don't get lost," Chester calls. Stacey lands a kick on his leg.

It's a pleasure to be outside. We walk through the town and find the goats by following the sound of their bells. Goat kids spring around the field making sweet noises. We try to count them but can't be exact. We've been in the sun long enough; it's time to make tracks to the post office for homemade ice cream. I presume the young girl serving is family. I point. "One chocolate and mint chip and one strawberry and vanilla." We share the shade of the umbrella where I sat earlier.

"Do you like England?" I ask Blake, who looks more vulnerable than I feel.

"I miss the sun and the beach and my dad... but it's all right, I suppose. Chester's boring."

I nod with approval, what I haven't said in words can't be repeated. We save some crumbled ice cream cone to take for the goats. The joy of separation is over too soon; Chester and Stacey have come to join us.

"I've rung Gerry and let him know we've got you. He sounded very pleased. He's bound to get better quicker if he can concentrate on himself." Chester hitches up his trousers around his too-much-food-and-drink abdomen.

"Thanks, Chester. I won't bother to ring him again today... as long as he knows what's happening."

"I hope you're not sulking, Nat. We can do without that. Why don't you take Blake to the park area? I'll order early evening drinks in the hotel garden for later. Stacey and I need to wash and brush up. Spike will be OK with us."

"Let's see if we can find a ball for sale." Blake and I can relax and play together in spite of Chester.

When the two of them are out of earshot, Blake starts to talk. "I wish I could play with my dad sometimes." I squeeze his hand. At seven, he's learning to cope with the difficult problems of relationships.

"My mum gave up her acting career to be with Chester."

"I'm in goal," I chirp, throwing the ball.

Chester and Stacey drift by, checking up on us. They have brought Spike with them. "We're all staying at the hotel tonight and leaving first thing in the morning. I've booked a table for supper. See you later." Chester looks pleased to shelve Blake with me.

"Who is your dad, Blake?"

"Nothin' but a surfin' bum." Blake echoes his mother's voice.

It's time to concentrate on the game. He has quite a kick for a little lad, but I manage to save some of the goals. A group of local children join in, and where sport is concerned language is no divider. When a boy of about twelve turns up, I pass the task of goalie over and kick the ball past him on at least one occasion. Dishevelled, we return a little late to the hotel.

Drinks are served and – silly me – I decided to change afterwards. My grubby knees are showing below cut-off jeans. Mistake.

The white wine is beautifully chilled, and delicate cheese biscuits are served on a saucer with a doily. The biscuits are not the pre-packed type, but individually shaped ones from the baker.

Stacey is wearing white, which looks terrific with her dyed blonde hair. Damn it. Is it money, time or magic that gives some women the ability to appear that neat? Something must be wrong with me for studying her outfit, willing it to have a dirty spot somewhere. It doesn't.

I dash upstairs to change. Make-up on, hair brushed – and the best outfit from a limited wardrobe – I'm ready for arriving downstairs a second time. Sarah's midi skirt was getting too tight for her. Beige is a colour that goes with my blue blouse and I don't mind second-hand clothes. I imagine Stacey does.

The evening is pleasant until Blake has gone to bed. We adjourn to the bar area and sit in leather seats for an after-diner coffee and handmade mint chocolates. Chester takes Stacey's hand.

"We've been trying for a baby. We've been checked out and they say there's no reason why we shouldn't have children, and I think we've been lucky."

I fumble in my bag, find my wallet and take out my photo.

"This was my son." I can see it's embarrassing them but I didn't intend it to. I genuinely wanted to share my experience and the difficult time Gerry and I had. "Life isn't always straightforward, but it's good to believe it is until it isn't. I loved my son," I say.

From their faces, I can see I'm on the wrong track; they wanted something superficial and cheery.

"Sorry," I say. I put his photo away and walk across the room to study the carved wooden plates on the walls and the pictures made of dried edelweiss.

"Your sister really is difficult, Chester. There was no need for that." Stacey's whispering is very audible.

"Good luck, you two. I'd better get to bed." I can't manage to force a smile.

I catch up with Katy before turning in. Gramps has found a chess-set exactly the same as his, in an Eastleigh charity shop. Her reaction to Chester being here is laughter and I lighten up.

"Don't come home yet, Mum. I've got another week on the school radio and the lost mother story is going brilliantly."

The night is restless, as I have an I'm-being-chased nightmare again. I'm running through the jungle but mysteriously I grow wings and fly away from danger. I'm telling everyone I can fly. They don't believe me, but I'm showing them I can. Once airborne I keep going and going over the jungle, then the power goes out of my wings and I land with a thud on the floor.

It's 4 a.m. and I pack my case ready for the morning. There's nothing else to do but read, and the hours will pass. Spike whimpers his way through his own dreams.

By seven, I've packed the car and returned for breakfast. When the others come down I've finished, including a third cup of espresso coffee. I excuse myself and arrange to meet them in the foyer at nine. I suggest it will be good for them to share a relaxing time at the hotel before we start driving on the long journey home.

"Taking Spike for a walk before leaving," I say. I smile and excuse myself as they tuck into their cereals. With food uppermost in their minds, they almost ignore me. Off we go to the car park, catching the fresh mountain air tainted with goat smell.

We return to our Fiat and Spike jumps on to the back seat. I go to the front and start the engine. Like the small cars zooming around the town yesterday, I speed away. Will they chase me? How long before they discover I've gone? I remind myself I'm an adult, free to make my own decisions and go where I like. My head understands but my heart does not. It thumps hard, trying to escape my chest.

A few miles down the road there is time to stop, put fuel in the tank and take off again... and drive, drive, drive. When will it be all right to slow down and to stop looking in the mirror? I consult the Madonna magnet, hoping for another wink of reassurance, but it doesn't happen. The scenery flashes past. I would like to stop, but not yet. What will Chester and the family do if they catch up with me? Have me arrested and taken back to England like a child? I think of being yelled and shouted at. Chester is a big red balloon that pops, shedding tiny rubber pieces into the far atmosphere.

The Spanish border is ahead. If I can get into Spain there will be time to stop and think. Chester won't follow me that far.

"Consequences," I hear my mother's voice saying. "Natalie, if you behave impulsively there will be consequences." When did I do anything that was not reserved and well thought out? When have I done anything outside my box? Mum was kind and loving, and everything she taught me I swallowed whole like good children should.

"Natalie, you're nearly forty," I say to myself, but I'm still afraid of being told off. I resolve to finish my pilgrimage wherever and whenever I want to. Only then will I return to Eastleigh, my family and the bingo hall, reuniting with Gerry on the way. The nearest to change I can see myself getting is the photographic course but I expect a put-down on that. I don't want to end my journey with my tail between my legs like a naughty dog.

I'm finding something; it's the ability to be strong in myself and for myself. This is going to mean that other people will need to respect me for that. Easily said – but after the music I've created is faced, then what?

Border control ahead.

"Down, Spike." He knows the routine and crouches on the back floor as I adjust his blanket. The inside of a Spanish prison resembling Alcatraz and full of screams whizzes past my inner eye. This is one way I can end up in trouble – I have a dog without vaccination certificates. For a disbeliever prayer comes readily, and so does sweat at the nape of my neck.

No border control comes and I have slipped into Spain, all thanks to the EU. I sail along the roads until the Spanish traffic police stop me.

"Passport?" As I try to hand it out of the window it disappears down the side of my seat. I squeeze my fingers down to retrieve it.

"What is your reason for coming to Spain?"

"Pilgrimage," I reply, and try to control my hand from shaking as I show my passport. *Don't move, Spike. Please don't move,* I think.

"Documents? Insurance? Driving licence?" I'm noticeably sweating. A policeman peers in at my Madonna on the dashboard. That satisfies him. The passport is returned and we are on our way. Another miracle.

Spain, Spain… I'm in Spain. The excitement makes me forget the problems of Gerry and Chester.

Chester doesn't matter. He will go home and he and Stacey will mutter about me for a while. They can't collect Gerry and his bike because they don't have room, and that pleases me. I regret not saying goodbye to Blake because I would like to have had more of his company. Now his parents will write me off as nuts and deter further contact.

Dad went to Los Angeles with Chester after mum died. In fairness to Chester, Katy and I were invited but before I could open my mouth Gerry decided it wasn't a good idea. At the time I agreed. Why would I want to see LA? When Dad came back he said he enjoyed the beaches and Santa Monica. He spent a lot of time on his own because Stacey and Chester were both working. Blake was sent off to the child-minder each day. Dad missed Mum a lot. When he came back he said the big problem was that the place was full of Americans and he didn't understand them.

I asked him what Americans were like. He said they were such a mixed bag there was no way of telling. They all said "Hi," and "Have a nice day." He said there wasn't anything like a decent English war museum to be found in LA.

Dad does like cowboy and Indian films. He took a trip to the desert where filming a scene was played out on a set, including stunt men jumping between horses. He read stories about American history that he thought had been sanitised by time and by Hollywood. The trip had its bright spots, but he couldn't appreciate anything without Mum.

Dad was in LA when the election campaign for George Bush or Al Gore was running, and it left an impression on him of the razzamatazz. He mentioned it when I told him I had travelled to Lourdes with George Bush. The phone connection wasn't clear so I said I would explain about John Lennon when I got home. He was with Gerry on sending Chester out to get me after that.

The road twists and turns as it rises. There's time to take photos of the distant mountains. I want to remember this forever. The sun is coming towards me, making it difficult for a professional-looking shot, and shadows are over the valley below, but for my own pleasure the views should make great pictures. I'm not an expert yet. I've learned there is software available to improve the shades of colour. I'd like to try something like that.

I stay longer than I should. I've been trying to work out what to say to Gerry. The breeze catches my hair as I look up at the wide-wing spanned birds, soaring. The warm air is rising, taking them higher and higher. Dark clouds are gathering over the mountain tops and a double rainbow arcs over the valley. The red, orange, yellow, green, indigo and violet in the main arc are more vivid than anything I've seen at home. I don't take a photo because I want to observe it as it evaporates. Rainbows aren't forever.

I'm sure to find somewhere to stay, but not up here. I'd better get moving. Just past noon I drive into the nearest town with untidy commercial buildings and a dingy-looking bar. On scrutiny, it smells of stale beer, but serves eggs and chips. Five hours have passed since breakfast and I'm hungry and thirsty.

The fried eggs are cooked to perfection, the yolks are just right to dip the chips. I shake on black pepper and eat until the plate can be wiped clean with bread. Spike is unhappy; this is not his kind of place. We don't waste time and soon queue to pay. A short unshaven Spanish man leans forward and tries to shove money for my meal to the cashier. He leers towards me, showing his lack of teeth. My heart grips me inside my chest and I'm missing the protection of Gerry. I need help and there is no one vaguely interested. I force my euros on to the cashier's desk. The man grabs at my arm, making me face him. Spike nips his fingers, causing him to ease his hold. I shake him off and flee for the second time today. Laughter erupts behind me.

"Dumb, dumb, dumb, Natalie," I say out loud. Tears of fear wash my face. Running away from Chester could have bad consequences.

This grubby town is a thoroughfare for lorries trundling up and down and a few lost tourists looking for something that isn't here. Language is a problem along with my naivety. I'm pleased to be on my way to somewhere.

Down and down the mountain roads I drive to join a busier road at the bottom. This is farming country, with horses chasing in fields, cows hanging around milking sheds and sheep with no interest in life but eating grass. I feel safer.

Pilgrims are dotted along the roadside, following the signs. They walk in clusters or lines. I follow a sign for Santa Cilia de Jaca. It's posted on the pilgrimage route and hopefully this place is for me. I now have a group identity. The sign shows an aerodrome but it's in the middle of nowhere. I guess I'll discover what it's all about when I get there. Flying saucers are possible with my agitated brain.

I pull over to check my phone. It's a text, so it's safe. A conversation with Gerry needs more preparation and can't be avoided for much longer. Thank goodness it's not his number.

I open it:

Bloody brilliant, Nat. Didn't know you had it in you.
Yr B F Lisa.

Admiration well received.

8

Flying Like Eagles

In Santa de Cilia people wander around the square taking time to move from one foot to the other, ready for rest and recuperation. Some have walking sticks to go with their hiking shoes. I'm in serious walking country, and this village is a suitable place to stay.

The village is unremarkable; there are no shops, but a choice of simple places for bed and breakfast. I decide on an unpretentious hostel and book in.

"Walking, gliding or visiting?" asks the proprietor.

"I'm a pilgrim in a Fiat," I reply.

"So you're off to Santiago de Compostela then?"

"I'm not sure where I am or where I'm going yet."

"I see a lot like that," he replies, without expression.

"Your key. Room 18. Supper 7.30. *Buenas tardes.*"

Thank God he spoke English. I should learn a smattering of Spanish and Catalonian even if it is just greetings and a few numbers.

My room is basic but Spike can stay; it isn't a problem. Pilgrimage place it may be, but there are not the Catholic trappings of Lourdes. A few dried flowers are neatly placed in a vase on a plain wooden bedside cabinet. The showers and toilets are shared on the landing, and it's cheap.

A husband and wife team run the hostel, with the elderly mother doing what she can. It's orderly, simple and comes with the enforced company of others. If you want to make tea or get a cold drink in the unmanned bar area, help yourself. It works on trust, you put your money in the cardboard box provided.

We've only had one bad incident with money at bingo. Harry was going to the bank six months ago when three young men approached him, one brandishing a knife. He handed over a bag but it wasn't until later that they would have realised it contained the used bingo cards he kept for the records. It shook him up, so now we hire a proper security firm to take care of banking. Harry is no match for thieves; he's much too skinny. For a moment, I miss work. I have been there a long time and expect to be there for a few years yet.

After helping myself to tea and muttering "Hello" to a few strangers, there's time to explore outside before supper. Spike and I stroll to the river at the bottom of the village; we are the only ones here. The water rolls over the pure white stones; they are round and of all sizes. It's crystal clear and numbingly cold as it runs down from the mountains. I kneel at the edge and gather up a handful of the coldness; it drips down my arms before I splash the residue of melted snow on my face.

Spike runs around until he spots vultures above us. He's happier in my arms as we watch the birds together. I don't think they want Spike for supper, but the fish from the river. They might be tempted to try him as he's not much bigger than a rabbit, and they do take local lambs.

At the top of the hills on the other side of the river, I catch sight of white glider planes coming into land. Like silent birds they gracefully lower themselves from the heights and disappear behind the hills on to the airfield I saw signposted.

The evening sun carries vestiges of warmth. I find a seat to glance through a well-thumbed travellers' guide borrowed from the hostel. Places to go, things to do: Zaragoza, monasteries, skiing, white water rafting, hang-gliding. I can see why this is Gerry's idea of paradise without me.

I'll ring Gerry this evening. I know he was thinking of me when he sent Chester but I was managed and manipulated, and I didn't like it.

It's time to return up the narrow shaded street to the hostel. I hope to meet friendly English-speaking people. I still feel shaken by the lunchtime experience in that horrid town and worry about what could have happened.

The restaurant starts serving at 7.30 precisely, by which time we are all queuing outside. The bar is closed until after supper, when someone will be free to attend it. The proprietor arrives to open the door. We file in and squeeze on to benches at long wooden tables marked with age but scrubbed clean. There's cutlery wrapped in a paper serviette at each place and baskets of bread and garlic dip to share. The ratio of men to women is five to one but we are not so outnumbered that I can't find other women to talk to.

The saintly type is not for me. They look clean, don't wear make-up, they have wonderful skin, and deep, genuine smiles. I choose to slide in on a bench opposite a young couple and next door to a man with a handlebar moustache and open hand gestures of welcome.

The food is substantial and straightforward, there's plenty of pasta with a tomato-based sauce and a sprinkling of grated hard cheese. There's a jug of water and an allowance of one glass of red or white wine each. Dessert is a lemon curd pastry. The bar is next door if anyone wants more drinks, but only when you've finished eating. The restaurant is run on the, 'Get them in, get them fed and get them out again' principle. A bell rings for silence. If you want a packed lunch tomorrow, this is the time to order it. No key held in the air; no packed lunch.

I like this togetherness for now. I can get lonely left to myself. This way I have no choice but to chat, it's all part of the experience. I discover people have different reasons for their journey; to come to terms with something or for the pleasure of the scenery and companionship. Some are more religious in their quest.

I'm here by accident but pleased I came. If life throws any more brickbats my way I won't go to the doctor for pills; I'll travel and go for long walks in beautiful places.

During supper, Spike is in the bedroom. The sound of clattering cutlery and plates mixed with laughter and unfamiliar voices would make him agitated.

I chat with the young girl sitting opposite.

"Dan and I are pilgrims," she proffers, indicating to the young man next to her. "We're walking to Santiago de Compostela."

"Are you doing it for a reason or for fun?" I admire their choice of vacation.

"Dan's respectable. He's a gardener. Mum doesn't like him. She interferes and we need space. We want to be together, don't we?"

Dan edges about on his part of the bench while concentrating on his plate, "Oh, yeah. Yeah."

"You must like gardening, Dan?"

Nothing is the reply. I study them for a moment until names in neon lights appear above their heads: *KATY and MATT.* I help myself to a glass of water with ice.

Hector has a voice just the right depth for a man with greying hair and a handlebar moustache.

"I fly one of those big white birds from the airfield. I saw you watching them from the river."

Dan is suddenly interested. "You mean you fly a glider?"

"That's it. If you want to come up to the airfield tomorrow I'll show you around. You too, of course, Natalie," Hector encourages.

"So, Natalie, why are you here?"

Hector is like a long-lost uncle and I can't help but warm to him. "I'm a bit lost. I was completely lost, but I'm getting an idea of where I'm meant to be. When that happened, I decided to go in the opposite direction."

A chocolate cake arrives at the end of the table and, with a slip into spontaneity, 'Happy Birthday' resounds around the room. The elderly mother takes a bow.

"Ninety-six," the son admiringly announces, and everyone claps… the kind of thing we do at bingo.

"How old are you?" I ask the girl as we eat cake.

"Seventeen," is the coy reply.

She looks a young seventeen to me. I wonder if she might consider me as a temporary stand-in for the mother I think she has spurned.

"Why don't you walk with us?" she asks.

"Thank you, but I've got my little dog. We drive and stop where we want to. I'll figure my way on or back as and when I'm ready."

"Unreal."

"That's what my daughter says," I say.

The girl pulls out a shell hanging on a string from her bag. "You need one of these." She stands up and places it around my neck. "That makes you a pilgrim. Follow the signs with a shell on like this one." Dan jerks her to her seat with embarrassed abruptness.

My instinct is to keep an eye on them because somewhere a mum like me will be grateful. I might hang around them while I'm here; if they want to talk they can. We all agree to meet at the airfield in the morning.

Hector wipes his mouth with his serviette and stands, ready to leave. There are bits of blue tissue stuck to his moustache. I think Roald Dahl would have liked him and recreated him in one of his stories.

"Meet me by the third door down on the right in the main street... 9.30 in the morning. I'll see if I can sort you out." Hector speaks closely to my ear and gives me an affectionate pat on my shoulder. Is his smile lustful as Monsieur Jacques's was on the ferry or playful like the artist in Montmartre? I feel neither, and think I'll be safe.

For all Monsieur Jacques's faults, if it wasn't for him I would still be circling round the Arc de Triomphe. I'm going to give Hector the benefit of the doubt.

"Zocco, anyone?" The bar tender cum waiter cum assistant cook is waiting to clear the dining area, so we are herded into the bar and spill outside on to the narrow street. A shot glass is filled with Zocco for us all. As Indians called whisky firewater, so this is fiery and goes straight up my nose as I try to swallow. The need of a good cough sends me scuttling up the stairs to my room, where I rush for the water jug by the bed and take fast gulps. Spike is disturbed and needs a comfort cuddle so I scratch his ear gently and he settles back to sleep.

Gerry is increasingly on my mind and I can't put off ringing him any longer. I'm sure we'll manage a reasonable conversation, as neither of us likes an argument, least of all on the phone.

"I'm still in the Pyrenees, but on the Spanish side."

"I'd like some visitors. Chester couldn't come. They spent ages waiting around for you and then had to rush for the ferry. My bike needs sorting out. I went cycling once near where you are."

"Why didn't you take me?"

"Don't be silly. You can't ride a bike. You're more of a Cornwall person. You've got Katy and your dad, and I go cycling."

"What if your leg doesn't mend properly, and you can't ride a bike again?"

"Golf. You know I've always wanted to play golf," he states.

"Goodnight, Gerry, I'll be with you soon." There's a lot we haven't said.

I think about my friend Susie who married a golfer when she thought she'd married a man. After three years and the fact that he didn't want children, she couldn't stand it any more and left. Then she married a vicar and became a mother, infant school teacher and unpaid church worker. When she wanted to be reminded of the carefree girl she had been we'd meet at Lisa's house, sit on the floor and share a bottle of Chardonnay and a pizza. We would be sixteen again and fall around laughing at nothing. With my friends on my mind, I drift off to sleep.

As I take Spike for an early morning walk by the river a light chill wind blows down the valley. The snow-capped mountains rise in the distance and the intensity of the sun hurts my eyes.

I wonder why some people get to live here and others are chosen for Eastleigh. Eastleigh is a decent, friendly place and there are places a whole lot worse, but scenic it isn't. I need more beautiful places and things in my life. I take out my camera and capture the morning, making a promise to myself that I won't stay in Eastleigh forever – but such promises are often forgotten with the need to work and pay bills.

At the hostel, I pop my head around the dining hall door to see if breakfast is ready. The old lady is putting out serviettes with a portion of bread at each place. She looks up, taps her watch – and points her finger at me, then the door. She's right. I'm half an hour early. This regime would only be fun for so long. Unfortunately, there's nowhere else to go, so I return to my room and wait.

Hector doesn't appear at breakfast. After I've wiped the residue of jam from my fingers I leave the dining hall and make my way to the heavy oak door at 9.30 a.m. as instructed. I hold on to the large brass handle and begin to push. Hector comes from inside and pulls. My eyes are adjusting to the dim light when Hector reaches for the main light switch. Should I have brought Spike? I'll be OK.

"Come on, my dear." He leads me by the hand to a row of desks and sits me down by one of ten computers. He presses the on switch and it whirs into action.

"Now tell me, where do you want to go? Rouen in Normandy, is it?"

"Well, yes. Maybe."

"Where is it you want to go?"

"Barcelona." I blurt out.

"Barcelona?" Hector ticks away on the keys and turns on the printer. "Why Barcelona?" I detect a genuine interest.

"Queen. I love Freddie singing 'Barcelona' with the opera singer Montserrat Caballé." I become aware of sucking my tongue then pursing my lips. "Then Rouen

Hospital. I'd better go to Rouen soon. My life is waiting for me there."

"You're lucky to have a life to get back to. Hold on to it." He hands me the printouts of maps and directions. "Barcelona, Rouen… take your pick. If it's Barcelona, I have a cousin there. Her husband is Spanish. Linda would love female company from the UK."

"Is your cousin nice?"

"Sure. Why else would I send you? Meet you at the airfield at 11.00." He points to the sky. "Wave clouds are forming. It's going to be a brilliant flying day."

"See you later," I reply. Hector heads off; the clouds are calling him.

I return to the sunlight and walk down the street, turning off to visit the church. The bells in the tower are silent. I'm alone. I tread softly and listen to my shoes creeping over the old stone floor. It's simply built with soft curved arches and I like that. The altar is made of stone with a white cloth and two heavy brass candlesticks. A plain wooden cross is hung on the wall and I'm tempted to say a short prayer.

"They're OK without me, aren't they? Look after everyone, and don't forget the contestants at bingo. I'll be there soon. Thanks." A lady has come to tend the flowers; tweaking the arrangements while looking at me without expression.

Oh, help, I think. Spike is still in the room. What if the door is locked all day? Will there be anyone to let me in? A quick dash and I'm at the hostel. Stragglers are still milling in the doorway, staring knowledgably at maps and pointing all over the place. I put my head down and rush towards the stairs, hoping no one asks me if I can help direct them. Spike is waiting, and barks.

I scoop him up and bundle him downstairs, grabbing the last packed lunch from Reception as I pass. It's time to hike up to the airfield. The road is steep and twisting and my floppy sun hat is essential. The sky is empty apart from a line of clouds.

As I turn a corner, the clubhouse appears ahead of me. Hector sees me coming and beckons. "Come with me. I'll show you something wonderful," he says.

Briefly, I stop at the swimming pool to ask Dan and his girlfriend how they're getting on.

"Dan's had a bloody bucketful and wants to go home," the girl says. They both look equally bored. I guess Dan hasn't come up to expectation.

"If you want to go to Zaragoza airport I can take you. We'll talk later." From the look on their faces I take that as "Yes." I'm relying on the computer to give me a printout on how to get there without driving through Zaragoza town. My hope is that Dan has some sense underneath his facade of a dimwit.

Hector leads the way through the clubhouse and I trip along behind him, trying to keep up. A kind lady from behind the bar whisks Spike away as we pass. With a backward glance, I see Spike is being made a fuss of. We half run half walk across the field, to a row of ten gliders, and there are more being pulled from the hanger with human force. They're bigger close up and I can't resist stroking a shiny nose and running my fingertips along the edge of a wing. Hector reaches over me and into the small cockpit of a two-seater and hands me a red bag to strap on.

"Parachute," he explains. "You are up for flying? Got your sunglasses?"

I copy Hector as he straps himself up.

"I'm not jumping out when we're in the air." I have no idea what I'm letting myself in for and wonder what the hell the consequences of this will be.

"Safety precaution. We all wear them. You're safe in my hands. Trust me. I've never had cause to use one yet." There's no opportunity to argue.

"Climb in." Hector helps me step up to the front seat and I slide myself in. The cockpit smells of men, and sweet wrappers are stuffed in odd places. The controls on the dashboard mean nothing to me.

"I can't fly this." I'm all for getting out.

"Of course not. I'll be in control from behind you. We can talk with ground control on the radio and listen to the variometer. It measures our speed up and down. There's an altimeter on the dashboard, that tells you your height." Before I can argue we are both strapped in, the canopy is fixed over us… and I'm not aware of when I agreed to this.

The glider is hooked up to the tug plane that purrs away in front of us. Hector is on the radio.

"Juliet Bravo, take up slack." The tow-rope tightens and we move slowly along the runway. The tug plane is making all the engine noise.

I shuffle around, checking to see if there's a sick bag just in case – but there's nothing obvious. What if I want to wee? There's no answer to that apart from hold on.

"All out at your discretion." Hector is talking to the tug pilot. The engine roars and we're off, it's too late to change my mind. We are pulled along before taking off and then pulled higher and higher, nearer the sky and mountains. My stomach rises and falls with the movement.

As we cross the foothills, the glider bucks and jumps, hitting lively air pockets, ever rising, and heading for the trees beyond. We are lifted over the treetops. After a clunk I watch the tow-rope snake away, and watch the tug turn towards the airfield. We are gliding with the sound of the wind passing over us. The white wings are shimmering in the atmosphere.

"Relax. Your shoulders are hunched. Look around… enjoy. I'll trim her up. There should be lift hereabouts."

I've entered a new world.

"In stable flight," Hector informs ground control. We are close enough to see the pine needles on the trees that cling to the mountains, and the variometer bleeps away. Hector turns the glider almost on its wing tip and I stare down the wing. We straighten up and soar above the valley between mountains.

Concentration is total. Hector claps his hands near my ear; my heightened nerves make me shudder.

"It will soon be your turn to take control."

Is this man mad? He really is a Roald Dahl character – completely bonkers. The height of the snow-capped peaks above the Aragon Valley and river below are so breathtakingly beautiful that I abandon fear. If I'm going to die… what a way to go. The parachute sticks in my back. What was it I was supposed to pull if I have to bail out?

It's exciting and quietly lonely soaring in the mountain peaks with only air with thermals to hold us here. Hector's chat, punctuated with the occasional "Whahee," when suddenly rising, is comforting.

"Are we going over that mountain?"

"Monte Perdido is too high; we can't manage without oxygen. Tempting, isn't it? Here, would you like a biscuit or sweet?"

That would be taking a risk too far with my stomach, and Hector has picked up on my feelings.

"Look ahead. That's another thermal, look at the vultures soaring in it… beautiful in flight, aren't they? Look at that big white one. You only see them in this part of the world. That's where we'll go… follow the birds. You OK?"

"I think so," is my feeble reply.

"Now do as I say. Hold the control and look straight ahead. Push it forward gently." The nose of the glider tips down. "Now e… ease it back slowly." Because I'm nervous and I think it's like the car handbrake on an old Fiat, I drag it right back hard, and learn that you don't get a second chance with that kind of force. My brain has nothing in it but mush.

The nose goes up. I shove the control forward hard to rectify things and the glider begins to twist round and round. I lose sense of where we are. I think I'm in one of Dad's World War II dogfight films. Mountains, valleys, buildings and sky spin so fast they're merging into each other. My voice won't scream. Closing my eyes, I concentrate on keeping vomit in and what death will feel like.

"Oh, shit. Shit. I have control. I have control." Hector's steady hand takes us out of the spin until we glide forward. The sickness is going to stay around, hopefully inside my stomach, but I'm alive.

Recovery and the avoidance of heavy swearing takes concentration and effort. Hector's voice of sanity washes over me.

"It's OK to spin, but you're supposed to plan it. Fortunately, we're trained to deal with emergencies." He erupts with a good belly laugh. I think I'll be the talk of the clubhouse and hope it will soon be time to head for land and the hostel. "Are you good for a bit longer?"

"Yes," I squeak, dreaming of lying on my bed. "No more controls please." We fly towards Ordesa Gorge, and Hector explains that it has a drop of 4,000 feet. Roller coasters at fun parks have nothing on this, and nothing of the view. We sail along to Mount Oriel and practically touch the climbers standing on the top. They wave, with no knowledge of how dangerous I can be.

I'm emotionally exhausted when we turn in the direction of the airfield. Hector's on the radio, "Juliet Bravo… landing in ten minutes." Vultures share one last thermal with us, flying near our wing tip. We wave goodbye and return to the runway.

Hector's strong hand steadies me, as my legs shake badly while I attempt to climb out of the cockpit. Trying to release the parachute is impossible. I've never been much of a drinker but I could be tempted to try Zocco again. In fact, I crave it. In the event I become one of the boys and take the beer offered, swigging it back at speed. Telling them about the spin causes so much laughter, you could hear it from the top of Mount Oriel, and that's kilometers away.

"If there's a next time don't scare me. Here's my cousin's number in Barcelona. They're expecting you." Hector is nothing but calm and cheerful.

"Barcelona." I grasp the scrap of paper.

My attention is drawn to the young couple still sitting by the pool. When I can move from the security of the bar and I'm sure my legs can carry me, I'll go and try to encourage them home.

Hector fumbles in his pocket; he brings out a small silver compass and places it in my hand.

"Thanks, Hector. I'll keep it to remember you. Where's north? Where's south?"

"You still don't know? Here, let me show you. Now listen up." The magnetic hand rests facing north, and he proceeds with a lecture. What Hector has missed is that even if I know where north and south are that doesn't explain in which direction I'm supposed to go.

Katy says I need a gadget that's just on the market and will get cheaper and better in time. It would tell me which way to go; it has a talking voice announcing the twists and turns. It sometimes gets things wrong but it could be an investment worth having. It sounds as if it was made with people like me in mind but only if I keep travelling, and there's not much chance of that.

The gadget would have taken me straight to Rouen Hospital. I'd have spent all this time hanging around for Gerry – the story of my life. I'm pleased I haven't got one right now.

"Thanks, Hector." I kiss him on the cheek, feeling a tickle from his moustache. There's a glint in his eyes; no doubt, he's dwelling on my mistake in the glider.

Spike brushes himself on my legs as we start towards the pool. I pick him up and whisper, "They'll never believe me at bingo."

I dangle my feet over the side of the pool.

"You're brave," Dan says, coming closer and stroking Spike.

"Brave or crackers? Is it time you told me your name?" I'm speaking to the top of the girl's head as she hugs her knees and stares at her feet.

"Scarlett," she mumbles. "And no, my mum wasn't reading *Gone with the Wind*. She named me after my aunty

– and yes, Grandma loved the whole Scarlett story and I get sick of telling people."

"So, Scarlett and Dan, am I taking you to the airport tomorrow? If so, we need to sort out your flight and you need to arrange your journey from Heathrow home." They don't have mobile phones, which is odd.

With my packed lunch and extra cakes bought at the clubhouse, there's enough to share. Lunch is amicable but silence rules over attempts at conversation. We take a walk to the river before collecting the key to the computer room. I go with them to the door. Scarlett is with me and Dan straggles behind. He stands as if in line as I unlock, and then he files in past me.

We sort out a ticket and a map that shows I can avoid the town on the way to the airport, but I'll still need support from Dan. We go our own ways for the rest of the day and agree to be ready to leave at 9.30 a.m. tomorrow.

In the computer room, I check my emails. Alex has been efficient; he has sent me a list of interesting websites and asks when I would like to visit the BBC studios.

By the way, it was very nice to meet you, he writes.

The BBC visit is an awkward question. I can't go without Gerry, and Gerry won't be interested in coming unless there is a sporting connection. I don't have to give an answer right away.

There's someone I need to speak to before leaving Santa Cilia. He stands in the square; he's made of grey metal and is twice as tall as me. He has a pouch and I wonder if he's a pardoner who collected money so that people could die sin-free. I take off my shell necklace and give it to him, thanking him for my pilgrimage. I've found more self-confidence, and a sense of fun and friendship with strangers; that's enough seeking for now. I have the desire to make it to Barcelona before returning home.

I'm changing and Gerry is staying the same. I won't be left at home again when he goes off doing his sports-related things. I need more of him. If I live until I'm eighty I don't want to spend most of the next forty years on my own, but married. Then only end up with his company, if he becomes decrepit. That isn't a life together.

The morning brings more than I bargained for. Scarlett, Dan and I meet after breakfast and pack everything, including Spike, into my little car. Dan sits in the front and I give him the map as well as the printed directions. We are going to need them.

I've known one other person who lined up when he approached a door and then filed in; he had spent time in prison. I've caught a glimpse of Scarlett's passport and she is only fifteen. I want to see her home safely. Dan doesn't strike me as dangerous, more the easily led type. I also know that bad people don't have three eyes and a warning sign.

We make it to the airport with reasonable ease. Dan isn't too bad at reading maps and directions, thank goodness. I'm not happy leaving them, so I park and go as far as check-in. Dan goes off to the toilets, leaving Scarlett and me alone. I take my mobile from my pocket, "You could ring your mum and tell her you're coming home. Trust me, she won't be cross."

Timidly she takes the phone and moves away, out of earshot. Dan returns and I keep him chatting until she comes back red-eyed. I know she has made the right contact. They head towards customs and I whisper to Dan, "Do the decent thing and leave her alone to grow up."

"Can't fucking wait to get rid of the daft kid."

Before they go through the gates Dan has fallen back in the queue, leaving Scarlett to board on her own. I have done what I can and wish them both well.

Spike and I are alone again.

9

Barcelona and a Question of Sex

"Sorry I didn't ring yesterday, but you could have rung me. I'm fine but I need two more days. I'm still in Spain; we're on the same bit of land." Gerry is in superior mood, and his sighing is on the increase.

"I picked up the *People's Post* today." There's a pause and a rustle of paper. "You're on the front page with Britney Spears. You spoke to a vision of John Lennon at Lourdes. Nat, you have to come back. We'll get you some pills and counselling. Ouch, some idiot tripped into my foot."

"It wasn't a vision. He was real."

"Are you m…?" Gerry controls his words. "I want to get my bike and go home. I need a new one. Is there anything left of your bonus? The insurance money won't cover the model I want. Katy's ordered some brochures for me. I can choose which one will be best to improve my speed."

I'm not interested in his bike. I know I should be more caring, but it isn't happening. If I'm guilty of anything wrong, I know I've spent the past week getting more and more wrapped up in myself.

"I'm going to Barcelona," I say to him.

"Why?" he shouts in my ear.

"Queen." I can feel the gulf between us has just become bigger, and over the phone isn't the way to put things right. "I'll ring you later. I promise." I'm pleased to put the phone away and start driving. It rains like a sudden cloudburst. The cosiness of the car and the swish of the wheels give me solace. I'm aware my situation has caused deep concern.

Scarlett has made me think more of Katy. I'll stop to eat my packed lunch and try to catch her on her mobile. I miss the chats we have at home.

When I stop in a lay-by, I see Harry has been trying to call me. It must be important so I ring back. I'm not expecting what he tells me. The bingo hall is closing. With bingo on the Internet and smart new bingo palaces, fewer people are coming to play at the old hall. I knew the numbers were down but I thought we would have a meeting and come up with ideas and everything would be all right again.

My pleasure in being away has disappeared. What about Joan, Fred, Joy and the others? Where will they go? For the young ones it will be the pub or nothing. Bingo is cheaper than the new cinema complex with expensive buckets of popcorn and drinks. That's what it all comes down to: money. My sadness turns to anger; they need me to fight for them and what's right.

I know Harry has no fight in him and therefore no job. If he isn't at the hall working, who will employ him? He changes light bulbs, checks on the cleaners, counts the cash and smokes. He's fifty-five and lives in a council flat on his own. He had a wife once, but he had an affair. After that, neither wife nor woman wanted him. I have Katy, Dad and Gerry. Dad won't be around forever and Katy will spread her wings and fly before long. That leaves Gerry and me with possibly half our lives left.

I value Lisa and Susie like family, and I care about the people at bingo. Making new friends while travelling through France and Spain, has been fantastic. Some of the people I've met on my journey I'll be staying in touch with, and others I will never forget.

My plan is to work hard on the photography course. A bingo caller with photographic qualifications must fit somewhere. *Stay positive, Natalie,* I think.

It's easier to find my way with the computer map, especially with the directions written down the side as well. I'd have preferred human guidance but that isn't possible. Sometimes I have to turn around to find a road I've just missed, but that's not too bad. All the names are new to me.

The printout map says four hours twenty-five minutes; five and a half hours later I'm on the outskirts of Barcelona. That's good, bearing in mind that a two-day trip has taken ten. Things are definitely getting better.

The Olympic anthem, *'Barcelona',* is ready to belt out of my CD player. I sing along, pretending to be Montserrat Caballé singing with Freddie Mercury. The sound reflects my triumph. I follow the signs to the car park where I've agreed to meet José, who should be waiting to show me the way to their apartment. When I get there I can't see him so, I ring Harry again to pass the time.

"What's that music? Where are you?" Harry asks. I turn the music down, especially as people in the car parked next to me are distracted by the noise. This conversation is important; old-established businesses in Eastleigh are realising the ripple effect of planning decisions.

Harry has found out more. Our hall, the hairdressers and the newsagents are going to be demolished so that the three-screen cinema complex with restaurants can be extended alongside the shopping mall. An entrance to the extra parking spaces is going where the newsagents is.

I feel bereft. Losing the bingo hall is bad enough, but I have used the hairdressers for twenty years and have always bought our paper and others things from Mr. and Mrs. Singh. They are part of my life and the community. We know one another's business; for good or bad.

What will Joan, Fred, Joy and their friends do with a three-screen cinema complex?

"How long have we got, Harry?"

"Just over a week. You'd better get back here quick if you think you can do something."

"What about Theresa's ashes buried under the cherry tree outside? They can't build over a grave."

"They can. If you remember, we didn't ask permission to bury them. Only her family and we two know she's there. The box they were in will have disintegrated."

"What will you do, Harry?"

"Don't know yet. They said I can have my cubicle and I'm going to erect it by my vegetable patch. It will be a mini greenhouse."

"You live in a flat, Harry."

"I've got an allotment."

"I didn't know that."

When Harry's cubicle is erected in the middle of a group of allotments, it will warrant a photograph. Perhaps I can sell it to the *Eastleigh Standard*. My first photography job? I have worked with Harry for ten years and never knew he grew his own veg. I've rarely seen him outside his cubicle. He's there when I arrive, and still there when I leave. Not a lot of conversation goes on through smoke and scratched plastic windows.

Occasionally I've found a bag of runner beans or fresh tomatoes left for me on the side of the stage. Fred is a keen gardener and I presumed they were from him. Three times this year there have been half a dozen eggs. Does he keep chickens as well? I always thanked Fred for the gifts but he's deaf. It's not surprising he just smiled. At bingo, Rose helps by writing the numbers down for him.

José's car has arrived and is waiting by the exit. I hurriedly say goodbye to Harry and pull up behind José. We acknowledge each other before venturing on to the road. I'm amazed and proud I've made it this far.

We weave our way through narrow, one-way streets and end up in a square surrounded by modern blocks of flats. Getting parked is a relief and having someone with me has been the only way to drive in a town like this.

Anyone from a different town or country has to learn new places. If I lived here I would learn my way around. I'm sure I would… maybe.

My unruly hair feels better for a shake. After unwinding my body from the cramped driving space I offer my hand to José, then he welcomes me with a big smile and three kisses. This friendly man takes my case, leaving me with Spike and his supplies. The lift quietly glides up to the fifth floor, where we enter a spacious and plush apartment. Gold and red decor glows all over the place.

Two of the lounge walls are covered with bullfighting paraphernalia; there are posters, photos, a spear and a full-size matador outfit. José doesn't look the type, but I'm filled with admiration for this smallish Spaniard taking on the mighty bull. Dressed in his matador costume, he does look bigger and bolder in the photos. The picture of a bull, with several banderillas in his shoulders, and blood on his body makes me feel sick. I take a second look at Spike, hoping it isn't all animals that José treats this way. His friendliness reassures me for now.

Linda appears with almost a skip.

"José found you. How's our Hector? Still has an eye for the ladies, I see. Drink? What would you like to do?"

José takes my bag to a distant bedroom. I sip freshly squeezed orange juice and hand Spike to Linda. "Would you take him for a while if I go to the City Centre?"

"If you want to get lost, go out on your own. Come on. I'll take you." Linda finds her bag and flat shoes. "We need to plan where we want to go and what we want to do, the bus is our best bet."

Linda hands me a guidebook with a map of Barcelona. "It's divided into six different areas," she explains. I'm lost before leaving the apartment and feel useless and deflated after my earlier success of driving here.

"What do you want to do the most? We've got a few hours before this evening and all day tomorrow, but we still can't cover it all."

"OK. Gaudi, Miro, Picasso, shopping," I gabble.

"Stop there. We can plan all those but your feet will ache and your head buzz. We can go to Gaudi's Sagrada Família this evening. It's at its best lit up. Right now, there's time for shopping. We can pass some Gaudi buildings and Miro sculptures."

My heart is racing; we're ready to go. Before leaving the house, I watch as Linda kisses José passionately. I put it down to keeping close to a matador in case someone else arrives on the scene. I can't imagine kissing Gerry like that when I leave the house, or do I mean ever? When were we last passionate? If he was something more exciting than a sports shop manager, would I be more passionate? He doesn't encourage me, or I don't think he does. Does he find me exciting? The unanswered questions hang with me.

155

I haven't thought about it before; I take our love as it comes. My shoulders hunch at the thought of Gerry and home.

"I'll treat you to a coffee in my favourite cafe. You'll get a feel for Barcelona and we can get to know each other better before the stresses of roaming around hit us."

The cafe is part of a bakery with freshly baked bread, big doughnuts and iced cakes. We are in a side street where traffic doesn't come. At the table, I study the guide. Linda speaks fluent Catalan to friends passing by, the result of living here for eighteen years.

"How old were you when you met and married José?" I ask her.

"We met at a bullfight when I was eighteen. We married a year later. I was pregnant. You have our daughter's room. She left to study in London a year ago."

These two have no children at home and openly love each other. Is that what happens with the empty nest syndrome? Do you find each other all over again?

A crisp filo pastry filled with apple and a touch of liqueur, then covered with whipped cream, arrives with my coffee. The waiter knows Linda and the pastry is a gift – his speciality. How can I refuse it? The delicate spoon that comes with it is reassuring; many little mouthfuls taken slowly can't have as many calories as big ones wolfed down with speed.

"Have you thought of having your hair cut and styled?" Linda is staring at my head. Before I can answer she's on her mobile asking if her stylist will take a look at my hair and make some suggestions as to what would suit me.

There's nothing wrong with my hair. It's dark brown with a natural light tinge and sits in curls on my shoulders. There was no time to visit my usual lady before I left. What will she think if I change my style without chatting it over with her first?

The argument is swung when I remember my hairdresser is under the same compulsory purchase order as the bingo hall. In a week it will have gone. It's easy and cheap to go there and has nothing too smart about it. My style has been the same for years. I hope my stylist will stay in a salon close by.

Half an hour later, my curls fall to the floor. Anton is going on at length about what wonderful thick hair I have, but it needs thinning out to look chic. Anton leaves my ears covered but my neck is showing bright white where it hasn't been exposed to the sun. Gerry likes my hair the way it was but Katy thinks I should have changed it years ago. 'If it's OK why change', has been my philosophy. The mirror shows a different me and Anton is prancing around with delight at his new creation.

The nail therapist works on my nails and I have to choose between fifty different colours of varnish. I stare at the black and wonder. Pale pink might be safe. I pick up the bottle and hold it to the light from the window. Pink makes me feel feminine. Sparkling turquoise catches my eye. I hesitate then point.

The hand therapist wears long nail extensions with tiny black sequins. She tidies my cuticles and massages my hands before putting on a coat of polish. We're ushered to a row of chairs near the window to wait for my nails to dry. When she's finished all three coats, my nails look amazing and blue. I observe the various stages of hair washing and cutting in the main salon. I would love my hairdresser to see it. This place would be too big and luxurious even for the new Eastleigh.

Coffee is provided free.

"Mind your nails," says the young girl. I take a large handled mug that is easy to hold. This is shopping Linda-style and I'm wondering what the bill will be. Finally, we're served tiny biscuits, and I'm careful not to rub or catch crumbs on my nails as I eat.

"How's your sex life?"

"Pardon, Linda?" I reply, playing for time.

"Lingerie shopping… substantial knickers, medium-size knickers, or thongs and lacy bits?"

"Oh… medium."

"English women are like that. That's why I married José – excitement."

"So you wear thongs and lacy bits?"

"All the way. You should try it."

I study the bill and it's expensive. It's three times what a haircut would cost at home, plus the nails. Fancy spending this much on something that is going to disappear after a couple of weeks…

Losing a baby and my inability to have children has affected how I think about myself. What will the fact that I'm forty bring to my life? What's it going to be like? With shiny hair that moves as I walk and nails I can't stop looking at I feel more like thirty.

We're heading for the lingerie shop. I'll look around, but intend to leave with my usual style of comfortable pants and reasonably priced bra. The rule is, if it's not in a sale don't buy it.

I look at pink or cream matching sets. Linda picks up red. I venture into blue medium-size knickers and she picks up shiny black thongs. We go to the desk to pay. My purchases are wrapped in fine white tissue paper before being placed in a spacious box.

Linda says something to the assistant, and all the items are parceled up into one bag and tied with yellow ribbon. They are all mine.

"Are you ready for Picasso tomorrow?"

Ready? No more pressure about sex inflicted on me would be a relief. An art gallery should be safe ground, except Picasso was into sex big time.

"We'll go home for a quick supper, then José will drive us out to see Gaudi's church."

I'm not sure if I find Linda's approach intrusive or fun. Either way, girl talk is making me think. I've discussed sex on Chardonnay evenings with Lisa and Susie. Lisa said, "Do what you want and enjoy it. If you don't want what he wants then tell him to sod off." Susie reckoned God said married people should share a positive attitude to sex, and there were plenty of Christian books that told you how. Her second husband banned sex on Saturday nights, as he wanted to concentrate on his sermon for the next day. His congregation was entitled to his full attention, like a footballer playing football. Lisa and I had our own private view that he might be concentrating elsewhere.

"Playing away," Lisa said.

I regard myself as ordinary and normal and Gerry is happy enough. When Susie said she would lend me one of her Christian books Lisa said, "You don't need it. Just go by what you feel," but she thinks I could do with freeing up, and she's probably right.

I text Lisa: *Bought black shiny thong, a bra and matching red lace knickers. What will G think?*

I'm sure he likes thgs and lc, came the reply. *Try them.*

To see Gaudi's church at night is fantastic. After driving nearby, we park and walk about. The spires and architecture are between the impression of a Gothic castle and part of a film set. You have to look closely to see it's a Christian church. To see such art and sculpture fills me with desire to know more, to see more. How will I put this genie back in its bottle? I take photographs and more photographs to take home.

The galleries of Picasso and Miro are for tomorrow, but another shopping trip is important to me. Linda is all for it and knows just the shop.

Before bed I use Linda and José's computer. I set myself up on The Facebook and request Katy and Alex as friends, then hit the privacy button. I check my emails and Alex has sent to me again. He's remembering my company and hopes to meet in London. Why would he say that? He might be married and I certainly am. This is casual computer speak. Press reply:

I am not going to meet you as anything other than a friend and… and… No. Stop there. I can't send it. It's too complicated and we will stop communicating soon, anyway. There's no reason to tell him or anyone else that I can't have any more children. What was I thinking of? I'm tired.

Next morning I'm in a shop with beautiful antique fans displayed on the walls, racks of dancing shoes and – what I've secretly wanted for ages – a flamenco dress. I try on an expensive one for fun. I put on the shoes and hold a fan. The assistant encourages me, but this is too much in money and style. Now I try something simpler in style – one red and one turquoise. They are wrapped in tissue paper for me, and placed in a fan-shaped carrier bag. The dresses aren't too flouncy or dancey. I can wear them out occasionally, or dream of wearing them if I have the right place to go. They make me feel like dancing.

Picasso was off his head; weird but exciting. Miro made lots of shapes with colours, turning his back on the art establishment. I try to make up my mind which artist I like the best, but they're so different. My life is richer for my visit here. Thank you, Freddie Mercury. You planted a seed that grew. Thank you, Barcelona, for inspirational art.

The Picasso house that is also a gallery takes leg power going from room to room. It's spacious, and I can take time to absorb the ambience of paintings and read some of the information. Picasso thought we needed to understand a painting to truly appreciate it, but if I waited to understand each one I would spend all day not seeing much. Through his art, he says lots about himself and his view of the world. He has a mixed-up view of sex, but that's my opinion and I don't think it counts for much. I can read more about Picasso later.

Look, Natalie. Look, I impress upon myself.

His paintings went through a blue phase and a rose phase. He changed and developed his art over the years and his life changed in parallel. What colour phase is my life in right now? Turquoise – from the look of my nails, my car, the flamenco dress and the underwear I just bought.

Reflecting on my own art and photography, it has remained the same for years – and that says a lot about me.

I need to see more art. I need to paint and take photographs. At least I'll have different ways to express myself, especially if the rest of life stays the same.

A hundred years ago Picasso went from Barcelona to Paris. If I take time in Paris, again one day I *will* look for more of him. Who was that sculptor? Rodin. I fancy going to his place in Paris; that would be totally amazing. There's so much to cram into the rest of my life, making the fragments of learning from the past into something more tangible. Light bulbs flash and flash in my brain.

I can hear the sober voice of Gerry saying, "Money, Nat," and, "Who do you think you are?"

We stop for coffee and I thank Linda for the great time I'm having. I need this break to prepare myself for Miro, and his creations with colour.

I don't understand the abstract artwork, but it's fun to bend myself at different angles to change the view.

"I don't think you're supposed to do that," Linda suggests as I practically fall on my head.

In a big white building, I drift from Miro's paintings to his sculptures and back again, feeling as if the colours have jumped inside me. I want to stay longer in Barcelona but can't justify more time away to Gerry.

Back at the apartment, a familiar face greets me. Hector has come to join us. I'm genuinely pleased to see him.

"Try on your new clothes, Natalie," José and Linda coax. I rush to my room and open the bags. I hesitate, taking time to run my fingers over the tissue paper and stroking the fan-shaped carrier bag.

I throw the dresses on the bed; the choice is red or turquoise. I choose red to model for the men. It comes to mid calf with frills across the bust, and has flounces around the waved hem of the skirt. There were other dresses of that were fuller in the skirt, but the two I've chosen look wearable for a special occasion.

The long mirror at the end of the hall flatters me. My new hairstyle sets the outfit off perfectly. I dance through the lounge and make a stance at the door to show off. Linda strikes up a flamenco note. She throws me castanets and holds on to a pair. We dance together as she sings ever louder, moving from table to chair to sofa. It's fun to dance the flamenco, which I learned four years ago. It isn't much, but I improvise.

José picks up his guitar to add to the flamenco rhythm.

"Find the gypsy in your soul," Linda enthuses, and shows off her talent with the castanets. Hector joins in, clapping loudly to the beat. The spirit of the flamenco has released its wild side.

Hector drops the rhythm and applauds as we fall back in the chairs. "Well, what are your plans, Natalie? I see you got here just fine."

"It wasn't too difficult. I reached the outskirts… just a sec, I need to catch my breath… José was waiting for me, like you said. He drove slowly and all I had to do was follow. Tomorrow I must make my way to Paris, then on to Rouen. Frankly, I've no idea how." I didn't add that right now I didn't care.

"José will help. He'd love a trip to France. He can take some photos." Linda sits back, lifting her hair from the nape of her neck, and waits for us to sort something out between us.

"It's too hot, I'll put the air con up," José says. The room cools at the flick of a switch.

"What do you like to take photos of, José?" I'm hoping to find a kindred spirit who might teach me something about the art of photography.

Linda looks at José, who looks at Linda, who looks at José. I wonder if I've said something wrong when José stutters, "I take photos of electricity pylons."

A short silence holds in the air before I blurt out, "Pylons? Is that something to do with your job? You're a bullfighter." I draw José's attention to the bullfighting memorabilia.

"That's my dad. The bull got even. They have horns, remember, and one got to gore Dad in the groin. He died of blood loss. I won't go near beef, dead or alive."

"I see." At least I think I do.

"Mum said she'd been thinking of knifing him in the groin for years. Matadors have quite a reputation and Dad was no exception. He was married to my mum but there are various half-brothers and half-sisters around. Mum said she was better off financially when Dad had gone, but underneath she was extremely sad. She visited his grave often, but there were always flowers from women and children she didn't know. She didn't want me to go into the ring." José reaches into a drawer, takes out a pile of photo albums and firmly lands them in my lap. "Look at these, if you like."

An album wobbles on my knee as I put the others to one side to stop them sliding to the floor. I turn the neatly set-out pages. There are 300 or more photos of electricity pylons set behind cellophane protective sheets.

"I like electricity. I belong to an Internet club where we swap photos. I took about 150 of those myself. The rest I downloaded and printed. I've got friends all over the world. France has great pylons. I could show you some then send you on your way." I watch the excitement in his eyes.

"If you know where you're going, I'd be grateful. It's my birthday tomorrow. I'm forty." I struggle to hand back the albums. I've given them inadequate attention I know, but after twenty or thirty photos, I'm aware of wanting to sleep.

"See you in the morning," I say. I take a sandwich and drink to my room, mull over the day and – importantly –

ring Gerry. Tomorrow I will make sure Linda understands that I don't want to break free from Gerry. I still love him very much, and loyalty could be my middle name.

Spike appears happy, if less bouncy from what I would have considered normal a few weeks ago. He doesn't go out, apart from quick visits to the park. He walks around the apartment with his head in the air, looking as if he owns it. This is another place he must hide, as animals are not allowed in the apartments.

I phone Gerry, looking for love and companionship in his voice. It isn't there. He has an easy knack of crushing my warmth and sympathy.

"José's going to lead you, you say. Concentrate on following him; you need a man to look after you. Thank him from me. What does this José do?"

"He's a bullfighter, a famous one. Tomorrow I'm running with bulls."

"Bloody hell. You can't do that. Ouch. Fuck." Gerry is sucking in air. He must have hurt himself.

"Don't get so irate. It isn't doing you any good."

"Your mum was odd, Nat, you're just like her. I wasn't expecting this at your age."

"Joke, Gerry. Joke. Goodnight. See you soon. Be happy." I find the photo of Dad, Katy and Spike and the one of Lisa, Gerry and me, and put them on my bedside table. Spike is sitting close to Katy; she must be missing him.

I try to ring Katy, but the phone's engaged. Gerry must be speaking to her.

I don't usually fish for information; I don't have reason to, but I want to know what he's saying.

"Hi, Mum. Dad said you're travelling back with a python hunter. I've been speaking to the *Eastleigh Standard* and now the *People's Post*. Dad's read the articles they've published, and I think he's proud of me, but I'm not sure what he thinks of you. I talk to journalists all the time you carry on getting lost. I've told them about the pythons in France. Make sure you take photos, but don't get too close for your own safety. They hug too much. I don't want both parents in hospital."

I don't want to let her down, I'm sure that will happen when she sees pictures of electricity pylons. I could do with a hug, but not from a python.

"Dad said there's something really wrong with you, and he wants to know if you watch too many TV soaps and daytime TV. He's worried they might be sending you crazy. I told him he was grumpy. He needs to get out of hospital and on his bike."

The phone calls are making my head buzz. I wonder if they're right. Is there something wrong with me? Katy says I'm going to be on radio and TV when I get home: *The Lost Mother Returns*. I put it down to her vivid imagination and misplaced sense of humour.

"Gramps is pleased with the chess set from the charity shop. It's exactly like his old one, and he's playing with Matt most evenings again." Dad's doing a good job of keeping Matt downstairs. Teenage sexual experimentation is not a thought I want in my head right now.

Sleep comes easily after a day in Barcelona. First thing in the morning, I really will be driving in the right direction for Gerry and home. It marks the end of my journey, but I wish I didn't have mixed feelings. It's always difficult to resettle into daily routines after having a great time discovering new places and things. It will be all right when I'm in Eastleigh, and I have my birthday party to organise.

It's time to leave the apartment. My baggage has increased and the lack of room for Spike in the back of the car places him in danger of being crushed. Gerry travels light, but there's the question of his bike.

10

Safari in France

It's my fortieth birthday. I need to show everyone today is special, so I wear my new red dress to get noticed. Hector is joining us on our pylon safari and then driving on to Paris. He has no one to go home to, he is his own master.

Linda has come to the car park to say goodbye. She pats Spike goodbye, as I place him on what little space is available on the back seat. I look at him and reflect on how he has been these last few days. Perhaps he's sulking at the unfamiliar surroundings. He's sleeping more than usual and not eating properly. His age and the heat could also be plausible reasons. My car is too old for air con, but even indoors he's not so lively.

"We'll stop at the first great pylon," José calls.

"Hector, take the picnic," Linda remarks, standing by a pile of bags and boxes. I'm glad it's all going in his car. Soft bread rolls, paper plates, serviettes, a picnic rug, packets of crisps, bottles of fresh orange juice and lemonade and still more food is all lifted into Hector's car. We thank Linda, and again she and José share an affectionate kiss and cuddle.

It isn't because he's an exciting bullfighter; I found out he's a sewage engineer. It's because of who they are together, and they make a habit of affection. I'm jealous of what they have. Hector turns away to get in his car. Linda clocks his feelings and rushes to hug him and say goodbye.

Hector lost his wife seven years ago. She died of cancer, and he's never really got over it. Gliding and travelling has helped to fill the gap, but it's not a substitute. Apart from the time he's in the sky, he's making an emotional effort.

"See you again," Linda says. Now I'm the recipient of affection I'm strangely grateful for the warmth shown to me.

Until I glanced at José's photos, I hadn't noticed how many different pylons there are. They can look like giant ladies, men and families, with arms outstretched ready to walk or dance. He had a special French pylon album with photos taken across French fields. Pylons lined up three deep and ten across, making an orchestra. I'll be dreaming of pylons moving around and partying together.

We convoy out of Barcelona. It's only eight o'clock and I'm not sure how many hours it will take to get to Paris, if that is what we intended to do. Time has to be added for driving through the countryside to find the best pylons and stopping for our picnic. I figure I should make Paris by early evening. There's every point in trying to make it to Rouen this evening. If I don't they may put Gerry out and leave him to fend for himself. I'll do my best, but old Fiats don't go fast.

I try to speak to Gerry. He is losing patience, and it's in his tone of voice. It's humiliating and I wish I could communicate better. Is it him or is it me? I switch from one view to another and think of Picasso's faces divided by shape and colour.

Lisa has texted that Eldred wants to get married and start a family. She has decided she needs time to think it over. I can't imagine Lisa doing the marriage and motherhood thing but hope it works for her, if that's what she wants.

Eldred certainly wants the whole family life thing. Forty isn't necessarily too late.

Lisa said Susie is struggling. Can't wait to get home and have a girlie night, this time I'll have lots to talk about. I have no relationship problems, thank goodness, Gerry and I are always stable, but we're suffering from being apart. He may need to make adjustments to take in my new self-confidence and find time to listen to my stories. When I told him about gliding with birds he said nothing, he thought I was making it up. I didn't mention the spin.

The morning passes quickly and concentration ensures I keep up with the others. We turn off the road to follow a row of pylons along a country lane, until José turns in to a lay-by. Pylon hunters have maps showing where to park and which pylons to see. The first important pylon turns out to be a giant in a field on its own with loads of heavy wires swinging from its arms. It's painted red and white and has a head that's too small. I expect it to take off and walk at any minute. It would make a great kids' horror film – *Pylons Take Over the World* – with scary music thumping a rhythm to its steps.

We gather the picnic, and all carrying something, climb the fence and trail across the field. Telltale pats of cow dung and the accompanying brown flies have to be stepped around. I wish I'd worn something more practical than my red flamenco dress and flat lightweight driving shoes. Flies have taken to landing on my legs; they're adding fuel to my horror-film thoughts.

Pylons are bigger close up, hissing and buzzing in pylon language. José starts taking photos from different angles. Joining in the madness, I give him my camera to take a shot of me, with as much of the pylon he can manage in the background.

Hector spreads the picnic blanket and sets out the salad, rolls and individual apple pies. Flies don't concern him. We drink real orange juice from Spain and settle down to relish the feast. I continue swatting flies here and there, against the wishes of the rest of the party. As I eat the last of the cheese Hector puts his hand behind his back, brings out a small chocolate birthday cake and lights a candle that plays 'Happy Birthday' repeatedly. This is a party I won't forget.

With José scared silly of bulls, the cowpats have unsettled him. Spike is twitchy and has his nose turned up, smelling the breeze. I give José the job of feeding Spike to take his mind off things.

"There are no cows in the field now, José. Trust me. Those cowpats are dry and full of dung beetles." Hector's deep voice would steady anyone's nerves in the same way as it steadied mine in the glider.

"What made you choose to be a sewage engineer?" I ask.

"I'm safe underground and it's a job that has to be done. These days I work in the office on design. I worked underground for the Olympic Games in 1992. Someone had to keep the sewers flowing... all that shit... I should have had a lap of honour for the work I did."

José turns on a hand-held radio cassette player. It crackles with electrical interference. My hair is standing on end, sticking to my hand, as I run my fingers over the top. I'm contemplating the strange effects of electricity when I catch a look in Hector's eye and follow his line of view. In the field is a heavy black bull.

It's nearer to us than we are to the fence and it's plodding in our direction. It's easy to mistake his lack of speed for possible friendliness. Spike has perked up and is looking around, he growls before starting to bark. His bark isn't loud enough to scare a rat. We watch, not blinking, as the bull gathers speed. Huddled together in the centre of the pylon we're unprotected. We look at each other to see which one will be sacrificed.

The bull's nostrils are mesmerising, and his hooves reverberate through the ground. He hesitates, scraping the ground with his front hoof. Should we run around the pylon legs to try and confuse him?

José and Hector tug at my skirt. With a penknife, Hector splits the length of the material.

Armed with a red skirt José steps forward and the sewage engineer turns toreador while the pylon buzzes louder. I can hear the bullring cheers and hope this nightmare will stop.

The cassette player crackles its way through Spanish guitar music and José is manoeuvring the bull with a twirl of my skirt above his head and a flash by his side. I wish I could take photos, but there's too much angst in my brain to concentrate on getting the camera out. How long can José keep this up?

In a cloud of dust the farmer appears over the horizon, driving a big old tractor and yelling in French. He is using the same hand gestures as the man with the chickens who fell off his bike in the Loire Valley. Hector and I make our way to the edge of the field, leaving José and the farmer to sort things out.

The bull is attached with a rope to the tractor, but not before it has trampled all over the chocolate cake and eaten the candle. I imagine the candle still playing 'Happy Birthday' in its stomach until the battery runs out. We didn't get to share the cake, but we are alive and unhurt. José the hero comes to join us.

Spike is in my arms, to keep him clear of the muck he would love to roll in. Hector hands over the picnic rug to cover my bare legs. I'm grateful I wore my medium-size knickers. What good would a thong have done me now? The pylon we have left behind has my red skirt attached and it's blowing in the wind. This is my photo opportunity.

I want to tell Gerry and Katy I was chased by a bull, but not in the streets of Barcelona. We go for a group hug to release the tension. Residual electricity sparkles between us, making us jump apart.

José is telling us how two of his friends were arrested in Greece for photographing an electricity station. They were charged with spying and, if it wasn't for the diplomacy of the British government, they would still be in prison there. No one in Greece believed that people took photos of pylons and that some visit electricity stations as well. It isn't something I'll be taking up as a hobby.

I rummage through my case and find my cut-off jeans. I'm sorry to abandon my skirt but no one, including José, is going back for it. Anyway, it's pretty ripped. How would I explain having a skirt ripped off in a field to Gerry?

"Sorry, José. It's time to be on our way. We'll leave you to photograph your pylons and return home to Linda. I'll follow Hector to Paris and we'll say our goodbyes there." I sit in my car, behind Hector, he has learned his lesson about trusting me in the front.

My phone rings. It must be Gerry wanting to know where I am and if my day is going well. I'll speak to him later, when I can confirm I'll make it to the hospital this evening.

It's three hours before I tune into the rattle coming from under the car. It was there earlier, but went away. It's there again, and getting worse. If I can get to Rouen, then Gerry can help me sort it out. The more I travel the louder the rattle. I can't slow down – Hector would be bothered or worse, lose me – so I keep going.

A horrid clunk happens and the rattle has stopped. I pull over to check and stare at my exhaust in the middle of the road. Men are for mending cars and catching spiders. I am not. This is another one of those consequences that crop up. It's a time when doubts about what I have done rush at me.

I wait for a clear road to retrieve the rusted exhaust and think: *Should I ring Gerry?* I hold the phone, debating, then decide that Dad might be a better bet.

"Keep driving to a garage, preferably an exhaust centre, and get it repaired there. They should do it quite quickly for you."

"Thanks, Dad. I'm on route to Gerry and was doing well until this happened. This damned exhaust has held me up."

"You shouldn't have taken an old car as far as you have. What will you do for a car if that one is no more use?" I'm in trouble and a little girl again. I need to fight the feeling off. I can do this; I need to find a garage and sort the problem out.

I lift Spike out of the car and give him a short break. He laps his drink then tries to vomit. Spike is more of a concern than the car, but soon he is better and we can go on. Now there's no Hector to follow.

I read the directions and think I can follow them. My new confidence pleases me. Five minutes down the road, I spot Hector coming back. His ready smile is a relief. We chat about the problem and he takes control. I'm grateful.

An hour later, all is well again. I have a new exhaust, but with that and the cost of the fuel, I'm aware of more and more money disappearing.

I wonder how long my skirt will stay on the pylon catching the wind, or if the farmer has taken it down. It's a shame because I liked that dress, but I still have the top of it.

11

Returning

We're on the Paris *Périphérique*. Hector points from his window and I exit at the Le Havre and Rouen junction. My computer printout is prominent on the passenger seat. The compass is at hand, but only for the entertainment value of watching it turn to north, south, east and west.

I am longing to see Gerry. I want to touch him, and smell his scent. We have been apart too long. It may be just a visit tonight, but I'm hoping he will be allowed out and we can share time on my birthday. We'll be going home together tomorrow.

I'm trying hard to follow the signs, but it isn't easy. My heart misses beats along with the stress of worrying what to do if I take the wrong turning. I hope I've made the right decisions. So far I've avoided accidents, which is surprising.

Katy and Gerry were right; Rouen has a major hospital, with many signs to it. How could I have missed it on the way? Sorting out directions and organising my route has become easier. There are mistakes, of course – but I can stop, look at the map and rectify my direction without panicking – even if it takes several attempts and gear crunches. I'm sure I wouldn't have made it back quite so easily without Hector and José.

I've booked a hotel near the hospital. The receptionist has promised to keep a room for me… it may be us. I hope so. The car park is practically empty, as all the other visitors have gone. The atmosphere has cooled and Spike is sleeping. He can stay here for now.

I run towards the hospital. Here at last. I leap up the steps with a few precious items in my bag. I imagine the look on Gerry's face when he sees me, and the big long hug we will have. He'll be so proud of me. Everything will be OK.

I've remembered the bottle and hold it tightly under my arm. I'm not going to drop this one and, anyway, it's plastic.

My reflection revolves with the door and I make a decision to look in mirrors more often, as they are there for a reason. Gerry won't mind what I look like, the important thing is that I'm here. The hospital echoes quietness. The light pad-pad from the nurses' shoes as they prepare the ward for the night accentuates the lack of real noise.

I want to dance down the corridor as I danced when leaving the Louvre in Paris and down the bank to the boat in Cognac – but this is a hospital, so I rush along with my head down.

I slow down and look around, directions have become a mystery again. I ride down in the lift and go too far, getting out at the kitchens. A weary-looking chef points the way to the stairs with a ladle dripping in sickly leftovers from supper.

The double doors of the ward are closed. They open in the middle as I approach. I stand tall, looking around for Gerry. He is sitting by the third bed down on the right, packed ready to come out and somber-faced. I wait for a smile but it doesn't come. Of course, he is in pain and has been unwell, while I've been travelling around all over the place. How could I be so selfish?

I look at my shoes, cut-off jeans, and red top that is half of my dress. Did I brush my hair? It looks different after my haircut. Will Gerry like it? Salvation comes as I remember the bottle under my arm. Patients sitting in chairs at the end of the ward raise empty glasses. Gerry must have said I was bringing a bottle.

"Thank goodness I bought the Lourdes water," I mutter, and take it out of its plastic bag with a picture of baby Jesus and Mother Mary on. These poor sick people will be so pleased that a little bit of Lourdes has come to them. I feel like a missionary as I hand the bottle to Gerry; my whole body has a warm glow.

"Vodka?" he asks, studying the bottle's clear liquid.

"No, silly. Look." I slide the button on the bottom and it starts to play 'Ave Maria'.

Gerry's face is grim; he looks at me and then at the patients holding up their glasses.

"Let's get out of here," he says without expression. The waving of plastered arms and legs becomes frantic. "Take these." He thrusts a carrier bag holding his toiletries into my hands and I try to hold them. No kiss, no cuddle… not even a smile. I'm a failure.

Balancing himself on a crutch, he puts his hand behind my shoulders, turns me around and pushes me forward towards the ward doors. He's still strong, for a man with a broken leg. Clonk, clonk, is all I hear as we attempt to hurry away.

Leaving the hospital, he stares at me.

"What do you look like?"

I laugh, realising how odd I must look.

"I've had the most amazing time." Our eyes meet. Surely he can show some sign of pleasure at seeing me?

"Finally, you made it," he says, touching my shoulder more gently.

"I've booked that hotel on the far side of the car park. I've borrowed a wheelchair. Sit in and I'll push." He sits down and I pile the baggage on his lap. The bottle of holy water is with me, out of his sight.

How long can I stay happy if Gerry keeps his straight face? He's got a spot or two from spending too much time without fresh air and sunshine.

We gather up our sleeping bundle of fur from the back seat. Gerry is pleased to see Spike, and holds him up to check he looks all right. The car can stay in the park until morning. At the hotel we take the lift to level seven. I open our door and stand behind him holding on to the wheelchair, waiting again for a smile. He is clocking the champagne, the fruit and the candle. The view of the hospital isn't great, but this was all I could arrange at short notice.

"Natalie, what is this all about?" He only calls me Natalie when he's frustrated.

"It's my birthday," I shout. "You can't have forgotten my fortieth."

"Of course; I'm sorry. I've been worried about my bike, and you getting lost and behaving weirdly, especially towards Chester."

Is he beginning to realise that he has left the hospital behind and is coming back to the outside world?

Gerry opens the bottle of champagne and we sit back in quiet reflection as we so often do at home. Everything will be all right and I feel a sense of relief. The alcohol circulates and goes down well with the French strawberries. My poor man needs to rest his leg on the bed; he stretches out and falls asleep on top of the covers. I finish the bottle sitting by myself.

With no one to talk to, I sit and think; in a few days, my job at the bingo hall will be at an end. Lisa has rung and said she has decided to marry Eldred and they are going to start the family they want with the help of IVF. He is buying a house with four bedrooms in a village close to a river on the south coast. They hope we will visit loads. The wedding is going to be low key but she doesn't want to get married without her two best friends so to make sure the date is in my diary for early next year. Susie is looking forward to it. The three of us will be together as always.

The wedding is a secret, as Anita is unaware of definite plans. Eldred is away working on a building contract and they are going to share their news with her together. Anita is now in her twenties and making her life as a beautician, specialising in advising women with olive skin and black hair. She has made a request that if her mum decides to marry Eldred they can go to Thailand together before the wedding happens. She isn't going to look for her dad or any of his family, but wants to know where half her roots are from.

Lisa said something else that surprised me, and only now have I got time to think about it. Would Katy and I go to Thailand with them? Well... um... err... is the only way I could think of responding. I don't think Gerry would approve, and where's the money coming from?

Lisa is concerned to know how Gerry is and what I'm going to do for a job without bingo. Photography and art are thoughts that take over my brain. I reflect on the art I've seen and the photos I've taken. What about working in an art gallery, or in a photographic business? I'd like that, but

I'm not good enough and have no relevant references. Something must… something will crop up.

Gerry is sleeping and snoring loudly. He has raised a glass to me on my special day and crashed out after drinking champagne. As he sleeps I watch him, pleased he is with me. I finish the last of my glass and lift Spike from sleeping on my toes to the end of the bed. The tiredness from driving and having had such an eventful day, wash over me in sleep.

Fortunately, Gerry is flat out on top of the covers. The night would be uncomfortable sleeping next to a plaster cast. The plaster has been reduced and more will be taken off when there isn't as much chance of him jarring the leg.

At breakfast, Gerry wants to know if I think he should buy two bikes or one bike and a set of golf clubs. I can't answer as neither interests me, and when I mention Thailand, it clearly doesn't interest him, as he doesn't take the suggestion seriously. He does say that Lisa has her own life and should be left to get on with it – and that she was being polite, asking me to tag along.

He's brighter when we go to the car. Our bags are in the wheelchair and Gerry is walking with crutches. I've washed and brushed my hair and put on my blue blouse. On scrutiny in the mirror, I notice a rough edge on the collar. I need to shop for clothes and wish Linda could be around to join in.

The gendarmes have delivered a mangled bike and we struggle to fix it on the roof rack. A passer-by stops to help, and starts pulling at bits to stop them falling off on the journey. There's a touch of emotional pain on Gerry's face as metal clatters to the ground.

The bike is firmly fixed and Gerry opens the boot to put our things away. He smiles.

"That's better," I say. He runs his hand over two boxes of wine from the chateau in the Loire.

"Harry is helping organise the bingo hall for my party. I thought the wine was a good idea," I say… and wait, unsure if Gerry's response is going to be positive or negative. Has it always been like this, or do I notice it because I've been away? The party is an event Harry wants to be involved in, as it will mark the end of bingo in Eastleigh. Because it's my birthday, no one will feel sad about it.

A new community hall is opening in three months and it will be available for the pensioners of Eastleigh and district to play bingo once a week. The sessions will be run on a charitable basis. I can work there as a volunteer. The old lottery ball is going spare if we want it, and the developers are going to hand over £1,000 to the project as a gesture of goodwill. I'm thinking about volunteering but, in all honesty, I don't want to.

Gerry pulls me back from my thoughts. "We need to talk about your job and what you plan to do. I think you can manage something better than a bingo caller," he says, as if complimenting me. "You can tell it wasn't a proper job; it's been relegated to volunteer status." Gerry is balancing on the car and pushing his crutches in the back. We abandon the wheelchair in a bay like a supermarket trolley and I'd like to abandon him with it.

"What do you call a proper job? Volunteering can… " My voice gets lost as he struggles into the front seat and sweeps his hand over the junk, as he calls it. An Eiffel Tower key ring, a Madonna magnet and a compass land in his lap, and he hides them away in the glove compartment. He has to jam them in on top of a plate with a toreador and bull painted on it. It's a copy of a painting by Picasso.

Nostalgia made me buy it. Mum had a tea towel on the wall with a toreador printed on. One of their friends brought it back from a Spanish holiday. By hanging it on the wall visitors knew that if Mum and Dad hadn't been to Spain then they had friends who had.

"What's that guitar doing in the back? Couldn't you have ditched it, knowing what little room we have?"

Now I'm annoyed, but he has no way of knowing everything that has happened to me since coming to France. It will take time to explain. He needs to see the photographs and meet some of my new friends.

"What would you like to do today? A birthday treat – name it." Yes, we need to settle back down together. It won't happen quickly, like I imagined.

"Honfleur," I say, feeling better. "Hector said I should go there before leaving France."

"Honfleur it is, then. We can talk about how to get over this when we get home." Gerry is furrowing his forehead.

"Over what?" I'm on an emotional switchback. He says something nice and then spoils it. Doesn't he know when to shut up?

Hector was right. Honfleur is beautiful, with so many small art exhibitions, boutique shops and lovely places to sit. We have our lunch seated by the harbour edge, watching the yachts and breathing in the sea air. Gerry manages a slow walk-about, looking in sailing shops He leans on my arm and complains of pain now and again, but he is making an effort for me. I like his dependence on my help and would like to be aware of it sometimes at home. He has agreed to sit on a bench while I look in fashion boutiques, and he will meet me in an hour.

A shop that is not too expensive is in a side street, and I

choose a pair of smart green trousers and a yellow top. I look at my bottom in the mirror and decide that the thong Linda bought for me will be great, as it won't show a panty line.

Standing outside on the pavement, I notice a tall thin house on the opposite side. It's squeezed between the shops. On the front wall is a brass plaque to Henri Marcel, who lived here. I liked my book about him, which was bought in the charity shop at home. He painted pictures – then ripped them up, repositioned them and painted a new picture. He's similar to Picasso and cubism, but not the same. The colours he used were bold, and the reconstructed vibrant paintings were full of activity. Some of his paintings are of people, others of buildings. He lived here for twenty years until he died in 1996.

I am always doing what I thought I couldn't do, because I learn something, is the quote under his name.

"Yes, Henri," I say out loud. I mustn't let Gerry see me talking to myself and clasping my hands with excitement.

Gerry has walked a short distance to join me. He turns away from the fishing tackle shop window, and we drift back to the harbour. While we look at the yachts we pause to ring Katy to tell her we will be on the ferry soon and will be returning home in the early evening. She has done lots to get ready for her trip to Japan – and Gramps is upset he spent hours teaching Matt to play chess and now she's ditched him and is going out with Luke, who is still at the snakes and ladders stage of life.

BBC Radio 4's *Woman's Hour* want to arrange an interview with me, and Katy wants to be my agent. I put this down to fantasy or a joke.

New clothes, sunshine, and we were heading home. It feels good.

"Before we go can we walk along by the sea wall?" I ask. Once he's there his mood mellows. I decide to bring something important up.

"You know you said I could do anything I wanted on my birthday. Well, this is it." I take my purse from my bag and open it where the cards and photos are kept. I pull out my photo of our baby. "I want to talk about him." I get a sideways look and his hand goes to his face. I know I've made another mistake.

Then he is kind and gives me a rare long hug. "Put it away, love. Just put it away."

So that is that. The silence of the years is clear.

"I met the chef, Gary Blain," I say, changing the subject.

"Really?" Gerry is full of doubt, which underlies his attempt at interest.

"Yes," and I show him the photos on my new camera. "You know that dog of his? It can do a little dance. Here, look." Gerry studies my mini video and turns the camera round and round, getting the measure of my new possession.

"I want to do a photography course in September. What do you think?"

"I'm sure that'll be fine. I was thinking about golf lessons. If I play, I want to reach a reasonable standard. You were right; I will need another interest. Cycling won't go on forever. It's time to go to the ferry. Katy's getting excited about seeing us, and she has missed Spike."

At the ferry it feels like a war zone with everyone trying to escape the country. A large man in his big lorry with a toothy grin looks down at me. I wave enthusiastically.

"Stop it, Nat." Gerry practically smacks my hand. "You don't know him."

"Yes, I do," I state rather too loudly. We watch and wait for the cars to board.

"If they ask any questions about Spike, remember he's nothing to do with me. You brought him to France without vaccinations. What a daft thing to do."

"I wasn't coming here for so long – only a night – and then time went by and I didn't know what else to do. I had to keep him with me. He knows when to hide."

"Promise to take him to the vet. What if he picked up rabies and bit Katy?"

I know he's right on this one. I've been stupid and I will take him straight to the vet.

"I've got some photos of Tony Blair," I say meekly.

"With or without Cherie?" he asks, as if Cherie was a type of tomato ketchup.

"With, of course, and a double helping of chips," I say.

"Pardon?" Gerry puts his hand to his face again and puffs wind. It's time to drive on to the ship. Gerry watches to make sure I don't hit anything and park where I'm directed.

On board I sit outside on the deck, away from prying eyes that might see Spike. I have mixed feelings as we leave Le Havre and France.

Gerry has collected the cabin key and come to join us. I think there's something he wants to say, but is avoiding the issue. He's spending too much time staring at the cartoons and signatures on his plaster when he's not staring at the sea.

"Nat, it's your dad. Nothing serious, love, but I know you're going to miss him. We all know you're unstable, at the moment, but we can't avoid this one. He's moving."

"Why? Isn't he happy living near us?"

"It's nothing to do with being happy. He wants a change."

"Not an old people's home? He's too young in himself for that. Is it because I left him for a couple of weeks?" The optimism I've found is frittering away, leaving a void.

"No, of course not. He's been offered a voluntary job on the Watercress Line, working on the train station as a ticket collector. He's so excited, like a kid."

"Volunteering will be good for Dad," I say. "I'll miss him. Why is he moving? Alresford isn't far away. He could commute." I wonder if I can make him change his mind.

Gerry consoles me. "He has a flat in Alresford within easy walking distance of the railway. He'll be happy. It isn't a problem, we'll still see him lots. He said he was lonely for company of his own age and is finding it difficult to relate to Katy's friends."

"Not just him," I utter. "How many frogs will visit home before her prince arrives?"

"You're not upset, then?"

"No. I don't fancy sorting out his house, but it was going to have to be done one day. There's still some of Mum's stuff around. It'll need a coat of paint before he sells it."

"He's got that in hand. He's planning to get someone round to do everything because you shouldn't have to do it. I'm sure he would like it if you were there to help."

I should have steadily helped him clear out over the last four years, but sometimes it's easier not to disturb things and to leave it for another day. It hasn't mattered because he has never thought of moving on.

"Any other changes happening?"

"No, Nat. Only you. We need to get you home and back to normal. It's surprising what your own environment can do." The sea breeze is getting up so we go inside, with me feeling on edge.

For most of the journey, we hide away with Spike, in the cabin. We read the papers, do a crossword or doze. There's nothing to look at but walls, listen to the droning sound of the engine and feel the roll of the ship. Spike can curl up on his blanket.

Nowhere on the boat have I bumped into Monsieur Jacques. Introducing him to Gerry as my rescuing angel in Paris would be a strained situation.

I reflect on Dad moving, Katy growing, and my job at the bingo hall that has all but disappeared. Lisa is moving and Susie is returning to her parents until she finds somewhere to live with her two children. The marriage to the vicar is over. Her house belongs to the church so she has to move out. A kind lady parishioner, who looks busty in a pink fluffy twinset, is looking after her husband. Perhaps you can be too thin for some roles in life.

Susie vowed she would never set foot inside a church again. That would be a shame. I long to spend more time in the churches and cathedrals of France and Spain. They aren't religious buildings to me, but places of history and architecture – monuments to the people who built them. They are art and they move me.

Gerry and I talk about the familiar things of home, where everything can return to normal. The conversation is disjointed, and we have difficulty stretching ourselves over a communication divide.

Linda mentioned in passing that I might look a little closer at Alex. I told her I wasn't looking and was returning to Gerry, definitely. One marriage: one husband. It might not be exciting but it's right, and the best thing for Katy and me.

Spike is giving a rhythm of little snores, and we drift to sleep for a while. When I wake up Gerry is happy reading the paper, resting on the bunk bed, so I go for a wander about the ship. It rolls more now we are out at sea. I catch sight of Monsieur Jacques in the bar, just finishing his beer. I gesture to him as I write a note to let him know about my party. Not wise – but I owe him, and he might like to come if he's anywhere close.

I relax on my own for a while. Later Gerry hobbles up the stairs and sways towards me as the ship hits the top of a wave and rolls down the other side. I turn from reading and watching the sea go by through the window. He says Spike is restless and I need to go to the cabin. He isn't a dog that barks much, but we have to be sure no one knows he is there. It would be too easy to relax our guard. We aren't on English soil yet, and I panic if I think too much about the consequences of what I've done.

"A criminal offence," Gerry has remarked several times. He suggested, caught or not, that I should be careful I don't develop criminal tendencies along with poor judgement. He doesn't want any more nasty surprises.

Chatting in the ship's lounge while trying to steady a glass of lemonade, Gerry's contacts with Chester become clearer. Did I know Chester had problems at work? No I didn't. That was my fault because I don't speak to him properly. No one would think he was my brother. He was arrested last week and questioned for two hours and there was more questioning to come.

Suddenly my attention is focused. He might be involved

in a scam to activate a virus that takes money from the bank accounts of rich people and lands it in the accounts of the poor. A modern-day Robin Hood.

"It's a crackpot idea… probably started by Chester to make himself look more interesting than he actually is," I say.

"You don't think much of your brother, do you?" Gerry states, while reading the sports pages for the third time in case he has missed something important.

"We have a mutual lack of admiration since the Tracey and Stacey mix-up. It was a mistake, but he presumed I was judging him. Things may change, but sending him to find me didn't help."

"What about you, running away like that?"

"Why are we arguing?" My voice carries across the ship's lounge area. "Sorry, but I don't see the point in discussing Chester." I drop my voice and Gerry doesn't look up from his paper.

I return to my book, I like a good romance to get lost in. What I haven't got I read about.

Following the announcement to vacate our cabin, we put Spike in his basket. I have forgotten which deck we parked on and which exit we need. Damn. Now I'm looking an idiot again, but when Gerry is around I don't have to bother about directions. I make hiding Spike the excuse for following in his shadow until we find our way to car deck C 3. He spots our car first because he is taller. Spike shuffles in his basket and I glance around to see who must be looking, but everyone has their own business to concentrate on.

We drive and clatter our way out of the ship and customs looms ahead. Our passports are checked. Two officers open the boot and glance around, shut it again and pat the roof for us to go. Spike is coming home with us. I can't bear the thought of him in quarantine, he would be lonely, and we don't have the money to pay for him, or for a fine.

12

Coming Home

"You're in the wrong lane, Nat. Over. Over." Gerry wants to grab the wheel.

"Stop being a nervous passenger. I can see all the other cars and they can see me."

"Bloody hell. Can't you read signs?" He shakes his head and stares out of his window.

Spike pokes his nose between the seats and Gerry makes a fuss of him. This is more like my man. Waiting at the lights, I touch his arm with affection.

I remember the thoughts of myself naked on a billboard that I had when leaving Portsmouth. Then the thought horrified me. Now I wish it had happened. Imagining how Gerry would react makes me laugh quietly. I'm in danger of appearing to laugh without a reason.

Before I went away, I was careful that everything I said and did was acceptable to Gerry. Mostly I stayed in my box.

"What's this about having a party and not inviting Chester and Stacey? You can't do that."

"I have to, because Tracey won't come if they do – and yes, I do prefer her."

"Chester has moved on and you have to. Stacey said counselling would be good for you and she will find the right person for you to see. In California they all have a counsellor and she has lots of experience of choosing the right one."

The worst thing is happening. Tears fall down my cheeks. I think of myself in the glider high above the world, and know I've received all the mind-straightening I'm likely to need. The tears confirm to Gerry that I'm unbalanced and that I do need help. I can see from his face he's reading in all sorts of background issues that aren't there. He's thinking of our baby, my mother, the bingo hall closing. He's wrong. I'm crying with frustration at his lack of comprehension of who I am and because there is a huge distance between us.

"How about marriage guidance, Gerry?" I dry my eyes and concentrate after I've clipped a traffic cone and sent it rolling around the motorway behind me.

Gerry doesn't often get angry, but I can tell he's had enough and would be much happier if he could get out of the car and ride his bike.

"There's a race in September. I'm planning on being on my bike by then."

"Good."

He picks up my mobile and scrolls through. "Who's Alex?"

"A girl I met." I can't remember lying to Gerry before. It doesn't matter, because I don't intend to see Alex again. It saves trouble if he thinks he's female.

"She's a camerawoman with Gary Blain's crew. Remember I told you about meeting them on the river? She's invited us to the BBC studios."

Gerry rests his head back and closes his eyes. I look at his furrowed forehead and I'm filled with love and sympathy. He has struggled through his time in hospital and has an uncomfortable plaster on. He's a caged animal, unable to live his life at speed.

Gerry's phone rings. It's Chester. A, *we're best buddies,* conversation follows.

"Yes, she's here now. I'll tell you about it after we get home. We'll have that drink you were talking about. Has Nat mentioned her party to you?"

"No, I haven't," I mutter. I knew I would have to invite him but I wasn't going to until the last minute. With luck he'll have made other arrangements. I'm still cross with Chester for turning up in the Pyrenees.

There were times when we were friends. When we were in our teens he dated Susie, and the only way to be in touch with my friend was for him to be extra nice to me. A go-between was not a role I liked, but I did it for Susie as she was struck with him.

After I was married, I found out about their secret. Susie had gone away after her exams. She was the clever one, passing eight subjects at A or B level. At sixteen she went to stay with her aunty in Aberdeen and didn't get in touch for months. When she came back she was different, not as chatty, and she gave up coming dancing with us.

One night, years after, we were round at Lisa's house sitting on the carpet in front of the electric fire. We put candles around and shared our bottle of Chardonnay. We played a game where you each had to share a secret. Lisa said there was someone she had always loved and wasn't going to tell us who. It wasn't playing the game by the rules, but there was no moving her. I had an exciting secret; I was pregnant. The mood had settled to melancholic. Wasn't anybody going to get excited for me?

"I had a baby," muttered Susie. We both stared. We waited, expecting her to deny it as a joke.

"When?" Lisa challenged.

"That time I went to Aberdeen. I went to a Catholic place where they send girls like me."

"I thought those places were wiped out in the fifties." Lisa looked sad for Susie. Lisa had kept Anita and had always known she had done the right thing for them both.

"It was horrid. Horrid," Susie cried.

We let her carry on and waited for her to indicate when it might be safe to speak. When her crying subsided, I asked where the baby was.

"She went to a good home – a doctor and his wife. There wasn't enough money to keep her. I didn't have a job, and the sort of spare cash my parents had wouldn't stretch to bringing up another child. Dad's health wasn't good and some things can't be changed. It was for the best."

"Who was the dad?" I stupidly ask.

"You should know." With that, Susie picked up her coat and left.

"Does that mean I have a niece somewhere?" I asked Lisa, already knowing the answer.

"Dear sweet Natalie, you expect love, marriage and children to be so straightforward. It isn't. That's only for the chosen few," Lisa replied.

I wondered if Mum and Dad ever knew, but I don't think so. Did Chester know? I had Susie's secret and there was no one I could ask for more information, so I tucked it away.

When Katy was born, pink and wrinkled, I thought about the cousin she would never see. My own happiness sent sad thoughts away, and Susie was about to marry. I hoped she would have more children one day, and in her second marriage she did.

"Did you know about Susie and Chester having a baby?" I can tell Gerry wants to get out of the car. "Well?"

"Yes, I knew. Chester told me. When our baby died he was very supporting to me, and I haven't forgotten it." Gerry is now reflective.

"Chester was nineteen. Do you think he's forgotten about the baby or the scars it left on Susie?" I ask.

"No. You never forget your children. Now can we drop the subject? Do you want a live group or a DJ?"

"Well I don't want a dead group," I quip, thinking I'm being funny.

"Don't be silly." He releases one of his well-practised sighs and I let the subject go. We sit with our own thoughts to travel the last three miles of the motorway. Spike senses we are near home so he sits up and watches out of the window. Gerry leans over to pick him up. For the last few minutes, he sits on Gerry's lap and turns towards a ruffle behind the ears. I wonder if he senses the bad atmosphere floating around.

"Are you going to take him to the vet tomorrow?"

"Yes, of course I will. He's getting older and could do with an all-over health check as well as making sure he hasn't picked up anything nasty from our journey."

"Good idea, love. Dad seemed well when I spoke to him, and Katy is happy enough. You do a good job of looking after everyone. I'm sorry for being a pain. I didn't like being in hospital and I was worried about you."

"I made mistakes, I know… but everything turned out all right in the end and here we are, nearly home. Can't wait to tell you more about it and explain who the people and places are in my photos."

"When we get home… that's what we need, to get home." Gerry stretches out as far as he is able, making himself so handsome and tempting.

I put my foot down. The tired Fiat argues but eventually

responds. From the boot of the car come a few gentle notes of 'Ave Maria'. We are laughing together and it feels good. Perhaps the Lourdes water can perform a miracle and make our marriage right. I look down to consult the Madonna magnet then I remember it's in the glove compartment where Gerry shoved it.

"I had promised them all a drink of cognac and the ward sister was going to turn a blind eye. I don't think the French will forgive me." Now he's splitting his sides laughing. "That was a classic."

It's a relief that Katy will see us happy when we get out of the car.

"What's that?" Gerry asks as he looks in the direction of the sound.

"It's the Big Ben chimes. Alan changed my ringtone when I was on the boat." Gerry picks up my phone from the well by the handbrake and presses buttons at random.

"Would you like a new phone for your birthday? Ah, found a message. *Filming Victory. Portsmouth dockyard, next week. Want to come? A.*" There is so much more going on in Gerry's head that he ignores the message and puts the phone away.

I know I'm blushing, so I open the window, complaining about the lack of air con. I've done nothing but chat happily at length, share my dreams and enjoy Alex's company. Now we are texting.

"Playing with fire," comes my mother's voice.

Gerry has always worn his hair very short as he doesn't want it to get in his face when cycling. It's grown and is flicked across his forehead and it makes him look softer and younger.

"What happened to your cycling pants?"

"They cut them off. I can get new ones practically free through the shop. It's the bike that's the problem."

Pylons are along the side of the motorway; they are giants, and architecturally beautiful. I decide not to point that out to Gerry as I'm already beyond his understanding. I'll go for a walk some time, take photos for José, upload them and email. Should be easy enough to learn how.

We're at the turning for Eastleigh at last.

"Ring Katy. Tell her two minutes. Can't wait to see her." My phone feels like dangerous ground, but there's nothing incriminating on it. There's nothing incriminating full stop.

"Your dad has helped us taking care of Katy. We'll miss him."

"He doesn't need to move. He's always been a few doors away."

Gerry rests his hand on my knee and the traffic lights change to green. I daydream until several loud blasts on horns make me stall. I quickly recover and, with a jump or two, the car makes it through the junction.

"He's moving on, Nat, and you have to let him. He's found a flat near the steam railway. That's what he wants. I think we will see a positive change in him."

Dad has talked about moving but I didn't think he meant it.

"What's he going to do with his house? I feel it's my house, I was brought up there. It was Mum's house."

We take the first exit from the roundabout and approach Market Street.

"What do you think of white leather sofas, Gerry?"

"Haven't thought about it. Why? Do you want one?"

"Yes. I still have half my bonus left and I want to cheer up our front room."

"I don't see why not, as long as I can still have a decent bike. I'll find out how much I need. Did I say I like your hair like that?" Gerry adjusts Spike on his lap, accidently touching my hand as it rests on the gearstick. It's an accidental touch and he doesn't notice.

Alex brushed the back of my hand when we sat on the riverbank. Was that an accident? Then Alex held my hand and pulled me to my feet. Wow... no accident.

As we swing round the corner into Market Street my braking skills are tested with a screech. People with cameras mob the car. Flashes spark off in our faces. A TV cameraman stands outside our house and a blush quickly rises on my face. Of course, it isn't Alex, it just makes me think of him.

I can't park among the crush of people and vehicles; abandonment in the middle of the road is the only option. Hippies are outside our house, forming a circle and chanting. There's no way of driving past.

The multicoloured women's skirts touch the ground as they tip forwards then backwards. They raise, and float their hands, twirling their bodies around slowly. I fancy joining in, but there's no chance. There are now two of me, the other Natalie is somewhere else.

"Go inside, Gerry. Can you take Spike? I'll come behind you with whatever I can carry. I'll move the car as soon as I can." Gerry hobbles along the path towards the door. The paparazzi take photos of everything, including the crumpled bike. With Gerry indoors, I get my camera and photograph the bright skirts and headscarves worn by the women dancers. The men have scarves around their necks and bits of string in their hair, men and women are all dancing with trancelike movements. Tattoos are across both genders.

Clapping and bongo drums set up the rhythm.

"You saw John Lennon at Lourdes," a man shouts to me. They sit in the middle of the road and sing John Lennon's '*Give peace a chance*'. Then they sing the last song of John/George at Lourdes: '*The world needs love. The world needs peace*'. A free spirit is clambering around inside me, trying to get out.

How could the Pope explain a vision of John Lennon? Might I be like Bernadette and be made a saint along with John Lennon? More likely Saint Tony Blair. I wonder at what strange things can happen in life.

Gerry is staring out of the lounge window and knocking on the glass. The cameras are still taking photos and filming. I nod at the hippies and raise my hand in the V sign of peace. There isn't much peace waiting for me in the house.

"Get rid of them, Nat. Get rid of them."

I take a sheet of A4 paper from beside the computer and write:

It wasn't John Lennon. It was George Bush.

I pull back the net curtain and stick it on the window. Hippies file up and read it, looking disappointed. They gradually disperse towards the town. Katy follows them to the bus station and, in journalistic style, takes photographs and statements before they leave Eastleigh and go back to their own anonymity.

"Good. We can sort ourselves out without interference." Gerry sinks into the lumpy sofa and raises his plastered leg as I push the stool under his ankle. He points to the cushion that he wants for extra comfort. He flicks through the TV channels looking for sport and finally settles for golf, complaining that he's in the mood for football but there's none on.

I thought I would be thrilled to be home. I'm pleased to see Katy and want to see Dad, but the house feels small and restrictive; I want to be going somewhere else. I understand how Gerry wants to be on his bike, but I've never felt this way before.

Tea from my mug slops on the carpet as I try to bump my case upstairs with the other hand. I'm about to annoy Gerry, but the decision I took on the boat on my way to Saintes is not forgotten. The photo is only three inches by two and a half. I've found a frame in the drawer and our baby looks so beautiful and right resting on the top of the chest of drawers. With my fingers, I draw an affectionate line across the top of the frame and then turn to the task of unpacking.

I don't have a lot of clothes, but we only have one wardrobe between us and it's difficult to squeeze in the turquoise flamenco dress. Gerry's shirts are sticking out, a problem solved by kicking the door shut.

"Phone for you, Mum. It's Harry," Katy calls up the stairs.

He wants me at work tonight. There's only a few more days and the hall will be closed. A contented feeling eludes me. It had better come back soon, because this is life as I know it. Everyone probably feels the same when they return from holiday.

"Give it a day or two." I hear another of Mum's sayings ring out.

It is all very well planning a photography course but I need a job, and fast. We don't earn much between us, and Katy needs our support for a few years yet. We've managed so far, but haven't had to extend our income to paying for university. A marriage is far into the future. Really, we should save something for her... Oops... I've forgotten the phone, and run downstairs.

"Harry, how's it going? Any chance that the bingo hall can be saved?"

"None. Bingo finishes on Friday. You can have the hall for your party on Saturday, then the doors are closed for good."

"What are the oldies going to do? They need the bingo hall, and us."

"No they don't, Nat. They're looking forward to coming to your party and have made plans to meet up for coffee mornings. They realise the prizes are crap and it's the same old thing."

This remark strikes hard. What is happening to my life? I escape to the mountains of the Pyrenees, and my spirit lifts.

"There's lots to sort out, Harry. I'll be there tonight as usual."

Dad is making his way through the hall. As he passes he gives me an hug. He isn't usually the demonstrative type, but I always know he cares.

"What's this about you moving, Dad?" I ask.

"I had my name on the list for volunteers on the railway and it's my turn. If I don't do it now I'll be too old. I've found a nice little flat overlooking the station. I'll be moving at the end of the month. We need to talk about my house."

"What really brought this on?" I ask, as kindly as I can.

"Katy will only be at home for two more years. Then what? Chester and Stacey are expecting a little one, I'm told it's a boy. When he is a little boy, he can come on the railway.

I can take him on the Santa Claus train and to the *Thomas the Tank Engine* day. It all happens when they get to two."

"When's it due?" I can't help thinking this is a dramatic change of life because of a baby that isn't here yet.

"January." I offer him tea. Dad sits and Spike jumps on his lap and needs to be chased down. "They are going to call him Jack, after me."

I gasp, "That's the name of my baby."

"What baby?" Dad looks lost, and then it comes back to him. "It's after your baby, too. Our family will have another Jack." He pats my arm. I forgive him, but I don't forgive Chester and Stacey. Surely Gerry would have something to say about this.

Gerry's still watching golf, when Katy comes and stands beside me. I must have looked in need of support. It's time to get ready for work.

I've lost weight and my trousers are too big – no more struggling with the zip, it's easy. Next my handbag needs sorting out. I swap holiday odds and ends for work requirements. The Eiffel Tower is a handy key ring.

"Hold on to the memory, Natalie," I whisper to myself, and tighten my grip before releasing this treasured object into my pocket.

I was restless before my journey. Now, I'm feeling trapped. I expect to feel better when I'm calling the bingo numbers; there's something about being in the bright lights and on stage. After my party, the hall will be closed for ever. Then what?

"Mum, it's for you again. Can't you get people to ring on your mobile?" Katy says.

"Hello. Sorry… who?" I say to the unknown person on the phone.

"Miss Frogmore. I'm the editor of *AWAY*, the travel magazine, affiliated to the *People's Post* newspaper. Mrs. Kenning, would you be willing to speak to us about an exclusive?"

"An exclusive what?"

"Not a cold caller, Nat. Don't talk to them. Put the phone down." Gerry doesn't look up from the TV.

"We are willing to pay a competitive rate. Please don't take other offers until we have spoken. Agents will want you on their books, and they can be pushy."

"I'll ring you tomorrow, if you don't mind. I don't know what my husband will say. I need to talk to him about your generous offer." Gerry should be pleased when I mention that sort of money in his ear.

"Mrs. Kenning, can I call you Natalie? Please consider a meeting with me at your earliest convenience."

"I will. Thank you," I say, not sure of the reality of this conversation.

I say nothing to the family. Instead, I collect my things and hurry down the street to bingo. It's odd being stared at where no one has taken much notice of me before. These things soon die down, and I'm the same Natalie. Nothing will be exactly, the same, but probably close to it. People and places have changed me. I have to find a way to fit into my old life. I'm trying to adjust, with so many new thoughts floating around in my head.

Dad has plans for his house. His new flat will be a rented property, and he wants me to have his house a.s.a.p. I'd like to keep it for at least a month once the papers are signed. Chester isn't interested, and what cash Dad has will be his when he passes on. I think he doesn't want any hassle and is happy to let me get on and deal with parent issues as usual. I am pleased the house will be mine.

I can decide what to do once the papers are signed, meanwhile mulling over ideas is exciting. I can make the changes I would like to have made to our place, but have never been able to.

These old railway workers' houses are very welcoming when brought up to modern standards. The ceilings are comparatively high and the rooms a good size apart from the kitchen. There is the space to extend. It's hard to believe that 33A was once home to a family of eight children. The gardens are long and narrow, with plenty of room to grow veg if you want to.

I could add an attic room at Dad's house, and modernize the bathroom and kitchen, then sell it. The project could occupy my time and I'd have some cash at the end. First, I must be satisfied that selling his house is really what Dad wants me to do. He sounds as if he's made up his mind to walk away and that's it.

The exclusive could help pay for the materials I'll need, and help me keep up with the bills for a while. There could be enough money to make a good job of it.

Am I dreaming in the same way as if I might win the lottery, knowing it will never happen? If I give it freshly painted white walls we could move there, then do up our place and decide which to sell. There are all sorts of possibilities.

Dad is giving me the independence I need to feel more confident about my situation and myself. I think he knew this when he made up his mind to give me the house. I'll be able to contribute more financially to the life I share with Gerry and Katy. The future could be good.

For now, though, I must concentrate on bingo. I must leave the thoughts that have come with me along the walk to work, outside. I open the doors; the familiar dusty smell of the bingo hall and the sound of chairs scraping hits me.

13

Bingo is Over

The contestants are restless as they face the inevitable. I have to call the numbers repeatedly. They have been offered the new community hall one night a week for bingo and have asked if I will be their caller.

The lottery ball makes more noise than usual as it clatters round. It won't last much longer, but it's only going to be thrown out so we are free to take it. It's too big to keep in the community hall cupboard so they want me to take it home each week and look after it.

It's sounding a little crazy, and I'm not up for it. Not to let them down, I agree to put a notice on the supermarket community board and see if a volunteer would like to take over. Perhaps they could devise a system and do it themselves.

The truth is that I don't want to see the ping-pong balls of red, yellow, green and blue again. This is the end for me. I turn the ball off this last time.

The walk home passes unnoticed as I drift along in my own world. One thing I register is the board outside a house on the opposite side. The number of the loft conversion company is clear, so I make a note. I'll ring them next week; there's no harm in asking for a quote.

Ahead is the photography course, and my mind constantly turns to decorating Dad's place. I could put up some Picasso prints. I like Toulouse-Lautrec's pictures of cats. How great would that be? What about creative photo collages on canvas? I can make those if I learn how.

Katy says I shouldn't make the house mine but leave it as a blank canvas for buyers to imagine their own things in. She is right, but the ideas for the look I want to create are growing. She also wants to know if I mind if she has a belly button stud – and yes, I do. She says it doesn't matter as she'll have one in a month's time on her birthday, and a yellow jewel is what she's chosen.

Bamboo blinds don't twitch like the old nets, but I feel that several pairs of eyes are watching me. Gerry is right. I've become the subject of neighbourhood gossip.

"Enjoy your celebrity status. It won't last." I turn to see Harry catching up. His company is welcome.

"Don't you mind losing your job?" I ask.

"Why should I? I'll get some pay-off money and, living in a council flat, I won't lose my home. Anyway, something will turn up… and I can spend the rest of the summer on my allotment."

We enter the house together to find Gerry pacing the floor with his plastered leg, making a rhythmic clonk like a ghoul. He appears to be reading the paper, but his eyes don't focus on the page.

"Nothing about you today, that must be it. The bombs we are showering on Iraq are more important." It's strange watching an active man caged up.

"There's a candlelight walk in Winchester on Friday. I'm going. It's a walk against the war and for peace."

"You don't want to attract more attention to yourself. Stay home and look for a new job. Why don't you train to be a classroom assistant? That would suit you."

"Thanks for the suggestion. I want a job where I can get out and about." Perhaps it's an unrealistic goal but the need for money will dictate, I'm sure.

"You should be protesting against the war in Iraq with us. Why don't you come? You could find a place to sit." It would please me to have him there, although he won't come.

"You should stay away from Winchester. Any sort of protest will cause trouble, but you don't listen to me. Make Harry some coffee, love, and we can get the music for your party organised."

I'm not in the mood for this, it's been a full and tiring day, not to mention bingo tonight.

"OK," I say, and shoot Harry a smile. In the kitchen I count to ten and look out of the window at the clouds rolling overhead against a darkening sky. There's a half-dead chrysanthemum on the side by the kitchen sink. We are kindred spirits.

I walk around the space in the kitchen – three steps to the left, four steps to the right – and ask myself how many times I've walked it since we moved in seventeen years go. If we extended into the garden, the kitchen could be more light and airy.

Gerry isn't in a receptive mood. I'll pick a moment later and see if he agrees to my home improvements, money permitting.

Lists I've written are on the pad by the kettle: ring editor, find agent, kitchen roll, coffee.

I think about bingo. If nobody played a game or gambled a little, life would be more boring for those who like to play. If I make a fool of myself, what's new? I'll gamble and phone the editor in the morning.

Gerry is talking to Harry about the Tour de France – how I'd been so close in Paris and had not bothered to go and see the cyclists whizz by. They're nodding and looking into their mugs of tea, my childish way of rebelling when Gerry ordered coffee.

"How about a beer, Nat? Harry might like to stay for a bit."

"The exercise to the kitchen would do you good." The uncharitable quip has fallen out of my mouth and on deaf ears.

The trouble with a house this size is you can't get out of each other's way. You're forced into conversation unless you make yourself busy. We sit together but we are not together, in the front room. They drink their beer and discuss muscle wastage and physiotherapy in preparation for getting Gerry back on a bike a.s.a.p.

"Tell me about the Cup game between Millwall and Manchester United in May," I ask the two men, who stare at me.

"Why?" they both reply.

"I'm interested."

Bemused, they change the subject.

"I see you're getting ready for Saturday." Harry nods at the boxes of French wine in the corner. "They'll have cleared the bingo hall by then. Perfect timing."

"Forty. My wife's forty. Can you believe it? I get to meet these new friends of hers."

The doorbell rings. "Do I have to answer that?" Katy calls.

"It'll be for you, Katy. No one calls on us late in the evening." Gerry turns up the TV sound, and I pour myself a G and T. It's becoming a habit in stormier times. Harry says, "Goodnight," and Gerry indicates to Katy.

"Told you so. Me again," she states, showing Harry to the door as she answers the caller.

I wave at Harry as he passes the window. Katy pops her head round the door.

"Something about an agent who wants to speak to Mum. He'll call again tomorrow. Looked like the bloke from the newsagents, but smarter. Have you missed paying the papers?"

"At this time of night? What did you tell him?" I ask a fed-up Katy.

"You were out."

"Bed now. You've got a busy week."

"I know when to go to bed. How do you think I've managed for the last two weeks without a mother or father? Going up, anyway. Friends to chat to," and she takes the phone."

We fall into the old routine of comfortable silence for what little is left of the evening.

Gerry proudly makes his way up the stairs first, attempting a skip at the top. His plaster hits the side of the banister. At a slower pace, he makes his way to the bedroom door.

"Come on, Nat. I'm back on form."

"Be up later. There's mail I want to attend to." I wonder why he tried to skip upstairs, as the time for the big reunion has passed. Just me and Spike together again.

The post looks like a bundle of bills except one I twirl in my fingers. Advertising rubbish? It heads to join the rest of the junk mail in the bin.

What about decorating your dad's house? You might be interested in advertising leaflets, says my inner voice. I stare at the envelope balancing on the edge of the bin. *You may as well take a peek*, I hear, and click my fingers. The letter flies back from the bin:

> *Dear Natalie Kenning,*
>
> *Please telephone the number on the letterhead at your earliest convenience. We would like to discuss the possibility of work with our travel team on our weekend AWAY magazine. We look forward to hearing from you and send our congratulations on such an interesting visit to France and Spain. We would like you to consider our offer before accepting other offers that will come your way.*
>
> *Yours sincerely,*
> *Leanne Frogmore.*
> *Editor.*
> *People's Post. AWAY magazine*

Is this someone's idea of a joke? There's something going on here, and I wonder if Katy knows more than she has said. The phone call… the letter. The morning may clarify what it's about. I need sleep.

Gerry is snoring gently. He looks in his twenties again… content, and the Gerry I long to be with. I kiss him lightly on the forehead and get into bed beside him. I'm happy to feel him here again.

After my morning coffee I make tracks to the newsagent, purse in hand. "You called last night, I'm sorry to have missed you. How much do I owe?"

"Nothing, Mrs. Kenning, I stopped your papers and magazine when I heard you and Mr. Kenning were away." He hands me the paper. "You've heard we are going to close? We can't compete with the supermarket, and the developers want the land the shop is on. I'm selling up and going to live in London, near our children. It's a dream the missus and I have had for a long time."

"I'm sorry to hear that," I say with genuine feeling. "But good luck." I fold the paper under my arm and walk towards the door, putting the change away.

Two elderly ladies gossip in loud voices by the cards. "She's a bit mad, you know," one says.

"Poor Mr. Kenning," says the other.

"Good morning, ladies," I call from the other side of the shop, and add a sideways glance which they can interpret however they want.

On returning home, I ring Miss Frogmore's office. "Who's calling?"

"Natalie Kenning," I whisper.

"Natalie who?"

"Kenning," I state louder, and wish I hadn't rung.

"I'll see if she's free." Classical music follows.

"Coffee, Nat?" Gerry requests while glued to his chair.

"Natalie, Leanne Frogmore here, I'm pleased you've rung so soon. We should meet. Are you free tomorrow?"

"Yes," I say feeling that my brain is out of gear.

"Shall we say 11.00? Come to Reception. I will have booked you in. Hand in your expenses claim and it will be ready for you when you leave."

I've promised to meet Harry at the bingo hall tomorrow to organise the chairs and tables, plus a bar area and the acoustics for the stage for my party. There's so much to do, and so little time.

I need to buy a smart skirt from the local shops as there's no time to go anywhere else. I'm not sure what to wear for someone named Miss Frogmore.

I feel important going to London, even if it turns out to

be a waste of time. Gerry is less than enthusiastic, and he's right. I shouldn't get excited over nothing, but it is a happening. I want different things to happen in my life.

My outfit won't be designer, and I know it will look Eastleigh. I will sit opposite Miss Frogmore across a wide desk. I will shrink to a metre tall and look so tiny sitting on a huge chair. The London magazine world is taking me out of my depth. I might drown. There will probably only be one story. It will be fun for me, even if it's minor for the rest of the world. They have gone to a lot of effort to acquire no more than one exclusive story.

"Work on the team," Miss Frogmore mentioned on the phone. What the heck does that mean?

"Gerry, can you help Harry with the party? I've decided to go to London tomorrow. If I don't go and see what's what with this magazine thing I won't know what I've turned down. It's a day out."

I disappear out the door with Spike, deliberately forgetting the coffee – something I would not have done three weeks ago. I think Spike knows he's going to the vet and is subdued.

Susie wants to meet for a drink. She needs to talk. She's taken a summer job in a travel agency; she might be able to give me advice if I need it.

I can get on a train by 9.30 in the morning to be at the offices by 11.00. I could meet Alex later. I haven't decided yet, and he might change his mind about wanting to see me. There's a possibility I'll have to return to the office for a further chat, so I'm told. I'll be home around 5.00 to be with Katy and Gerry. I'll meet with Susie over the next couple of days.

I couldn't work in the earthy smell of animals that is

always present at Pets and Pals, the vet's. I wait my turn while planning the arrival of friends and family in Eastleigh. After my turn, things have changed.

The vet has insisted on keeping Spike to check him out. She was cross and gave me a lecture about rabies, plus a leaflet or two. She said she should report me and I started to cry, but there was little sympathy. Spike has stayed and I have to go home and have words with Gerry about what to do next. Poor Spike. I hope he's comfortable and that the kind nurse remembers everything I told her about his routine.

I've only been home an hour when I'm called back by the vet. Gerry's at the hospital, having his plaster reduced and visiting the physio department, so I go alone.

The veterinary nurse offers me tea and says I can sit in the back office. My brain is butterflying again, I'm concerned the police are going to arrive. I'm relieved when the vet comes and sits down alone. She shuffles some papers.

"It's bad news, I'm afraid, Mrs. Kenning."

Rabies, my brain screams internally.

The vet gives me a second or two.

"Spike is old for a little dog. We should keep him in quarantine but I have to be honest, his liver isn't in good condition. In fact he won't live for more than a few weeks."

"Stop there," I want to shout, but she ploughs on.

"You have to make a decision, and the right decision is to say goodbye and leave him with me."

"I can't. I mean I can, but I need to talk to the rest of the family. Can I see him?"

"Of course. The nurse will take you through." I cuddle him close stroking his ears. I've noticed how unresponsive he has become. I put it down to the journey and expected him to be his old self once he was at home. Instead, he's been going downhill fast.

"I'll see you before you go," I whisper, then run out through the waiting room, tripping over a hedgehog, curled up in an open shoebox and causing its protector to catch the rolling ball of bristles.

The house is empty. I sit in Spike's chair, fumbling with the ragged edges of the arms. Before I know it I've dropped off to sleep, the emotion has drained me.

The sound of Gerry's key in the door disturbs me, and reality kicks in.

"Gerry," I call. He comes to sit down, looking into my distressed face. "It's Spike. He has to be put to sleep."

"I told you, Nat. I told you. This is all your fault."

"No. No, it isn't. He's old and his liver is packing up. He has three weeks at the most – and yes, it is my fault that he needs to stay at the vet's right now."

"Sorry," he says, putting his arm around my shoulders as I sob.

"I want to know what to do. When shall I say to go ahead?"

"We need to tell Katy. She has to be a part of this." Gerry is right. Poor Katy. Spike has been a friend to all of us and she has to say her own goodbye.

Kids are often the strongest ones. Katy wants to see him and Anita is going with her. After that, it will be right for Spike not to suffer.

Tomorrow it will be over and I need to collect the ashes. This will blur into a day in London. I want to talk and I want to listen to my own words and come to terms with all the changes. I want to meet up with Susie.

We try the new coffee shop in the mall. Susie is looking sorry for herself. It isn't easy to concentrate when she tells me about losing her husband and her house (as it was a church property), but it sounds awful. I mull over how everything has changed for we three friends.

Susie should have been the rich one with the gorgeous, successful husband. Now she'll have to start over. Susie's choices of men weren't right but she tried. Lisa was the wild one and now she's settling for marriage and a new house on a small housing development by a river, and trying IVF for a baby. I was the boring one and now life is bursting with interest. At least, that's my take on things. I'm challenged and feel stupid on the Spike issue. I know I was wrong. I still feel pleased he came on my journey.

What other people might have considered boring still represents my stability. I think of Gerry, Katy and Dad and I love them. Eastleigh is very much a part of me. Whatever else happens in my life these are my roots.

"It isn't fair, Natalie. He has everything and I tried my best. I have two great kids but we can't live at Mum and Dad's forever. What can I do?" Susie wipes her tears with the palm of her hand.

"What are you good at? Make a list, mix it all up and see if a job comes out. If you don't want to stay teaching and working your holidays at the agency, take time to find yourself, then let life take its course. You know I'm here if you want me. Friends for ever." We say goodbye.

"I haven't asked about your news," Susie calls out.

"Another time. See you at the party. If you see someone in a blue and white Millwall shirt, stay clear." I think of Alan and days on the river. "Have an interesting time at the travel agency this summer, one thing might lead to another."

Once in the door my thoughts move on to the party. I still have three days.

"Gerry, what did your mum and dad say about coming?" I ask, as soon as I see him.

"They want to stay in Spain. If it was somewhere else other than the bingo hall, they might have come. They said to have a nice time."

"Thanks."

I slip upstairs to catch up with Katy, there hasn't been time to talk about her last few weeks in school before going to college in September. She says how proud she is of me and is dead interested in how I get on in London. Then she says something odd.

"You and Dad still love each other, don't you?"

"Of course we do," I reassure her, and wonder why she has asked. She needs a dress for her prom night and doesn't want to shop in Eastleigh. Neither Matt nor Luke has asked her, so she's going with a group of girls. She still hopes Matt will ask her, boys sometimes assume without asking, and he's her first choice.

"This love thing is never easy, darling. Be yourself. Work hard to get good qualifications and make something of your life."

"Would you say you made something of yourself, Mum?"

"Yes and no. I don't know."

"Anita says she doesn't mind Eldred but she's glad she's moving out before her mum marries him. Says he doesn't smell like their house. She's used to girls. They've only got one bathroom and she doesn't want him in there."

"That makes sense. Why doesn't she talk to Lisa about it?"

"Doesn't want her mum to be unhappy, and she knows she has gone without a lot for her. They might move soon."

"Lisa and Anita can sort it out, but you can talk to me about anything that bothers you. OK?"

"I think so. I borrowed your phone earlier. Who's Alex?"

"She's a friend I met on the boat trip and hope to meet tomorrow in London. Goodnight."

14

Things Happen

The train clatters its way through Basingstoke and on to Waterloo. My mobile strikes Big Ben and, comparing phones around the carriage, I can see it's too big with no gadgets. I keep it as out of sight as much as possible. I don't recognise the number.

"Natalie, this is David Marston. I'm the organiser for the candlelight peace walk. Can you arrive at 6.30 and be ready to lead the procession?"

"Me? Why? What about the mayor or the dean from the cathedral?"

"We want someone to catch the attention of the press… reach a wider audience. It's important."

"Yes, of course it is. I'll be there. Do I need to bring a candle?"

"We're providing yours and other recognisable people will be walking with you. See you then."

I won't mention leading the walk to Gerry until after the event. Katy and Anita are going to join the walk and that pleases me. There's so much going on in my life that I skipped half of what David Marston was saying.

There's another consideration with Katy and Anita. They desperately want to go on a Thailand trip and for Lisa and me to go with them. Money and time are issues, but Katy isn't old enough to go without me. We have six months to plan. I would love to travel with family and friends, and share experiences. It would make a change from being in Cornwall without Gerry, although I loved being with Katy and Dad. I could try and find Gerry a sport to do in Thailand, then he might... just might... come with us. Scuba diving? I wouldn't mind trying that myself.

If Gerry's back on his bike then we could go when he's on one of his cycling trips, that's if he won't come. I don't think he would be happy at home without me. What would he do if we were away at Christmas? Maybe I'm worrying too much.

Dad's more than capable of looking after himself. He's mentioned someone called Margaret, but isn't forthcoming when I've tried to question him.

I watch the scenery passing the window, not really taking it in, when a hand pinches my knee. I turn towards an older lady with worse fashion sense than me. She's studying my face.

"You're that woman from the paper, aren't you?"

"Which woman exactly?" I ask.

"The one that got lost and met John Lennon from the dead. Will you sign this for me? Sorry, it's the only paper I've got."

I sign the torn envelope and hand it back with half a smile. A man from the other side of the carriage joins in.

"Are you that silly woman who can't read maps? You're all the same." I'm ready to argue but don't need to, every woman and a couple of men pitch in and no one can hear what's said. Eventually it quietens down and we all watch and wait for Waterloo.

I hope no one recognises me on the platform. I spot a man waiting to take me to my taxi, holding up his sign:

NATALIE KENNING. A few idle looks pass over me, everyone is too busy with their own lives to bother about mine. London is totally different from Eastleigh, where people gossip.

I like it in the taxi, even though the traffic is slow. I glance at Oxford Street with Selfridges, Top Shop and C&A. We take a right and arrive at a tall office building. A man in a bottle green suit opens the taxi door. I try hard to get out elegantly, but my bag and feet get in the way.

The reception area is mostly marble with tall ceilings and pillars. My heels echo – click, clack – across the floor. When I reach the desk, the receptionist offers to help. "Hello. Natalie Kenning, isn't it?" I was right, I have shrunk to a metre tall. "You are here to see Miss Frogmore. Third floor." She indicates towards the lift. I look around, half expecting Monsieur Jacques in case I need someone to come to my rescue. There's space between people here and they smell of designer perfume or expensive aftershave.

The spotless glass lift announces its arrival with a discreet ping. I want to let the doors close and run for the safety of the street. I need to get a grip of my nerves.

A secretary greets me. "This way. Sit down, please." I sit on the edge of the beige and green striped sofa. "Tea or coffee?" A simple decision, but what if I haven't drunk it when I'm called? Should I go for tea or coffee? What if it makes me want the loo again? Coffee sounds better than tea – less Eastleigh.

"Coffee, please."

"Espresso, cappuccino, latte? Cup or mug?"

"Um… cappuccino. Mug, please." Should I have asked for a cup with the security of a saucer to catch the drips?

"Large or medium?"

"Large or medium what?" My voice keeps disappearing.

"Mug?"

"Small, if you have one."

"That means cup. I'll get you one."

My coffee arrives, but the cup won't stop rattling on the saucer. The sugar is offered on twizzle sticks. I'll give those a miss, although they look very pretty.

The double frosted glass doors slide open. A lady my age in designer jeans and a black jacket holds out her hand.

"Come in, Natalie. Come in."

"Coffee?" I indicate.

"Bring it with you. We'll both have coffee in the office. Sit there." She points, and I sit on a dark brown leather chair; it's very comfortable. Miss Frogmore sits on a small matching sofa opposite me. We place our drinks on the glass and aluminium coffee table.

Half an hour later, I have the exclusive signed for a story about my recent journey, and I have the promise of a contract for my first assignment next week to Amsterdam.

"Go and see how you get along. Take a laptop and make notes. Email them. When you get back write the story, if someone else hasn't already done it for you."

The secretary wanted my bank details. I said I would email them. Gerry and I have always shared an account, now I want my own. It will help with checking what's going in and be a record for tax purposes. I can also check what I spend. Spending is on its way up.

I mentioned Katy to Miss Frogmore and her part in telling the story on the school radio, but she already knew. Miss Frogmore asked me to call her Leanne, and said to bring Katy up and show her around. She'd love it, I know. I was also introduced to my assistant, Rajit, who will help me write my articles.

"It's my article. Shouldn't I write it?" I ask.

"Only when you can. You will need an editor. Rajit will get to know you and fill in for you if you're busy. The important thing is to market *you* and keep the interest going. You will be good for *AWAY*. It's an exciting venture for both of us."

I must go to a hairdresser and a make-up artist, and return in two hours' time for a photo. The instruction is to keep a casual look. I put my hand on my phone and wonder if Alex could meet up around four. What if he doesn't like my new look? That isn't the point; he's just a friend. We could meet in a cafe for a chat. Why not?

"Hi, Natalie. Great to hear you. Did you try earlier? Your number came up."

"I had to cut off. Busy, sorry. I'd like that drink if you're still free."

"Sure can. I'll meet you in a great little wine bar I know off Regent Street. Look forward to it." His voice has a light-hearted roll to it.

If we have a drink at 4.00, when will I be home? Once the rush hour starts it will take longer to travel. I could be away by 3.30 and home by 5.00. If I stay it will be 7.00, or later.

What excuses will I have for being late? There's lots of news to tell everyone at home; my heart is pulling me that way.

I need to be back at the office tomorrow. I've been given the option of a hotel room if I want it, but I won't stop over. Staying feels OK to me but I'm worried about Gerry.

What would I go home early for? To get supper for Gerry? Katy managed perfectly well without me and she doesn't need me fussing, Gerry will have to get his own meals on occasions from now on. I'm going to have a drink with Alex, then go home. First, a visit to Selfridges feels like fun. Damn hiccups.

I move from the aisles of clothing through to the accessories. Handbags… is that the right price? This is a different world from mine. It's time to exit past the array of the beauty department sales assistants, who are spraying perfumes on the willing wrists of passers-by.

"Hmm… thank you." I sniff my wrist and it lifts me to clouds of fluffiness.

Alex is waiting for me, sitting on a bar stool and looking businesslike in a dark jacket and open-necked white shirt. He glances up, half smiles and slides off his seat, reaching out to rest his hand on my arm. He brushes my cheeks with a kiss. He's taller than I remember.

"Nice perfume. What would you like?" He pulls up a stool close to his. My lack of knowledge about wine clicks in and I don't know what to say.

"Red or white?… Shall I choose?" Alex prompts.

'Chardonnay' nearly left my lips, but I try to think of something else. "Sauvignon Blanc, please."

"Chilean? South African?"

"What do you recommend?" That did it. I have a glass of wine. The nuts arrive in a glass dish. I wonder how much this is going to cost, and do I pay for mine or let him? This worry habit is spoiling my pleasure. Hiccups have stopped, thank goodness.

Alex takes one leg from his stool and touches his foot on the floor. With a gun holster, he would make a great cowboy. *Sex, sex, sex,* I'm thinking.

I don't want to pry, but I ask about his family. He's happy to chat on. He's divorced and gets on well with his ex-wife and two daughters. His ex-wife is Corsican. She missed her home and family more as time went by. Eventually she made the decision to return, and Corsica wasn't for him. He visits them, and his daughters come to London regularly. He is friendly with his ex-wife's new husband and they all meet amicably on occasions.

"It's better this way," he casually remarks.

Alex had been away from home a lot, and was always shouted at when he got back. His wife was lonely. Eventually they had the conversation and worked it out. When his daughters were little they were their mum's focus but as they grew up she got a job, but she wanted a husband to come home to. He was in the wrong job for that; if he wasn't filming, he was working on a film, editing and writing. It's easier now, technology has moved on, but it came too late.

"Some break-ups are going to happen, but they're never easy. Hold on to what you have." He brushes my cheek gently with the back of his hand.

"Gerry's a lucky man," he says.

"Corsica? Where exactly is it?" Is that a dumb question?

"It's an island in the Mediterranean Sea, west of Italy, south-east of the French mainland and north of Sardinia."

Does he notice my eyes crossing? I'm full of admiration for the compass he carries in his head. Will I ever get the hang of navigation?

Alex wants to know what I'm up to, he genuinely does. I tell him about the photography course and a project I have to do before the course starts. I've chosen Picasso's picture of *Guernica*, with the suffering of war when the Basque people were bombed to bits. I'm going to take cuttings out of newspapers of wars where civilians have been maimed and died, make shapes and stick them on paper. When they're stuck on I need to photograph my finished work and make another collage that will reflect parts of the *Guernica* painting.

"Let me see it. I can help with the photographic equipment in the office." Alex sips his red wine and pushes the nuts along the counter in my direction. He doesn't let go of the bowl as I reach for a nut. We touch hands.

"That would be fantastic. It'll take a few weeks for me to do, especially as I have this job in Amsterdam. I can go where I like, do what I like and write about things that happen to someone on their own. Most of it will be unplanned." I stop to sip my wine to make sure I don't cough on a nut.

"Will I be good enough, or do you think my hopes will evaporate? My writing isn't good. I have to work hard to get it right. Do you always get filming right first time?"

"No, I don't – my work always goes through edit, often several times. Don't worry; you will be brilliant. You have loads of original ideas and the rest you can learn. You don't have to write it all yourself, I bet they gave you cover to help."

"I guess I'd better go. Thanks for meeting up." Time is dictating what I can do, against my will. We kiss again on the cheeks and I catch a slight smell of musk, the same as the last time we were this close, by the river. Better get home to Gerry.

He'll be excited about the longer-term contract; it can change our financial lives. I'll be waiting for the confirmation in the post every day. I don't want to rely on it working out in case they find someone better than me for the job – someone with more confidence with words. If I mess up in Amsterdam, that'll be it.

Alex is still holding my arm.

"Do you have to go? You should build a social life here for when you come up."

I could stay the night in the hotel room *AWAY* has held for me. They thought I might like to hang around the offices and get to know people. Their journalists often work late. Going home and coming back tomorrow is silly.

"Pop in and out when you want to. Sally on the front desk will look out for you," Leanne said. These people are a lot friendlier than I expected.

"I'll take you out for supper," Alex encourages.

"Where?"

"Let's go to Camden. I live in a houseboat at the lock. There are lots of people you can meet, and then you can take a taxi to the hotel. Welcome to London life."

My fun-loving self I found in France and Spain is paying a visit. Gerry's fed up when I tell him I've decided to stay. He thinks collecting Spike's ashes should be more important to me.

Chicken pie and chips in the pub tastes better than anywhere in Eastleigh, but it might be the ambience or the china dish the pie is served in. After a day worrying about eating and drinking in a new situation, I have finally relaxed and I like it, although I shouldn't.

We sit at our table in a packed pub. Friends of Alex stop by to say "Hello." At 9.00, it's time to go to the hotel and prepare for the practicalities of the morning. The interview is over. I can sign the necessary forms and find my way around the offices before going home.

We reach the door and watch as the rain pours down. Alex has ordered a taxi for me, but we must wait on the curb. We're getting wetter and colder. The heavens open and we are drowned. What will I look like when I arrive at the hotel?

Alex takes me back to the cover of the pub doorway where we stand dripping, and wait, but no taxi. I'd go for a bus or a tube but London is unforgiving for people like me with no sense of direction or experience. Gerry could have come, in spite of his leg. He could have supported me.

Alex pulls up his jacket collar and rests his arm on my shoulders.

"Come to my boat. You can dry off and we can find another taxi. Everyone's wanting one in this weather."

His arm resting round my waist is consoling, as we hurry through the rain along the side of Camden Lock. I wish I had time to take in Camden life: the lights, the noise, the crowds bustling around, the smells from the food stands and welcoming bars. Katy would love it; I must bring her. By mid evening in Eastleigh everyone's home or going there. This place must stay up all night.

An umbrella would have been useful, but I didn't think. Alex helps me aboard and unlocks the door. Inside he stokes up a central pot-bellied stove. He puts the kettle on, goes to his bedroom, and comes back with his dressing gown over his arm.

"I'll make tea. You can take a shower, and we'll hang your clothes by the fire."

Steamy water is a pleasure after my cold wet clothes. I'm not sure where the supply comes from, so I'm careful with what I use.

Alex has dried off and changed into a grey tracksuit. His hair is damp and swept back. We sit together by the stove, drinking warm tea. Wrapped in his soft velvet dressing gown I become aware of his life on the boat and something of who he is. His sofa takes the two of us and we curl up for an hour watching the fire and adding coal. Outside the rain continues to batter the roof. It's too late to go now. From the cupboard, he unfolds a spare blanket and tucks me in before going to his room to sleep the night.

I'm glad we didn't make love. It would have spoiled a deepening friendship and I couldn't live that sort of lie with Gerry. I've touched an emotion that's been missing from my life for a long time and it troubles me.

By 8 a.m. we've said goodbye and both left for work. By midday, I'll be on my way home.

The hotel gives me a preparation place. No one looks at me oddly as I ask for my key first thing in the morning. No one cares what I do. My skirt's much improved after a press with the iron provided. In the mirror I'm smart and smiling, ready to meet people in the main office.

If this comes to an abrupt end Gerry will have been right, I'll have made a fool of myself. Playing things down to friends and family is a good idea. Alex understands the media world and what I'm letting myself in for. He helps guide my thinking.

The phone rings, my taxi is here. I must learn the tube stations. I will not always be treated as important, even if work goes well.

I people watch as the taxi drives me to the office. I envy people walking their dogs. Home without Spike to greet me will be strange. Perhaps in time we'll get another dog, but now is too soon.

At my new place of work, I get to meet everyone and learn something of what makes the office tick. I'll be communicating with these offices as I travel.

Waiting on the platform for the train home, I ring Gerry. He tells me his mum and dad have been on the phone. They think they should come to my party and are willing to make the effort. They want to see Katy. Trev needs a hip replacement before the winter so he'll come to England to see his surgeon and make the necessary arrangements. Enid said that to sort the hip out would make their trip worthwhile. They're on their way.

Gerry obviously told them about Katy and Anita wanting to go to Thailand. The response wasn't good. Did Gerry think it was wise to trust her out there with me when I couldn't make it to Europe sensibly? Enid also wanted to know why he wasn't taking control of his family.

I look forward to telling them that *AWAY* magazine is willing to discuss supporting me for a Thailand trip. That might impress the family.

Up yours, my brain screams uncharacteristically. Where did that thought come from? It can't have been me. I'm drunk on freedom.

REM sleep takes over on the train. I wake up just before Eastleigh station feeling refreshed.

Dad tips the curtain back and waves as I pass his house, he appears to be looking for someone else.

Stuck in the front garden of 33A is Spike's old chair. I brush past it and open the door. Katy comes to the top of the stairs in a long royal blue velvet dress. Her hair is up in a twist. Her face is lightly made-up, and pride travels from my head to my toes. My daughter's preparing for her school prom.

"Hi, Mum. Glad you're back. Catch up tomorrow." Her friends have arrived and are laughing and chatting upstairs.

"Doesn't it look better?" Gerry greets me with a swish of his hand across the scene of the front room. He's put Spike's chair out for waste collection and changed the furniture around.

"No, it doesn't," I sigh. "I liked Spike's chair."

"Sit down. I'll make the tea and I'll tell you what else I've been doing. You know you wanted a white leather sofa. Well, I thought we would have a red one and I've bought it. It'll be delivered next week. You'll love it. With you working we can afford a lot of new things."

"I've always worked. Remember I only get fully paid every time I finish an article and it's printed. But it is enough money to make a difference. How about a holiday?" I feel a flip of my stomach as I imagine us having fun together on a beach somewhere.

"We could take Katy and Dad with us," Gerry volunteers. "Then if I couldn't come, what with needing to make up time at work and riding with the cycling club, you'd still have a good holiday."

"Yes, I suppose I would. Thanks for the tea." I take my mug upstairs to change into something lighter. Gerry turns on the golf. It seems such a funny thing to watch. So boring. The only time it was entertaining was when a group of famous golfers dressed up for charity, a reindeer team versus kangaroos. It should be made the compulsory dress code for golfers. I feel cross with Gerry over the holiday issue. My anger is hard to contain.

Katy's friends are milling around by the door and arranging to meet later. All she wants to do is spend time in front of the mirror.

I unwrap my guide to Amsterdam and start thumbing through the new pages. I'm soon absorbed in the architecture, the canals, the red light district and, of course, the art.

A call at the door reveals a young man in a suit. *That's more like it*, is my first thought. With a closer look, it turns out to be Matt. His lip ring gives him away. Katy and Matt walk towards his dad waiting in the car. Gerry and I stand by the window and watch in shared pride. He reaches out and holds my hand.

We gaze as the car drives up the road to turn around. I'm aware of a smart, elderly lady approaching Dad's house. I straighten my hair and rush for the door.

"Where are you going, Nat?"

"To see Dad and find out who that lady is."

"Why?"

"Because… I don't know." Gerry gently holds me back.

Rembrandt and van Gogh in Amsterdam fill my brain for the next half an hour, before looking at the bike magazines and receiving Gerry's attention. He tells me about which bikes are for various situations and explains the best ones to hire for cycling around Amsterdam.

"How did you pay for the sofa?" I ask, drinking the last of my cold tea.

Gerry takes out his wallet and produces a shiny gold card.

"Plastic," he announces proudly. "We can have things we want and pay later."

"Didn't take you long."

"I ordered it in France in case I needed it to get my bike. There's no way I am going to wait around once this leg is mended."

"Good job our income is going up, then," I say.

The picture of Alan sloshing a mop around the deck, proudly producing his credit cards has popped into my head. What else will come into our life with plastic? Gerry wants me to have a credit card. He says it'll be useful abroad. I point out that I didn't need one in France and Spain, so why would I need one now?

My phone dongs a loud Big Ben sound from the bottom of my bag and the temptation to own a card tickles my mind. A journalist might look better with a flash phone, but if it had too many buttons, I would lose the will to use it. The not-quite-with-it image is something I've been told to cultivate. If I become well off, and capable, no one will be interested in what I do.

I answer the phone. It's Katy.

"Mum, it's embarrassing you watching from the window. Please don't do it when I come home."

The room regains my attention. A red sofa would look fantastic on its own, but in our front room, it will offend the eye. Oh, well, Gerry's choice. At least he's taking an interest.

"Do you think I can go to Dad's yet?"

"Leave him alone, Nat. He's making his own life. When he's ready he'll invite you to meet her."

"I want to talk to him about moving. His house will be empty in three weeks and he wants the paperwork sorted."

Gerry wants me to sell the house right away, but I'm digging my heels in, as Katy wants to help do it up. We can have fun discussing the possibilities. Katy's name is to be on the deeds and she can have her share of the money when she reaches eighteen. The worry of Katy going to university has been sorted, thanks to Dad.

Spike always came for a walk late evening. I feel like going out anyway.

"Do you want to come for a short walk? We can go slowly," I call to Gerry.

"No thanks. Snooker's on in a minute."

The lead is missing from the hook by the front door. Gerry's done a good job of clearing Spike's things away.

There's a little metal box on the floor containing his ashes to be buried tomorrow.

With my hands stuffed firmly in my jacket pockets I set off down the road. The hippie dancers have left a scarf behind and litter is collecting in a wind circle.

Anita is making her own way in the world, so Lisa is moving to a house with Eldred. Would I move? My future, which looked set, is now open to question. Life on an estate – which is probably what we could afford – has its fears. What would the neighbours be like? Would they expect me to be neat and tidy all the time and fashionable in dress and house decor? Scary.

I could be a country girl with two large dogs. I imagine Gerry with me in a cottage with a log fire. We would go walking together and talk. Katy would visit regularly, and Dad would come to stay. Cornwall would be a great place to live, but we'd be better off staying in the Eastleigh area for getting to work.

My meandering thoughts come to an end outside the bingo hall. The lights are off. I wait for a pang of loss but it doesn't come, I wait... and again, nothing. There's been no major town uprising against its closure. I conclude that bingo here has had its day.

Changes in my life crept up on me, and now they're big: Spike; the job; Dad; travelling on my own.

"No more changes, please. I've had enough. I want stability." I'm talking into space.

15

Goodbye Spike

We gather in Dad's back garden. He's made a plaque from an old piece of wood and has written:

'Thank you for all you gave'.

We bury the casket of Spike's ashes and stare at the newly dug earth.

"Come on. We've made cakes." Katy moves us from the garden and into the kitchen. She still has mascara smudged across her face from last night, and from keeping back tears today. Anita runs her hand affectionately over her tousled hair.

"How was the prom?" I enquire, having received no ready feedback.

"Rubbish. Matt went off with Becky and we had a big row. Knew I shouldn't have gone with him, but did speak to Luke."

"What was it like, apart from the boys?"

"What?" Both girls say, staring at me. Then they serve drinks and cakes.

Dad and I stand quietly outside. The sun passes in and out of the old apple tree branches. It no longer produces the profusion of pink blossom and the abundance of apples it used to. Decking and a barbecue area might be better.

The individual cakes are topped with fluffy blue icing and the chocolate letters say *SPIKE*. They stick in my throat as I try to swallow. We are quiet, with thoughts of our loving little dog. We drink fizzy orange juice and lift our glasses to Spike having fun in his forever dreams.

"Can we go to Thailand, Mum? Can we?"

"Oh, I don't know, Katy. I don't know. You're going to Japan. That may be enough for now, but if you go I go."

"I need to go this year before I start a paid job instead of being self-employed, and can't get three weeks off when I want to." Anita has a point.

"I don't find it easy to be tied to exact dates. My job may dictate when and where I go." I'm realising how my time schedules will change. "Where in Thailand, Anita?"

"My dad came from Phuket. I want to go there – not to find him, but to see where he came from."

Lisa arrives, dressed in her usual style of a green and orange tabard covering her full figure and worn over uncomfortably tight jeans.

"I'm going to go, Nat. Looking forward to the sun, sea and anything else Thailand has to offer. I'd love you and Katy to join us. No pressure, though."

The girls gather the empty plates and take them to our house, giving me the opportunity to see how Lisa feels about Anita's Thai family. Anita's dad hasn't been heard of since before she was born, but Lisa wonders about Anita's grandparents. She can remember where they lived but they are probably unaware of Anita's existence.

Encouragement from my new job is a good reason to join them, but Gerry is an overriding consideration. Changing our family Christmas is not part of my plan. We always give each other stockings made of silly things. The tree always has many of the same decorations – some of them were Mum's. Christmas away from Eastleigh is proving a hard conflict. Gerry will be the decision-maker on this one.

"What about you, Jack?" Lisa turns on Dad. "What will you do at Christmas?"

Dad is a little coy. "I'll be all right, love. Don't worry about me."

"Gramps has got a girlfriend," Katy sings as she returns to gather up the dregs from the table, and listens in case she misses something important.

"Time for us to go and get on with the day. It's the candlelight peace walk tonight. I have to be there by six to meet with the other supporters." I look at Katy. "Home, please. We need a chat." A look of oh no, spreads over Katy's face.

We avoid conversation until we get to our door. "Now what?" she asks.

"Come and sit down a minute."

"That bad?"

"Now what's this about Gramps's friend?" Katy's shoulders relax to their normal level.

"He's all right, Mum. He hasn't had a chance to talk to you alone – and anyway, he thinks you might not approve because of Grandma."

"He's wrong. I would love him to have a companion. Mum would have, too."

"He's moving in with her in Alresford."

"Who is she? How did he meet her?"

"Her name is Margaret. She's a very nice person and she works in the ticket office at the steam train station."

"They could have waited a while before moving in together."

"Gramps is seventy-four, Mum. If you want to know

anything else why don't you ask him yourself?" A car pulls up and Katy takes the get out option and runs to greet Enid and Trev.

"Hi, Nana. Hi, Grandpa."

Is it that time already? They weren't supposed to arrive before twelve. They come in, leaving their cases in the car ready to go to Dad's house where they are staying the night. Apparently, our spare room is a bit poky for them.

Presents are spread out on the table. I haven't had time to open them, but there's always tomorrow.

"I'd love a cup of tea, Gerry," Enid announces, looking straight at me.

"Of course. Sit down, make yourself at home." I smile.

Soon I'm back with a tray of mugs steaming with strong tea, just how they like it.

"Here, Natalie. Open it now, and then you won't lose it." I'm handed an envelope to open under scrutiny. It's a card with a coach on the outside, and inside tickets for a trip to Hull.

"I thought it would suit you and Gerry, a couple of days in his dad's home town. As you're not a reliable driver and Gerry can't drive yet, coach trip will be ideal."

"I would have preferred Liverpool."

"Why, dear?" Enid asks, confused.

"John Lennon."

"Fuck John Lennon," announces Gerry.

Trevor tries to swallow a snigger and coughs it away. I'm not sure if he's mocking Enid or me. Enid is sure and gives him a sharp slap on the shoulder. My mouth drops and we wait as he coughs another snigger. He clasps his hands behind his back, and stares out the window. He roars a belly laugh. Gerry is first to catch it, and then I giggle, and finally so does Enid. We rock with laughter. Gerry opens a bottle and we drink each other's health.

The party atmosphere has begun, but I haven't planned supper. Fish and chips? Takeaway? I can't do that. They only come to see us once a year and I presume I'm expected to cook. I scribble a list: lamb shanks, onions, carrots, and potatoes. It's the meat and two veg option. I rush it up to Katy, desperately trying to think of a dessert.

"That jar of walnuts in honey from France, put it over some ice cream and you're there." I give her more money than is needed for the shopping and off she goes. By the time she returns Gerry has taken them to Dad's and I gear myself up for a session in the kitchen. The casserole can be cooked before the candlelight walk and warmed afterwards – perfect.

An hour later, they return to the wonderful smell of supper permeating the downstairs of our house. This is the moment to tell them I'll be out between six and half past eight, I might get back earlier. They inform me it will be too late for them to eat now they're getting older, especially if it has onions in it.

"You three can eat together when you like," I try apologetically.

"You know what, Enid," Trev says. "I fancy a nice plate of fish and chips from Mr. Plaice. You've got the best fish and chip shop ever here in Eastleigh, and I don't want to miss the opportunity of having some."

Now I have a large casserole of lamb shanks I don't know what to do with. I'll freeze them, they will do for Gerry during the four days or more I'm going to be away.

I don't think there will be much media coverage of our little walk for peace, and Gerry needn't be bothered about it. Katy is upstairs packing for the morning; it's an opportunity for time together.

We talk about Tokyo. They are going to visit the Trade Centre and have a planned visit to Hiroshima. Katy wants to light a candle at the Peace Memorial to remember the victims of the atomic bomb. She doesn't really understand what it was about. I guess it will come home to her when she stands there but I don't want it to. I wonder what it would be like to travel to Japan.

Uncle George was tortured in a prisoner of war camp by the Japanese, but we're at peace now and I'd love to see the sights. With my new job, I can suggest places, but the editor has the final word. Each new assignment will be reliant on the success of the last one. I can go anywhere in the world. I feel overwhelmed if I think like that. I must take one step at a time, unplanned is what I do best.

Becky and Matt are going to Japan and Katy wants to sit as far away from them as possible. Her worst fear was taking my red case, but Gerry has sorted that out and now she has her own black one.

In the front room, Gerry is looking at bike catalogues. He wants two bikes to replace the last one. I've looked at the magazines myself and had a chat with the man in our local bike shop. There's a lot more to buying the right one than I imagined.

Gerry has expressed his concern at involving Katy in the walk and pointed out that I should keep a low profile. He expects the police to be there and photos of us could be put on file as potential troublemakers. He's trying to scare me.

I begin to open my presents; the patterned paper, the sticky tape... I love it. A book about digital photography from Alan, I'm surprised I haven't fallen out with him forever, but he's coming tomorrow night. A new mobile phone from Dad, it isn't too technical looking. It will be handy when I've sorted out what I can do with it. Katy must have helped him choose it. In the corner of the room is a big box from Gerry. He nods at me expectantly and I struggle with the packaging. It turns out to be my own laptop computer. I can't believe he has thought so much about what to get me. He points out that we could all benefit and that I still might like to use it if my fancy job falls through.

"Thank you. Thank you so much." I run my fingers over its shiny exterior. I kiss him before kissing the computer, then slide it back in its box and think about where the money came from.

Delight fills me as I pick up a bunch of homegrown flowers and a box of eggs from among the pile of presents. Harry has been a good friend and I've never properly appreciated him until now. We are going to stay in touch. I have an open invitation to visit his allotment any time, and I will when I can.

A package delivered in the post is the last one I have time for. I open it, savouring the moment. Inside the smart blue wrapping is a book about Picasso. My heart is racing as I take in the pictures on the cover. No one has ever given me such a beautiful book. It's the story of Picasso's life, his paintings and quotations. I look all over it to find a message, but nothing. Then a photo falls from the pages to the floor, Whitey with Spike. They are running along together on the riverbank. On the back page is a message:

Good luck in your job. Be yourself. x.

I need to get ready and be out of the door. A taxi is due in thirty minutes. It will give the street something else to talk about. Not that I mind them talking about me, I've been a part of this community all my life, mostly unnoticed. Now I'm the centre of interest. It will pass soon, I'm sure. I would like to visit the newsagents without causing heads to turn, but that isn't going to happen before it closes.

Outside Winchester Cathedral, a small group is gathering. Students and the odd drunk are sitting on the grass, relaxing in the evening sun. David Marston hands us our candles encapsulated in safety glass, designed to make us stand out as leaders and to conform to safety regulations. Everyone else will be holding candles they've brought themselves.

We are given a briefing from a senior fire officer. He looks too respectable to behave like the firemen in Paris for Bastille Day. The police arrive and tell us our responsibilities and the danger of the protest being hijacked by people out to cause trouble. We are assured there are plenty of possible troublemakers around, and to stay within the lines of the crowd control police.

Crowd control? There's no crowd here, just six of us who have been organised to walk together. Katy and Anita have gone off to meet their friends.

Leaving the cathedral behind us, we walk towards the sound of voices in the high street. As we turn the corner by the Buttercross, hundreds of people are milling around the precinct.

"Right," says a police officer, "join together at the front and start moving immediately. A pace setter is in the line with you, watch and walk, not too fast and not too slow. In forty-five minutes, you will be back here, then disperse as quickly as you can. No hanging around."

Cameras flash and I try to keep my mind on why we are

here, and I give a thought to John/George. It's very emotional and my mind concentrates on the children who might be maimed or die in a war and who can't speak for themselves.

Not all voices are in support of us. Angry bystanders shout as we move forward.

"Traitors. What about our soldiers?"

"Friends of Saddam." The police move closer.

"You support Chemical Ali the Kurd killer." I can feel the mood changing and wonder where Katy is.

We wanted the walk to be silent but drums are playing in the crowd and raising the tension. Should I have listened to Gerry?

Alex is in the crowd; he stands back, watching. He has come from London to give support and to keep an eye out for me. Katy and Anita are not far away. They wave as I turn towards them. Slowly, a chorus rises, *'Give Peace a Chance'*. If John Lennon was a vision at Lourdes perhaps we could get him beatified for writing such a great mantra.

We reach our destination and David Marston stands on the law court steps giving a short speech questioning weapons of mass destruction and what our special relationship with America is about. As he finishes, a cauliflower passes close to his ear. Other than that there are no further problems.

It felt longer than a forty-five minute walk. At the end, I do as instructed and head back to the cathedral. Questions come from journalists and my photo is taken with various people, mostly I don't know who they are but they appear to be important. The main body of protestors and the crowd are off for a drink or going home.

A young girl has been hovering not far away. She moves forward.

"Hello," she says in a small voice. I reach out and give her a hug. "Scarlett, it's so nice to see you." In the distance, her mother gestures "Thank you."

I saw someone else earlier – Dan. He made no attempt to talk to Scarlett, or me, and disappeared quickly. I had no idea that news of the walk and my small part would spread around the south of England. People who know me felt it important to be interested and support the anti-Iraq war walk, apart from Gerry. Celebrity is a title I can't get my head around.

Gerry's mum and dad will be at home, forming an opinion of what I'm doing. Of more importance, Susie has been texting, she needs to talk again and there's little time. Susie has been a reliable friend over the years, especially when Mum died. Now I must make time for her. I message back and invite her to our place. We will disappear to the spare room and take what time there is. I'm sure Gerry and his mum and dad will be happy chatting without me. I can join them for a short time before bed.

I slip into the lounge and mention nothing of the past couple of hours while Gerry pours us all a glass of white wine and we relax.

"I hope you were careful not to be seen, Nat, especially with Katy around." I cross my fingers and toes. But the photos?

"How were the fish and chips?" I ask, sniffing at the pungent smell.

"Great. You don't get fish and chips like that in Spain." Trev pats his distended abdomen. "You didn't make any pudding, then? We did have a look."

"I'll make pancakes if you like," I say, hoping they turn down the offer.

Before Gerry can say yes, Trev says, "Too late for my digestion, but I would have done earlier."

"There's ice cream," I add. Enid looks put out.

The visit to Hull bugs me. The coach trip is not a natural present, as far I can see. Gerry was born there and they moved here when he was seven. He has shown no interest in going back. Enid still has a sister living there and we are invited to stay a couple of nights, but it's still a mystery.

"Gerry's aunty can put us all up, we could have a nice family time." Enid shows me Trev has tickets for a football match, along with their own coach tickets numbered adjacent to ours. Trev has also arranged a game of golf with Gerry if his leg is better. My heart sinks further than I could have imagined possible.

"Bring Katy. We'll pay for another ticket if she can come. We've booked the coach for two weeks' time before we disappear back to Spain, and while Gerry is still off work."

"Hull has a great modern bingo hall, it seats up to a thousand people, not like that poky old one of yours. We ladies could go to bingo… now you'd like that, wouldn't you?"

"I guess Hull is still home to you, but remember that your family moved over thirty years ago. I have a more demanding job now. Maybe Katy could use my ticket. She will be on a bit of a low when she returns from Japan. Time with you might cheer her up."

"You're not going to be away that much, Nat, this is a part-time job. I don't want you going off whenever you fancy. We'll talk about it and weigh things up. I was expecting you back Wednesday night but you chose to stay away." Gerry looks at his mother for support.

"We were wondering if Katy might like to come to Spain with us; we haven't seen much of her on this visit. Sorry... there are only two bedrooms, or we would invite you all. I was saying to Trev the other day... you managed to drift all over the place in Europe, but never thought to come to see us."

"I found places by mistake, not design, remember? If I'd come looking for you, I might not be back here now. Who was the invite to Spain for?"

"That reminds me, Nat. A guy with a big moustache dropped a present by for you. He said they are staying with the others at the Hilton and looking forward to tomorrow night. They'd like to see us for a drink if we've got the time."

A knock at the door, and it must be Susie. Oops... no, a delivery. I know what it is and ask the men to carry it through to the shed. It's covered in cardboard, but there's no denying the shape. Gerry has caught a glimpse but pretends not to notice; a beam slides across his face as he touches his ever-present bike catalogues.

There's time to open more presents. Linda has given me pretty-pink, short lacy pyjamas. I've come to expect this from her. They will be tucked away in the drawer for now. Firstly, it's rarely warm enough – and secondly, Gerry might think I have gone crazier. Come to think of it, my new thong knickers raised a knowing grin of approval.

They are surprisingly comfortable, with no panty line. Katy has been wearing fancy underwear since she's had her own pocket money to go clothes shopping. Anita is a big influence on her, not in a bad way, but what she has Katy wants.

Anita has a boyfriend who worships her and why not? She is beautiful, but there's a lot of her mum in her. She wants to go travelling when she's earned enough money. Katy would miss her but that's what happens in life… it changes.

Many times Anita has gone out without her and Katy would sulk for a while. Then she would become Anita's make-up model or get a free leg wax, and all was forgiven.

José has sent me a key ring with a bull and a toreador dangling from it. I text:

Great pylons M3, junctions 11 to 13. Drive at night. Take camera. Nat.

A card from Hector is a voucher for a gliding lesson and a book with aerial views of the Pyrenees with his name printed on the front cover. Oh boy, what a great gift, but he isn't taking me for the lesson, he's inflicting me on someone else.

I must remember to tell him about meeting Scarlett and her mum. It's satisfying to know they met up at Heathrow and she's back home in Basingstoke. They should try a pilgrimage together one day, walking, talking and meeting lots of people doing the same thing.

Maybe Gerry and I can go once we get the Hull thing out of the way and his leg is stronger. I could take him to some of the places I went, and we could drive to places he's ridden on his holidays. His cycling trips to the Pyrenees are more alive to me now. It would take legs like his to ride through those mountains. I'm not sure how we'd get the bike there without the club van, but he won't need it if we walk together.

I can't see Dad or Katy wanting to go to Cornwall in the same way again. Dad might take Margaret and they would have a great time. As for Katy, I'm not sure, she's not old enough to go places on her own, but is getting too grown up to come with just me. Gerry might take her with him one day. My heart is suddenly cold. What if I was left behind on my own? No Dad, no Katy, no Gerry and being forty. I'm grateful for the possibility of new things in my life.

Was that why Enid and Trev went to live in Spain, the proverbial empty nest syndrome? They certainly have a lot of friends there. Gerry is their only son and they couldn't keep visiting on the off chance of seeing us. They entertained friends in their Victorian detached house, but there was not a lot of dropping by or bumping into friends for a coffee. Their lifetime friends downsized or went abroad, life must have been dull sometimes.

I'm sure they planned on more grandchildren, but I couldn't help them with that. Gerry doesn't know why he was an only child. What would happen if I asked Enid?

"Nasty scratches you've got in the side of that car of yours, Son. How did that happen?" Trev's arms are folded, as he looks hard out of the window.

I take a large piece of chocolate cake with a cup of coffee, excuse myself and go to make the spare room upstairs comfy for Susie and me. Katy has left a stray sock on the stairs and I realise how much I'll miss her, Japan is a long way away. I take a bite of chocolate icing, scattering crumbs behind me.

Two navy-blue beanbags and a rug are all we need for relaxation. Except... except for Spike.

16

Visitors

"Mum, Susie's here."

"Send her up."

Susie looks smart in her tight trousers and skinny black T-shirt. She smiles through the muddle her life has turned out to be, but it's a cover-up.

"So sorry about Spike. You must really miss him. Are you going to have another dog?" Susie brushes a kiss on my cheek.

"I don't think so. It depends how Katy feels, but there will be times when no one's around to look after it, and that wouldn't be fair. Wine or coffee?"

"Coffee for now. I don't want to cry."

Leaning against a beanbag, Susie makes herself comfortable on the floor. The pretty-young girl has gained lines on her face and is another friend soon to reach forty. She should have had Mr. Rich-and-Gorgeous and a great family life, instead she has muddled through marriage and children hoping things would turn out right, and they haven't.

We both look up at the knock on the door and Enid enters, carrying a tray of coffee with two mugs. I already have mine and, in a flash, I understand Enid is coming to join us. She sits on the floor in spite of her A-line skirt and produces a packet of ginger nut biscuits from under her arm.

"So what are you girls talking about? Sex, love and marriage, or politics and religion?"

"Skip the politics and you're there," Susie says. "How do you keep a marriage going for a lifetime?"

Enid looks thoughtful, then picks a bit of ginger nut from between her teeth. "No sex. That's the answer, no sex."

Susie and I focus on the conversation, waiting for what she will say next.

"After I had Gerry I wanted something more out of life, if we had had more children I'd have been stuck like Natalie. Oh… I don't mean that rudely, dear – but with one child you've hardly made an effort. I wanted money and freedom to travel and to buy nice things; no more children gave us the chance. I did well in retail management, I liked being the boss, and it paid reasonably well. You and Gerry have never been ambitious, I was and I still am. Your generation had the pill, it was all more complicated when we married. My mother had nine children, and I helped bring them up. The pill was around when I married but there were a lot of reservations about it, and I didn't like sex. I was not part of the sixties' revolution."

"What about Trev?" Susie asks. I can see she is finding the conversation surreal.

"Has it done him any harm? No. He would do anything for me. Worships me. Now what about you two?"

This is weird. Since when did I discuss my sex life with my husband's mother? Maybe she does have a view that will help Susie in an odd sort of way.

Susie explains about marrying into the church, and how her life has been swallowed up by her duties there and a part-time job in the church school. Her husband made God an excuse for having sex with another woman he fancied. Susie was left to sort out the mess.

"Where's your forgiveness?" he asked her as she left, leaving her faith and husband behind her.

"Look to yourself, my dear. Get the best job you can and be strong. You can go up or down. Don't let any man knock you down. Stop talking and thinking about him. Make plans and move on. Decide how to be happy and go for it. I'm off, back to the men. Thanks for the chat."

"No sex, ever?" I find myself repeating.

"Not exactly. Birthdays and Christmas… and occasionally on holiday, but I was very careful. These days it's different – anything goes. I'm post-menopause and all that. A new era." Enid sweeps out the room and her shoes clop downstairs.

The gloom of our conversation has lifted as we discuss the future. Susie's holiday job in the travel agency could provide all sorts of opportunities. She is good at languages. She's applying for an air stewardess job, and she definitely has the looks.

Susie's parents are happy to help look after the children. They still go back to their father and the busty twinset partner. Soon he's to marry and she will become his new wife, which will legitimise everything. Susie is suffering from rejection, but hopes she will find happiness again one day.

There isn't much time to get everything done before the party tomorrow, so we finish our coffee and return downstairs. Susie lightly hugs Enid who shrugs it off in her usual fashion. I wonder if we might have more of a mother and daughter-in-law relationship brewing. I'd like to know exactly what she means by a new era.

I say goodbye to Susie on the doorstep and agree we'll meet up another time soon. I wish her well and note her sweet personality hasn't changed.

There's a skip in her step as she turns to wave, and then she picks a dandelion clock from our garden wall and blows at the seed head. Susie has many wishes. When it's her fortieth birthday, I'll talk to Lisa and arrange something very special. Perhaps being pretty and just the right size isn't a recipe for success in love.

Enid touches my shoulder and beckons me away from the men into the kitchen.

"You can see why I was so upset by what you've been up to. I wanted things to be good for the family, and you let us down. You won't do it again with this new job of yours, will you? You see, I'm not sure what to tell our friends."

Gerry is serving evening drinks. Saying nothing is the best option. I fear an improved relationship with Enid was a fleeting whim.

I consider the morning papers and what the family will read about the walk for peace. I comfort myself that it's local news and will only make the local papers. I might just get away with it. On reflection, there was a jostle of journalists there. If problems come they come – there's nothing I can do about it now.

I'd like some emotional support from Gerry, but he doesn't notice. He's busy handing round the crisps and topping up drinks. Bits from his bike have extended from the shed into the lounge, and a wheel waits in the corner to see if it can be salvaged.

"Katy tells me you've been going to the bike shop, Nat." Gerry's pleasure is encouraging.

"She had no right to tell you that." I wanted to keep it a

secret. I change the subject. "Party poppers or sparklers? What does everyone think?"

"Oh… party poppers, if you must." Enid sounds as if she might have more of an opinion on the subject, but I'm not in the mood to listen.

"Right. We need to make order from the chaos of boxes for the party that are scattered around the place. Harry will take them to the hall shortly," I say, putting one on top of the other. Gerry can't help much, but he pushes some boxes to one side.

Enid must have misunderstood, and sees the opportunity to rearrange the front room. In no time she has rubber gloves on, and is whipping round with a duster and polish. I shut my eyes, and momentarily wait to breathe again.

"Find the silver polish, Trev," she commands. "Try under the sink. You'll need to have a good rummage, but I'm sure I've seen it in there somewhere." Enid heads for Gerry's cups and photos and begins a good clean. I wonder at her enthusiasm for housework at this time of night. Thirty minutes later the cups on the sideboard shed light around the room.

"What do you think of white leather?" I ask, hoping to make a point to Gerry about the red sofa he's ordered.

"For what, dear? Leather always lacks taste. Why? You're not thinking of buying leather, are you?"

I back off, judging the dismissive look on her face.

"Oh… I don't think so." Hopefully the sofa won't come before they leave. Soon they're about to go to Dad's for the night. I must make an effort for Gerry's sake.

Trev prepares to leave. First he folds the newspaper and then his eye catches my map of Amsterdam. He isn't able to ignore it. He refolds it into the correct creases and pats it down neatly, having lost my position for me.

"You know when a woman's been touching a map, it's never folded properly and put away. There you are, Gerry. Where do you want it?"

"I need to sort out my dress for your party. We won't stay long at the hall but we will make an appearance." Enid points at the door for Trev's benefit.

Am I supposed to say thank you, or what?

"Sleep well," I half smile. Dad will make the best of their company. He's good at the welcoming thing, he always has been.

"Your mum's bought a special dress for my party? What sort of dress? It's a disco at the bingo hall," I say to Gerry after shutting the door behind them.

"You know what she's like. They'll make an entrance and leave after a drink or two, then come home to plan Dad's visit to his hip replacement consultant. Wearing a posh frock is Mum's way of making an effort, to her it's the right thing to do. By the way, where's Katy?"

"Asleep. I guess she can't wait for the morning."

We finish our drinks sitting in the front room together.

"We ought to go to France some time, Nat, you and me – but this time, I'll drive. Tell me about this job. Is it just a flash of something, or are you taking it seriously?" He stops to drink his coffee and stares at the electric bar fire that isn't on. "Do you think you will make proper money or do you need to be looking for something else? Wouldn't it be great to move on, like Lisa and Eldred?"

"We'll have Dad's house soon. Katy wants to do it up with me, and then we can sell it on. Our income is already up. I've been paid something for the London visit, an advance for Amsterdam and the exclusive, which was… well, you'll see." I don't disclose the amount – I can't believe it myself.

"You didn't tell me." Gerry turns the telly off. "How much?"

"Guess."

"Fifty? A hundred?"

"Way out. I've got my first contract, remember, and now I'm going to have an agent. I'm going to meet up with a couple next week then decide for definite which one. I'm going to be earning enough for an agent to come looking for me. Remember that one who came to the house and left his card? Seems I'm popular for now."

Gerry turns and studies me most oddly. I'm not sure what he's thinking, but for once, my confidence doesn't seep into the floor. I stare at my chubby feet and admire the bright blue nail varnish.

The *AWAY* magazine has arranged a choice of agents. They said it's easier to deal with them over finance and for me to be guided through contracts. I've already signed the exclusive deal. I'm signing for three trips, but there will probably be more. There are radio interviews and newspaper coverage. It will be much easier to have an agent to help me with things I don't understand.

I wonder where Alex is, I think he's been in London all this week. *He's just a friend*, I tell myself again, and there's nothing wrong with that. After all, Gerry knows nothing of writing, agents and art. His field is definitely sports.

It could be days since I carried a candle for peace through Winchester but it is only a few hours ago, and there has been little time to reflect. Tiredness sweeps over me, and it's time for bed.

I stop off at Katy's room, just as I did when she was little. Seeing her snuggled up in her duvet makes my heart flood with love. I so want her life to go well and I'll do anything to help and support her future.

I leave her to sleep and click her door shut behind me. Gerry is by my side, swinging his plastered leg; three more weeks before the plaster will be removed, and then there is physio.

Dad has announced he is moving in with Margaret next week, and the legal papers have been drawn up to transfer the house to me. It still feels a bit quick, but then it isn't about me, and I'm adjusting to the new situation. Mum wouldn't have minded, in fact, she would be pleased to see Dad with company. In reality she would have no idea, because that's how it was in the end, she didn't have a clue who any of us were.

Gerry is lucky to still have his mum. It's easy to see the funny side of things when she isn't in my space. Trev has my sympathy, although he never looks as though he needs it. I am sure Enid views Gerry in the same way.

"Mum. Mum." Bother, I must have woken Katy. I gather my dressing gown; throw it over my shoulders and head for her room.

"You will be all right when I'm away, won't you?" she mutters from beneath the cover.

"Of course I will. You can come and see the magazine offices when you get back. We have to think about you preparing for college, the holidays will go quickly."

"Goodnight. I love you Mum."

"Love you too. Goodnight."

Now Spike has gone it's bound to make her feel insecure. I'm aware that my job is changing and with it our home-life patterns. Leaving school and Gramps moving away is a lot for her to cope with. Now she's off to Japan.

With my new job the family will need to get used to me being away for at least a few days every month or even every week, and Dad isn't going to be close by. With all the excitement, I haven't thought through the implications fully, but I need to give this job a chance. At least between times I'll be home, but I don't know for how long. What experience does a bingo caller have for this?

My life is changing; Katy's life is changing... the same for Dad, but what about Gerry? I realise how stuck he is. His job must be boring at times, and sport absorbs him – but is it the only challenge in life he feels? When I'm settled in to my new life, we will talk and make sure he's going to be all right.

I've never looked at him this way before. His life has always appeared more interesting than mine and I have fed off that. He needs to know I still love him and we can move on and change together.

Alex is/was a flirtatious liaison and he understands the world I'm entering. He can be a friend, although he would like our relationship to be more than that. I know he won't interfere. If I manage the situation wisely, he can meet Gerry one day, and we could all be friends. Thoughts of Alex and the kindness he has shown me ease my mind into perfect rest.

17

Family Business

Gerry has been writing a diary and he wants to write his life history. His granddad filled three old exercise books writing about the family, his dad has done the same, and now he wants to follow them, but using the computer. I know he isn't good at expressing his feelings – like father, like son.

He has problems with writing at length, boredom sets in, but he has plenty of time to improve now he's restricted with his broken leg.

It was brave of him to ask for my opinion and I'm not sure if I'm the one able to criticise:

Page 1.

Nat says, "Start and keep going. Sort it out later." If I don't start I'll never get anywhere.

Sitting around with this damn leg in plaster, writing is giving me something to do. If Nat can do it I bet I can. I can't write everything. That's the trouble with writing about myself – honesty – and from whose point of view, apart from my own, do I see things?

I've read that events can be remembered differently by however many people were there. I'll do my best. I wish I had a brother or sister to help. I like having Chester around, but he doesn't share my family history.

I want to write about cycling, football and snooker but

Katy said, "Boring". Since it's Katy who will be reading it, I should listen. I'm going to write something about sport.

Meeting Nat at school was special. I was going to ask her out when she was eighteen, but I got impatient and asked her when she was only sixteen. No pushing the relationship for sex and all that. I got on with my own life, convinced we would be together eventually. I was right. Of course, there were other girls; some too loud, some too bossy and some talked too much, but Nat was just right.

We married and Katy arrived. She was part of the plan.

I'm only 5 ft 10 inches tall but Nat is 5 ft 5½, so I have a height advantage. She does wear heels, mainly when working at the bingo hall. There's a silver and black pair that come out if we are going out. They suit her.

Then there was our son. His death was not part of the plan, but we had to cope. We did well, considering, but I wonder what things might have been like… we could have gone to the footy together. I did ask Katy if she'd come once, but she said no.

I could have been a professional cyclist but you need money to back you up and freedom from responsibilities at crucial times of the year. It wasn't going to happen. I will list my sporting achievements at the end.

Nat is good with money and I don't know what all this job business is going to bring or if it will last. I'll keep the newspaper cuttings about her, as they may entertain future generations.

We live in Market Street, Eastleigh, but expect to move soon (fingers crossed).

That's it for now. I'm quite good at writing.

Forgot to write that Natalie has bought me a new bike. I hope she's got me the right one.

"Nat. Nat… you can read this and tell me what you think. What else should I write about?"

"Later. Katy needs to go to the coach and I'm popping into the bike shop," I reply.

I haven't discussed with Gerry that I need to ride a bike in Amsterdam. Without Alan, at Saintes, holding the saddle, I wouldn't know how to stay upright. The challenge is to get to Amsterdam and hire a bike, and tour the city without any help or pre-booked accommodation. I must write a diary, emailing it to the magazine every day. If the formula works then readers will be invited to send in suggestions of where they would like to see me go on my own. The only person who has any input into this trip is Alex, and that is small.

There are places to go and people to see right now. First I have to stop at the newsagents before dropping in on Harry, all this after saying goodbye to Katy.

Enid and Trev are volunteering to go to the school coach. I might get emotional and embarrass Katy in front of her friends, and God knows I've done enough of that lately.

Dad wants a quick chat with me while he is packing up his house. He wants help with decisions as to what things he might leave and what he should take to his and Margaret's new home.

The Amsterdam trip starts tomorrow. I need to have a good party, but not drink too much, so that my head is as clear as it ever will be. My short thank-you speech is written and ready in my bag. This is the last event to take place at the bingo hall; after the party the doors will be shut and the keys handed back. I've been thinking about applying for jobs in bigger, better bingo halls. I might have to travel further afield to somewhere like Bournemouth. If the journalism job fails, as Gerry assures me it might, then I can try for a job in one of those places. Would I be considered too old?

I'm going to register for the photography course and hope I'll have time to attend the classes.

On the way, I call in to the newsagents for extra crisps and party poppers. A glance at the local papers on the counter tells me that, yes, I am unavoidably on the front pages.

Do you know who I am, Mr. Blair? is the headline. I don't remember saying that, but I'm sure I thought it. *She was at Lourdes when the vagrant* (he was not a vagrant, he was a busker) *was shot dead instead of Mr. Blair*, continued the article. Otherwise, a good message and I feel proud, until I start thinking of yet more repercussions at home. I turn the papers over to show the back page. The nationals don't show anything obvious and I won't buy one for fear of what might be inside. The *People's Post*, for sure, will have covered the story; anything to build up their new *AWAY* journalist's profile.

In the *Eastleigh Standard,* I read: *Dead mice found behind the sinks at High Lites, the hairdressers.* It's about to be closed for redevelopment but Health and Safety should have shut it before. I thought it smelt funny at times, especially when my hair was washed.

Good. They have packets of party poppers. Harry will be waiting for the last bits and pieces. Thankfully, he can take over for the rest of the day. He said the new owners were not happy with the accounts when audited, but they appeared to let things go. They had only bought the business to close it down, clear the land, and then sell the space for development (in line with council guidance).

Whoopee for them. There's money to be made out of progress. I don't know why I feel cross, it's for the best, and I'm ready to move on. I reflect on how I like being a part of the local community, even if I am about to leave it behind.

At home, the hallway is empty of party stuff. Gerry is at Dad's having coffee with his parents, Katy has gone and Spike is no longer here. The house sounds empty, like I have never noticed before. If everyone is out; they are coming back, but this has a feeling of permanent change.

I start on the cards waiting to be opened. The first is from Anita: *Happy Birthday. I hope this will be the year you come to Thailand. It would be great if you, Katy and Mum came with me. Let's make it for Christmas.*

The trip to Thailand has slipped under the carpet of my mind, but it has gathered some pace in the minds of Anita and Katy and I haven't given an answer. This time it will depend not only on the family but also on my work diary. Gerry needs to come and, to my surprise, he has said he might as he could think of, "Nothing better than to be surrounded by four of his favourite women." Eldred said he doesn't want to come because of Lisa and Anita going on past family business. He will come if he's needed, but not otherwise. I'm hoping he will feel needed to keep Gerry company.

Enid and Trev have given me one of those big blousy cards with *Favourite Daughter-in-Law* written in big letters. What else could I be? Inside they have added an invitation to Spain when it suits us and an extra message: *Promise to tell our friends the things the press said are not true. Our friends support the Iraq war. You will bear that in mind, won't you? We look forward to you coming, and we will spoil you.*

Can't wait. This must have been an afterthought, as we

already have the invitation to Hull. Two holidays with them in one year is a new inroad. I would like to take time to decide, but decision-making is always immediate for Enid. I have a loophole on committing to them, as I can disappear on the pretext of work. The invitations are most likely aimed at Gerry and Katy, I'm sure they won't mind if I don't take up their kind offers.

The doorbell calls me. The last people I'm expecting are a couple of very sweet nuns. I look for their collecting box and try to remember where I left my purse.

"Might we just ask you dear, if you would be so kind as to give a talk at our ladies' meeting, on your visit to Lourdes?"

They look so lovely and friendly. I try to find the words to say "Leave me your number and I will check dates with my agent."

"Oh… you would be so interesting, especially the pilgrimage and your vision."

This talk is not for me, or rather not for them; mostly they have got the wrong end of the stick. I hand over a donation for whatever purpose they might see fit. As I shut the door, guilt springs its hand. There are always going to be mistakes and misunderstandings to deal with. I think Gerry is convinced that the whole thing is a mistake, and that even he might regret the closure of the bingo hall.

Two minutes, and the doorbell sounds again. This time it's a man to check the bike is ready to ride.

"Go through. It's in the shed," I request, "Please leave the wrapping off, I want to see it. Thank you."

It's like Christmas as a child. I imagined what it would be like to own a special blue bike, only I never had one. I would have bought Gerry his bike, but I wanted this one to get some cycling experience. I may need to ride one on trips in the future and right now, there's Amsterdam. I can claim it against tax. I don't think Gerry knows how much I've spent lately; money disappears when you're having fun.

"Have you forgotten that your dad wants to see you?" Gerry asks as he returns to the house. I'm grateful the bike is ready to ride and away in the shed. It isn't a secret, but I don't need a discussion – and least of all a detailed lesson on how I've bought the wrong one.

"Just taking a couple of minutes for myself. I'm off now; you can get some leg exercises done. Please don't go in the shed," I say, hoping he doesn't pick up on the conversation.

"Who are these flowers from Nat?"

"My friend Alex. She sent them as she couldn't come to the party… work, and all that."

"Expensive, aren't they, for a new friend? What did you say she did? Film crew at the BBC?"

"She has a secretary so they won't have been her direct choice, and they can be set against tax. When you have a job filming, time is of the essence."

"Why did she bother at all then?"

"Don't know." I leave the house for Dad's… where I find Enid in cleaning and tidying mode, which is useful. Dad needs a hand and I'm too busy right now.

"How much of this pile do you want? They were all your mother's." I stare at a mound of clothes and linens on the floor. I thought Dad had sorted it all out, he said he had.

"I don't know. Leave the piles there and I'll sort them when I get back from Amsterdam."

"No time like the present." Enid has bin bags at the

ready. "Personally I'd get rid of the lot, after all, you didn't know it was here. Left charity shop – right keep. OK... start."

I stare at the pile, and Mum's embroidered tablecloth catches my eye. I pick it up to keep, and announce, "Charity shop for anything worth selling." A difficult task is dealt with; sometimes the world needs more Enids. I imagine a whole army of Enids patrolling homes across the country.

I claim an envelope from the table before Enid whips it away. "Is this to do with the house, Dad?"

"Yes, it's papers the solicitor prepared. You'd better take a look. Chester's changed his mind and wants money from the house when it's sold. You two will have to discuss it. Stacey thought the money should go to the new baby, if not to him."

Poor Dad. He doesn't know which way to turn, but Chester and I are going to have this out. What about Tracey and Nicholas? Then Katy... she does have an interest. It sounded so easy, but these things never are. I have to make phone calls to the magazine and I'm not in a position to spend time going over the papers for the next few days.

I invite everyone along to our place for lunch. "Bring Margaret, Dad. I thought she might be here."

"She's coming later. She didn't think it was right to meet the family when we're busy. You will come and see us at the flat, won't you?"

"Of course I will, Dad," I reassure him. He too is missing Katy, and worries about her.

"You can have my old mobile phone so that you can both keep in touch when she comes back. If you can play chess, you can learn how to use a simple mobile. How are you getting on with Luke?"

"I miss Matt; he was doing well. Luke doesn't concentrate on Ludo – there's no hope there. Margaret plays bridge and I'm going to start going to bridge with her. What with that and my job on the train I'll be busy, but that doesn't mean I won't miss you." Dad has a tear in his eye as he turns away.

Like Enid and Trev, he's coming to the party for a short time and then leaving the young ones, as he calls us, to it. I hope they will enjoy themselves, although the music will be loud.

I return to our house with my head in a spin and feeling cross with Stacey. It isn't the money but the messing everyone around… or so it feels.

Yet more cards and parcels are on the table and it's my luck to pick up the one from Chester first.

Happy Birthday. All our love, from Chester, Stacey and Blake. It was written in Stacey's writing and I struggle with mixed feelings. They have gone to the beach for the day and are coming back to change. A phone call might stave off the effects of a necessary discussion. I get Chester with the sound of waves in the background.

"Dad said you wanted to change your mind about me having the house. We need to talk, mainly to put his mind at rest."

"Stacey and I thought that we couldn't ignore our baby, and we may need the money for his education, I'm sure you understand that that's fair and reasonable. The house needs a valuation. I should have arranged this in the first place. Sorry about that."

"That's OK, Chester, but Dad wants it sorted a.s.a.p.

Could you organise the valuation when I'm on my trip to Amsterdam?"

"To be honest, Sis, I'm busy too. I'll hand you over to Stacey, and you can sort it out with her."

"Tell you what, Chester. I'm busy. I'll hand Stacey over to Gerry, and they can sort out our business for us."

"I did say you might be difficult, and this isn't necessary. Stacey is capable of dealing with the sale of the house for us. Remember that she left her acting career for me. It will give her something to keep her mind occupied and help us all."

"This is *our dad*, and *we* will do it." I surprise myself at my firmness and fancy my first drink of the day. As I slump on the sofa, I start thinking about how grateful I am for my new life of challenges. It must work out. Enid was right when she told Susie to look after her own interests. Whatever else happens my anchor must be myself.

What has happened to my old comfort zones? Sometimes I feel glad they've gone. Getting up each day without having set plans is a better way to live. But there's still Gerry, still dependable. There's nothing in my history he doesn't know, and we have been through a lot together. I can't imagine our relationship changing fundamentally.

"What's up with you and Chester, Nat? Do you want me to help you sort it out?" Gerry tries to soothe the situation.

"No, I do not," I state.

"I only offered. It's time for lunch. What have we got?"

"There's plenty in the cupboards and fridge. I've filled the outside freezer for you in case I'm away longer than expected."

At this point we both remain seated. I'm expected to head for the kitchen. Over the years, Gerry has only been in the kitchen to eat from the fridge. He's reluctant to take on the shared roles of work and home.

"I'd like a ham sandwich," I say, and carry on looking through my cards.

"Oh… oh," Gerry mutters. "Uh, where's the butter?"

"Fridge. Where else? Sorry love, but you have to take this seriously, the kitchen is now our joint domain. Try your hand with fruit and veg, if you can't cope with recipes. I won't always be here. You'll find the new Gary Blain fish cookery book on the shelf. Most of those recipes are easy."

He looks at me oddly and hobbles to the kitchen. It will take time, but he might like cooking eventually. Takeaways have never been our regular thing and neither of us wants to live on ready-prepared food.

Enid would say, "It's your own fault for spoiling him," and she would be right. Our system has worked well enough until now. When I go to work in the evenings I have always organised supper first: fish pie and veg, cottage pie, etc., but now I'm going to be away for days at a time.

After twenty minutes, he hands me a plate of too many sandwiches.

"Thank you," I smile, and mean it.

Before I can reach my plate he holds out his hand, raises me to my feet and whispers in my ear, "How about coming upstairs?"

All I can think of is my desire to eat, and my mind is too busy to think of sex. Is this part of the way forward in his mind? Our sex life revamped? By the next magazine survey, we might have gone up in the ratings. I can never see us being in a Class A category again, nor do I want to be.

So he fancies sex, women expect so much more

269

emotion, unless you're Enid and take control. That doesn't sound a lot of fun to me. I glance over his shoulder towards the clock. Yes, we've got time… then I can treat myself to a slow bath and get in the right frame of mind for the rest of the day.

I'm looking forward to seeing Linda and José tonight… so pleased they've come. Will Linda approve of how I look?

We strip off, sex happens… and I think of Barcelona.

18

Getting Ready

By early afternoon, I'm in the bath with scented candles lit. Steam and gentle music mingle, and I'm dreaming of Alex. It's a shame he couldn't come. Gerry wouldn't understand, and I can't rely on Alan not to go on about meeting him on the boat on the River Charente. Anyway, he's a firm fixture as a female and becoming more of a secret.

There's a programme for helping young students to cook and sharing an evening meal with someone well known. It was started as an idea in the UK and is now going Europe-wide, with top chefs handing out advice and ideas. Alex is filming, and this means he can take time out and turn up in Amsterdam. He isn't going in my diary for the magazine, but if I'm in too much of a muddle he might be able to redirect me. A little company won't be cheating. I will play fair.

Drinking in cafes and eating in restaurants on my own will be a difficult part of my travelling life. Not even Spike will be with me. In my mind, I'll be sharing the experience with those people reading my diary. Should I try the cannabis cafes and wander the red light district? I will probably end up in these places by mistake.

I can look forward to one meal with Alex and a visit to the Rembrandt House on my own. That's assuming I arrive at the right place at the right time. The Zaanse Schans windmills sound like an amazing step back in time, but I will have to make my way out of town on the train to see them. First, my party is yet to come.

Gerry's voice rings out from the bedroom, "Where's my black shirt, Nat?"

"In the wash bin. Sorry, but I haven't had time."

"Yes, you have. You needn't have gone to Winchester on that parade, or whatever it was. It wasn't for your new job."

"There's time to get it washed, dried and ironed if you do it now." I try to make my point.

"I'll put it on the floor outside the bathroom door."

Is he joking? It isn't his fault if this is what I've made of him. There's a false security in making someone I love depend on me. I can't blame him completely.

"Ask your mum. She'll do it for you."

"You think so?" I hear him laughing. "Don't worry; I'll do it," he states, sounding put out.

"Well done." I try to encourage him but sound patronising. "Two more minutes and I'll be out of the bath."

Before I know it I've drifted into a doze, and family problems disappear behind a veil of steam smelling of rose petals.

Wrinkled, and cosy, wrapped in my pink dressing gown, I return to the bedroom and start to flick through the wardrobe. "Gerry, what shall I wear tonight?"

"Try your black dress. You always look good in that." Does he remember just how many times I've worn it? Something different is called for.

My phone rings. My guests are arriving in Eastleigh and meeting up. They want us to join them for drinks at the hotel. "Can we go, Gerry?"

"Why not? Who are these what's-its-names? Al, Pete, Sarah? Is that it?"

"I'll come back and finish getting ready. There's time. We won't stay long."

We are soon in the process of getting Gerry in the car. Adjusting the seats, and making room, is a fiddle; he will not be the only one grateful to get rid of the plaster cast. It frustrates him to sit in the passenger seat. He does that male thing of playing with every available knob on the dashboard as soon as he sits down. It might be helpful if they worked, but most of them don't. 'Chariots of Fire' starts to play and we share an affectionate glance.

Linda, José and Hector are at the hotel and have met Sarah, Pete and Alan. We kiss 'Hello', laughing with pleasure, and Gerry politely holds out his hand.

"Drink, Natalie?" asks Hector, putting his hand around my shoulder.

"Lemonade, please. Driving." I point to Gerry's plaster.

"You didn't tell us you came from a backwater like Eastleigh, Nat. I wouldn't have come if I'd known." Same old Alan, getting attention from trying to be offensive, or maybe he doesn't know how difficult to get on with he is.

"You gotta decent football team, though. Saints aren't bad, could do better. They've had good times."

"You're the Millwall man Natalie was telling me about. Come on, mate. I'll buy you a drink." Gerry has picked a friend. I wish it wasn't Alan, but it's good to see him getting on with someone.

"Hey, Nat. Anyone else we met coming? What about that bloke who was with Gary Blain?" I feel myself colour. I thought no one had noticed our flirtation on the riverbank, and that was all it was. Alan would never have known that we have kept in contact.

"What was his name?" Alan's thought cogs are turning and, since he is now sitting next to Gerry, there's no way of saving the day. "Aaron. That was it, Aaron."

"I can't remember," I reply.

This is silly. Truth would be better, but Gerry wouldn't understand. I have no intention of making a romantic connection. Marriage was for life with me, and the last thing I would ever want to do is hurt Gerry or upset Katy.

"So you're pregnant, Sarah. So pleased. I didn't want to ask when we were on the boat; I figured you would say when you were ready."

"Where did you say those pylons are, Natalie?"

"On the M3, José. You must get a photograph at night. Its a great road to drive and the pylons enhance it." Only Linda and Hector know what José and I are talking about, the comments go over everyone else's head.

Linda and José are thinking of coming to England to live, as their daughter is staying in London for good. Part of their time here will be spent house-hunting. They have the details of three houses near the New Forest, they all have a pylon in the garden. José can't wait to hear that comforting hiss day and night.

The conversation moves on and we chat until it's time to rush home and change.

"See you later." Gerry and I walk away, holding hands.

Chester and Stacey's car is outside our house and Enid is heading this way with Gerry's black shirt over her arm. My heart sinks, as my quiet time upstairs changing gets tighter. My best hope is that they will talk among themselves and leave me on my own, but Enid and Chester are not a natural mix. Gerry's not good at keeping the peace and he should get changed as well.

"I thought your mum wasn't going to do your black shirt for you," I say.

"I washed it, but she couldn't stand the way I was trying to iron. It was whisked away and I'm sure she has worked her magic and made it look perfect."

"Fairy or witch?" I mutter.

I like it when Gerry looks content, it brushes off on me, and this is one of those moments. He likes it when Chester is here and is pleased to have met Alan. Having his mum and dad around is a rare treat for him.

"Take the weight off that leg of yours, Gerry. I'll get the drinks." Chester moves towards the sideboard and shuffles the glasses, looking for matching sets he won't find. "Stacey would like fruit juice," he says, and he nods at me as if we understand the parts we need to play.

"Orange juice?" I ask, knowing it makes her sick. Then, feeling guilty for what I've just said, "Sorry, there's pineapple juice or lemonade."

"We won't talk about Dad's house until next week, Sis. Stacey has arranged for an estate agent to drop by. That will give us the foundation for a conversation." He continues to speak with his back to me.

My mind is elsewhere, racing through my wardrobe and limited make-up. One day I'll stop at the beauty counters in Selfridges and buy lots of lovely products. Do I have everything ready to slip on?

"I wouldn't leave things you can sort out now," Enid chips in.

"Mum… " Gerry throws her a controlling look.

Enid is busy inspecting the shirt to see if a single crease has been left in.

"There, dear: hang that up somewhere carefully, will

you?" Defiantly, I hold my hands behind my back and wait for Gerry to take it. Even with a plastered leg, I'm sure he can hang up a shirt.

"Where's that little dog of yours? So cute, if a bit smelly." Stacey is looking around as she speaks, expecting Spike to appear.

"He's dead, love. Gone. Remember… I told you," Chester whispers loudly, trying to appear sensitive.

I pour Stacey a large orange juice and leave the room.

"For Christ's sake, come and get Enid," I scream at Dad down the phone. "Chester and Stacey as well, if you can manage them all."

"Tell Enid I need her to help with a light supper before we go out."

"Thanks, Dad. See you later." I wish it was as easy to usher Chester and Stacey out the door.

"Can I come and keep you company while you change?" Stacey laughs lightly, patting her non-existent baby bump.

"I'm jumping in the shower first," I reply.

"You've just had a bath." Gerry is confused.

Can some men not read between the words you say? Alex would have understood, he has that sort of intuition.

Stacey follows me upstairs. "I want us to be the best of friends, Natalie," she enthuses. "Your dad wouldn't want his grandchild to have unnecessary financial problems. What if Chester and I split up? Not that we will, but you never know what's going to happen."

Stacey and Chester splitting up? How fantastic would that be? I stupidly smack my own hand, in the hope it will correct my selfish thoughts. "Fly," I say. "It's the time of year."

"You and Gerry are so sweet together," Stacey frowns. "He so cares about you." Stacey has such a high-pitched voice that it irritates.

Sweet. Eighteen years of marriage is not sweet. Right – moisturiser on, then foundation after my dress. Hair is looking too formal for me. It will fall out of place with the drizzle that has set in for the evening.

"Have you had your eyes done?" Stacey asks, studying my face.

"Done?" I question.

"Yes. You know… surgery. Everyone has things done in LA. If I need things sorted after the baby to get my figure back I'll visit my surgeon."

"And how much will that cost?" I mention, referring to money she might need for the baby.

"You have to prioritise, don't you think? You Brits will be doing the same as the Americans, in a few years. Catching us up… having a tweak here and a tweak there. Our thinking is always ahead of yours. Brits have never got the message about teeth, have they?" Stacey smiles broadly. On a second glance, I see there's a dot of lipstick on her front tooth.

I'm not going to change my pants and bra in front of Stacey. We are not that familiar, and I don't want my faults pointed out and told how a surgeon could improve me. I flash my perfect white teeth in her direction.

"Your eyes definitely have a sparkle they didn't have the day we came to find you and you disappeared. You were lost and confused. I understand. You're a whole lot better back in your own home. Chester and Gerry said you would be."

"Chester just called you." I stand my ground by the door, waiting for her to leave.

"Blake likes you and wants to know if you and Gerry can come and stay with us. Wouldn't that be just awesome, we'd be all together, like families should be?"

I'm saved by the Big Ben tone, on my phone. It's too much of a reminder of Alan, but beyond my technical skills to change.

"Hi," says a warm voice; my heart leaps. "Have a great party. I won't hold you up… see you in Amsterdam."

"Thank you," I whisper. Alex definitely helps my sanity and cheers me up.

"We're on our way," Chester shouts up the stairs. They promised to call in on Dad and they are going to the party from his house.

I slip on my dressing gown and go down to say goodbye, and a couple of other important things.

"We need to consider Katy and Nicholas and, most of all, Dad. This must be as easy as possible for him. He's giving away his house because he is still alive and wants to see us enjoy it. Please cancel the estate agent, Stacey." Chester looks irritated as I speak.

"You remember Susie, don't you Chester?" I say, and pause for my remark to sink in. "I will take charge next week and arrange for a solicitor to draw up papers. Susie needs to rent for a month or two; that will give me a chance to get the house ready for the market." I have made my point, I wouldn't have done that before I went away.

"Twenty minutes, Nat. Off you go and get dressed." Gerry gives Chester a sympathy glance as if I'm not going to see it. I hope his leg hurts.

"I won't wear my black dress. I have a new one." I have a smile rising inside me.

In my room, I open the box with a black thong and a

pretty bra, wrapped in tissue paper. I put on my turquoise dress from Barcelona and high heels… and head for the top of the stairs. Gerry looks up, "Black one, Nat? Black one?" His face looks quizzical. My dress is flamenco in style and I love it. I am going to my party the way I want to.

19

The Party of a Lifetime

I am walking tall, down Market Street, in a bright turquoise dress with flamenco overtones. Gerry is suffering the performance, but it isn't his party, it's mine.

Lisa is waiting on the corner. Eldred is working and will be joining us later. Anita would have come if Katy had been here, but preferred not to come alone. Lisa has a large black patent bag with her belly dancing outfit and all her rattly, shaky bits. After the cake cutting some of her friends are coming – and they are going to belly dance, which should be fun. The three of us join arms and walk towards the no-longer bingo hall.

The early evening light makes the hall look more inviting than it is. The signs are chipped and many of the outside light bulbs are dud. A stray black and white cat disappears from the small patch of grass as we approach and I take in the yesterday ambience.

It was sentimentality and the fact that it didn't cost anything that made it my choice of party venue. It's a community place where I've chatted to hundreds of contestants over the years. It feels like an extension of my home. It has its own musty smell from the mixture of years and from people who have left their mark on the faded and chipped plastic furniture.

Apart from Harry, we are first to arrive. My podium is

missing, of course. The space where Harry's cubicle was leaves extra room for dancing. He has made a good job of the stage. I stare at the flowers in vases from his allotment and catch the scent from large bouquets of orange blossom and carnations that stand in front of two large photographs. John/George's long poster is hung from the ceiling with his guitar leant against the bottom, and on the other side is a huge poster of Spike. In the background I can just see a dog's bottom walking away, it must be Gary Blain's dog, Whitey.

I look around the hall; tears begin to well up and my make-up is in danger. This part of my life has gone forever, but I have good memories of this place. Tonight is going to be a special ending, but also a new beginning.

"Here." Gerry hands me a tissue. "Come on. I'll get you a drink."

"Lisa reorganises the flower arrangements and chats to the elderly bingo contestants arriving.

"Calm down, Nat, and take it easy. You need more control." Gerry is speaking with affection, I think. I take a large swig of lemonade, enough to make bubbles go up my nose.

"I like your friends, especially Alan, but remember you haven't known them long." Gerry is wrinkling his nose and looking into the air. If he gets completely fed up, the wrinkles will spread across his forehead.

Lisa breezes over to the rescue. She leans across and kisses me on the cheek.

"I'm changing your drink, it's time for a G and T. Eldred will be here later, and the four of us will have a drink together. You must visit our new house. You'll love it." Lisa's perfume is drifting around me and threatening to make me sneeze.

"We might be house-hunting ourselves soon, Lisa. Eldred will be a useful man to know. Ah, more people are arriving. We'd better go and say Hello," Gerry announces.

The hall is filling up and Gerry steadies my arm as we walk towards the entrance.

"Now keep calm, Nat. Remember what I said, and control yourself." He winks and smiles at me.

I have the desire to kick him in his good leg. The strength of the desire is a surprise. I study my foot, willing it to stay on the floor. I've never felt this mad at him before. What is wrong with me?

The changes are going to my head, for sure they are, and I'm happy about that. Bad things are part of the past. I'm moving on and helping make a future for us, there is a lot happening at once and causing tensions.

Joan Littleton is here and looking lost. She wanders about, still with her slippers on. "Will you miss bingo?" I ask her.

"Oh yes, dear. We will miss you. You called the numbers so beautifully. But don't you worry, we'll be all right. So proud of you, and what you're doing, all those politics. Can we vote for you? We will, you know. Just tell us when."

The priest from Liverpool has come. It was a long journey for him, but there were visits to be made on the way. He wanted to tell me he tracked down a brother of John's and he's grateful for what I did. He's going to organise the burial of John's ashes in Liverpool and have a memorial service there. It turns out that John was in the army and had seen some bad stuff and couldn't settle after that.

The music is playing loudly and conversations have become shouting matches.

The priest finds his dancing feet and I'm taken back to the funeral service we shared in Lourdes. He dances on his own, apart from any companions in the close vicinity, throwing his legs about with abandon and enthusiasm.

Harry's doing a good job with the disco and, as the dancing hots up, dust puffs rise from the floorboards and spread more of a background musty smell than usual. I move to the back of the hall to watch. There are so few occasions in life to get so many friends together, and they are people I care about.

Weights are lifting from my mind, a process that started when I left Eastleigh for France. I'm sure it's from finding and listening to my own voice. I'm facing the problems and pleasures of life and embracing them.

I've always managed with Gerry away or tied up with sport. Now it's my life taking me away. I realise how much Gerry depends on me, and the stability I create.

The leg will soon be healed, but getting back to fitness will be his major challenge. He's leaning against the bar with his plastered heel resting on a stool rung. He rubs his thigh, trying to make it feel more comfortable.

Sometimes your future comes to find you and I know I want to reach out beyond where I am. There's no way back to the person I was three weeks ago, but what of my family?

Here in the bingo hall are my friends and family, but none of the new London business associates. This wouldn't be their scene. I wonder if they would enjoy watching belly dancing. Lisa is going to get some of us to have a go, and I expect that includes me.

A photographer disturbs my quiet moment. "*Eastleigh Standard,*" he says. He tips his head towards me and says, "Our local star." I stand back, expecting him to touch me as he tries to get a good shot without as much as a, "May I?" He must have invited himself, or was it Katy?

I offer an exaggerated acknowledgement and he nods back, I start to feel we are in a Jane Austen novel with our politeness. I ask if he's the one who suggested to Katy that I was silly, like most women who can't read maps. He visibly backs off but not before handing over his business card, which I leave on the nearest table.

"Best to try and stay friends with the media," I remind myself. If it wasn't for the local paper the nationals would never have heard of me and I wouldn't have a new job.

I glance over at the bingo contestants shuffling and dancing together on the other side of the hall. They are truly unbothered by the changes. When I'm twice my age I wonder what I'll look back on, and if changes will stop bothering me.

Gerry looks up at me from behind his beer and indicates to the cake Harry has placed on a table on the rostrum. It's a large iced square with my name *NATALIE 40* on it, and a miniature turquoise Cinquecento and forty candles.

"Speech. Speech," is a quiet call. I need the toilet. I slip from my corner of observation and make it to the ladies. They have seen better days, but are spacious and clean apart from graffiti here and there. In the days when the hall was packed every night for bingo or dances the six cubicles always had a queue outside.

Lisa's black bag is abandoned at the far end, on the floor. Her clothes are on top, from where she has changed into her dancing outfit. It was kind of her to say she would dance at my party. It's a while since I've seen her perform. She's moving on to teaching belly dancing and her standard is good.

The toilet doors are heavy and made of stainless steel with a gap at the top and bottom; they'll be useful for scrap metal. In a hurry, I use the first cubicle along the line. Soon I hear the voices of Susie and Lisa as they bustle down to the far-end. Two cubicle doors slam shut and costume jewellery jangles.

"You were asking what I thought." That was Susie's voice. "I didn't quite catch what you were on about. I didn't know you went to the Pyrenees. Doesn't sound like your kind of place."

"Shush. It isn't. That's when we slept together. He's great at sex... the thoughtful type." That was Lisa's voice, and the whispered words sex and Pyrenees are bouncing off the walls.

"Should I tell Natalie? ... Only I don't want to hurt her."

"Too late for that, Lisa. You shouldn't have done it," Susie replies.

"I don't want a lecture. It was only sex for him, and he returned to Natalie after that. Come on, we need to get back. I've always decided not to say anything. I love Natalie; she has always been my best friend. Why does this kind of thing stay around in your head? You'd think you could just forget it. I've been in love with Gerry for years. That's the problem."

The taps are turned on and I can't hear any more. I straighten my dress and stand with my back to the toilet wall. Tears drip steadily over the turquoise material, leaving salt-water marks as they travel to the floor.

As Susie and Lisa open the door on to the dance floor I hear Harry playing 'You've got to hide your love away' from the Beatles, and the voice of John/George sings to me.

I screw up the paper on which I've written my speech, and watch as it goes round in circles and flushes away. The pungent smell of old toilets fills my nostrils, pushing me out of the cubicle. The sound of 'Happy Birthday' floats in from the hall and mingles with the splashes from the tap as I wash my hands, and I wish I could stay here. It's time to return to my party.

I walk across the hall and the singing increases. Alan is thumping loudly on the makeshift bar. I look straight ahead, and walk slowly towards the stage and the flickering flames, struggling to stay alight, on the cake.

Harry silences the music and my guests settle down. The faces of friends quietly wait.

The little flames wobble as I lean over and try to find breath to extinguish them. It takes three attempts. Smoke rises and twists, a few long seconds pass… and I begin:

"To my new and old friends, thank you for coming. For those who have supported me on my journey, thank you. For those of you who think what I have done is funny or stupid, tell me what you have done that is better." My voice is getting stronger. I take a deep breath, raise my chin and continue. "I would like to make special mention of my husband and my best friend Lisa." I pause and watch them smile at each other in recognition. "I am sorry you both thought it was OK to have sex together in the Pyrenees."

An uneasy quiet holds in the air. Alan nudges Gerry. "That's your new bike gone, mate."

"I don't care about my bike. I care about my wife." His hand reaches out to me and I ignore it. I gather up the skirt of my dress to step down and try to avoid falling over.

"I know, mate." Alan carries on the conversation with

himself as Gerry moves closer to me. "I understand everything," Alan calls.

Gerry turns, "What do you know?"

"Women are easily lost, like football matches."

Gerry doesn't understand – and, for a moment, I want to laugh with nerves, but sympathetic faces around, trouble me. I glimpse Chester and Stacey and don't want to hear from them. It's time to go home. I want to leave alone, but it's impossible to walk away from your own party unnoticed.

Eldred brushes past me at the door.

"Sorry, Nat – missed the birthday speech, but I'll have some cake. Where are you going? Lisa having fun, I expect." I can only ignore him and turn away. Harry has put the music back on, but quietly.

Dad, Margaret, Enid and Trev are leaving, so I tuck myself in with them. I wait for conversation but none comes. We walk together in a silence that conveys everything for now.

The shock and the hurt are like tight shoes getting worse with every step, but I'm not going to be able to shake off the pain. I'm going to have to live right through it.

"Come home with us if you like." Dad puts his hand on my shoulder as we reach my front gate.

"No thanks, Dad. Tomorrow I leave for Amsterdam. Don't worry about me. I'll be all right. Goodnight." Poor Margaret. What an introduction to Dad's family.

My head swirls: Gerry, Lisa, work. I'm grateful for a pass out of here in the morning. Beyond Gerry and Lisa come thoughts of Katy and Anita. I want it to be all about me, so that I can curl up in a corner and feel sorry for myself, but it can't.

Gerry's key turns in the door. He comes and sits on the sofa with his head in his hands.

"What do you want to do, Nat?"

"I don't know," I reply. "I don't have a plan. How's everything going at the party?"

"Badly. There was no need to deal with everything the way you did and to involve all your friends, not to mention family. Too late now."

"Too late is something I feel. If you're staying here, I'm going back. I take it Lisa and Eldred have gone. I don't want to see her, but I want to say goodnight properly to everyone else... Sorry." I wait.

"Sorry for what, Nat?"

"Sorry. I thought the least you could say was sorry."

"How did you find out?"

"In the toilets, if it matters." I dash upstairs and jump into my cut-off jeans and blouse and head back to the bingo hall. The elderly contestants are determined to have a good time, dancing in a corner and eating cake at the same time. Everyone else is hanging around, having a drink and in subdued conversation. Harry has kept the music going a bit louder now, and I'm pleased.

"Let's all dance," I announce. There's slow movement from everyone. "Come on, for me," I encourage... and we all dance, moving from partner to partner. After a few numbers, it's midnight. Harry turns down the lights and it's time to close.

We all say goodnight.

"I'll lock up, Natalie. You go on. Come to the allotment whenever you want to. Here take your flowers." Harry presses a large bouquet, dripping with water, into my arms. I marvel at the beauty of them. They smell of the garden. I bury my head in the blooms and they comfort me.

I leave after one last look at the old hall, already stripped of much of its past. The background smell of dust lingers. I don't want to be here, and watch when the lights finally go out.

Susie falls in step with me and takes my arm.

"I'm so sorry, Nat. If I can help, I've got life's top qualification in relationship break-ups. What are you going to do?"

"I can't say right now, but I'll find my way. Did you know about Lisa and Gerry?"

"No, of course I didn't. Lisa was wrong. It took some planning and lies by both Gerry and Lisa, going all the way to the Pyrenees like that. How could they do that to you of all people?" Susie's voice is full of anger.

"Who am I, Susie? Just another forty-year-old? If I'm honest, it scares me."

We hold hands before saying goodnight and going our separate ways. It's a heavy touch of what a mess we're both in. My walk to the front door is laboured; it's not the happy return I imagined earlier. I listen to my key as it opens the front door. All is quiet inside and Gerry has gone upstairs. On the table I find a note:

My Natalie,

You know how much I love you. I am so sorry this happened. It wasn't love, just sex. You are my only true love. We can change, and build a better and a different life together. Think of Katy. I'm in the spare room for tonight. We can talk tomorrow. Remember I love you.

Gerry xxxx

PS I know it isn't the right time, but can I see my new bike in the morning?

My new bike? My new bike? Oh, he means *my* new bike. Nervous laughter escapes as I think of myself leaving for Amsterdam tomorrow when I haven't practised cycling. Thoughts of falling off too close to a canal spur me into planning an early start to the day. The saddle has been adjusted and the brakes tested. I'll go to the park where I'll be safe. I'm not sure about the safety of other people out walking or running and I don't want to look silly. For a second I wish Alan was here to help, and wonder if I should ring him?

Late morning I have to go to Southampton Airport, fly to Amsterdam, hire a bike and navigate my way around, keeping a diary as I go and sending the story to *AWAY*. I didn't tell them I couldn't ride a bike. Then again, they didn't ask.

Alan might offend me when I'm vulnerable so, as much as he might be useful, I decide to try this one on my own and hope I've benefited from my one and only past experience of cycling.

'I am always doing what I thought I couldn't do because I learn something'. I reflect on Henri Marcel's words.

Remember, Natalie, you made it through France and Spain. I pinch myself at the thought.

Alex pops into my head; he can be a friend, nothing else. I must sort out my own life. Thinking about a relationship and actually having one will take a lot of care in all directions. "Concentrate on your career, Natalie," I whisper. "Yes… but… hmm," is a voice I don't recognise.

I go to our room and try to sleep, the alcohol helps. Before closing my eyes, I glance at the photo of Jack and worry about his parents going their separate ways. It's cutting a tie.

When I get up, Gerry stays in the spare room. I go to the shed and take the last of the sticky tape and labels off my bike. As I push it through the house, there's still no sign of Gerry. He is being wise, as any attempt to talk to me right now might result in a plate-throwing episode.

I lean against my bike at the gate and survey the road. It's quiet and I must try to ride. I have gone for the basic gears and a basket on the front to hold my personal things. The silver bell fixed on the handlebars is an extra present I bought for myself. A little way from the house, and I ring it a few times, there's nothing like the sound of a bicycle bell to spread cheerfulness.

Before leaving home, I put my laptop and camera in my hand luggage and my personal stuff in a new grey case ready for the journey. The red case I have packed with personal things to take to Dad's house. I'm relieved at not facing Gerry; right now, there is nothing to be said. I just want to get away from him.

What possessed me to think I could cope with a bike? I try my best, wobbling and walking, wobbling and walking down the street. *Things can only get better*, I think.

I had no nerves going to France on my first trip as I thought it would be easy. Now I have no such illusion. Back then I drove my car and had a dog for company.

The article for *AWAY* will start on the flight and be in print next weekend. Gerry is not going to be on the other end of the phone this time… there used to be some comfort in his voice.

The papers will find out the truth about Gerry and me if they want to look, but fortunately, the local reporter left before the candles and cake scenario. With the media, it's what can make me more interesting and it's not necessarily the truth. I like to think I don't care, but I do. This job means much more to me now and I'm afraid of negative reviews.

When Alex turns up in Amsterdam there will be lots to tell him. His slightly tanned face with an edge of wrinkles doesn't go far from my thoughts. It would be comforting to talk if he's willing to listen, but faith in my judgement of relationships has been shaken by an earthquake.

I'm afraid of having loneliness as a friend more than of making a mistake. My future lies in not rushing at anything and making sure of Katy's security. Is Alex in the future? I don't know. It's early days.

The only problem at the park is dog walkers; the dogs view me with caution, moving out of the way with speed. My riding skills are better than I imagined, after about an hour I can watch the sky as I travel along. It's great, I should have tried it before. The breeze blows past me, taking with it a lot of my inner distress. Two birds shake their feathers and fly away. I shake my shoulders and straighten up. *I'm going to be like them*, I think.

I stop now and again to regain my balance. All too soon, it's time to go home.

Gerry is out and I don't care where he is. I take the chance to clear my stuff and tidy around before moving to Dad's. My bike has to find a space in his garden shed.

In my hand is a small package from Gerry, he left it on the table. I open it slowly, not wanting to confront bitter thoughts. Inside is a CD of John Lennon singing '*Stand By Me*'. He will find it in the bin on his return.

The taxi comes and I know I'm leaving more than my house behind. During the flight, I run over the events of the previous evening with monotonous repetition. The challenges ahead will force my thoughts to move on. I have a job to do that requires mental preparation. As I focus, the party and Gerry take second place.

Time can change things – I must give myself time.

20

A New Life

It's been two years since Gerry and I last spoke. I let the lawyers sort everything out. I have come down from London to go to Southampton Airport on my way to Dublin. I'm considering going to see if Gerry is at home, to say "Hello" for old time's sake.

There's no sign of where the bingo hall was, or the newsagents or hairdressers, but Market Street looks much the same. Dad's house has been sold, Chester and Stacey sorted it out. Susie lived there for a while with her children and Katy. I stayed there between jobs and they were good company. It took six months to sell without any redecorating being done, inside or out.

Susie has entered into the life of an air stewardess with enthusiasm. Her mum and dad look after the children when she's away, and if her ex-husband isn't around. Susie has turned down Enid's advice on relationships and is enjoying sex without commitment. I asked her if she would have a long-term partner again one day, and she said "What for?" The quiet wife, mother and teacher have disappeared like a puffball mushroom kicked in the air.

Katy is finishing her college course, studying media and communication, and living at her friend's house during the week. She comes to stay with me in London any time she wants to, and Gerry is just around the corner for her, in Eastleigh.

Telling her about the separation wasn't as difficult as expected. She was disappointed and sad but also pragmatic and an emotional survivor. More difficult was telling her about Lisa and her dad. For a sixteen-year-old coming to terms with her own sexuality, it was bad timing.

She went to Thailand that Christmas with Anita and Lisa. Anita looked at Thai men of the right age and thought, *Any one of them could be my dad, but none of them are.* She said, "I have a mum. I'm lucky." She helped Katy appreciate having her dad in spite of him making a big mistake in marriage terms. The best thing was visiting the country she felt a part of her belonged to. Anita said she knows her mum is all over the place sometimes, but she's her mum and she loves her. Overall, Lisa did me a favour, but it was a lousy way to do it.

Eldred and Lisa have survived the storm and he has stood by her. They moved to their four-bedroom house in a village in the New Forest. As far as I know, they are happy. Marriage hasn't happened for them yet, but I'm told she has a large diamond ring on her wedding finger. They have struggled unsuccessfully with IVF and are giving up. I've received texts from Lisa asking if we can still be friends and all I can think is, *Where is she coming from?*

Katy asked me if I minded her talking to Lisa, but it isn't her problem and I don't mind. I don't want her and Anita to fall out because of the rest of us. I've asked her not to mention me to Lisa, or think I was interested in Lisa any more. I still love Anita, although my contact is only through Katy.

Katy said the situation with her parents has put her off boyfriends for life. She wants to travel; Thailand and Japan were amazing places to capture her interest.

Katy and my dad accept Alex as my partner, and that is positive.

Dad and Margaret are getting along well, and Dad loves his job on the steam railway. He wants to work with the drivers but it's too much for him to shovel coal. He has taken the job of platform guard and his favourite days are when *Thomas the Tank Engine* comes and he sees the excited children.

A new wooden seat with its first signs of graffiti is outside the Eastleigh shopping mall... a place to gather my thoughts before doing what I've detoured this way to do – knock the door and talk to Gerry.

I'm aware of how different I look from when I left. I'm wearing a light grey, designer dress, with a tight black belt and high heels; large lime green beads sit around my neck and I've got a smart, short haircut. Will Gerry be thrown by the new me? Am I playing with a thread of dreams about an old flame and checking for both of us if the fire is out? I don't usually dress to impress when I'm travelling. Maybe I'm trying to rub his nose in the past, but what good would that do? Two years ago I shut the door and walked away for good,

"Don't play with fire, Natalie," my mum would have said.

I reflect on the divorce and philosophise. I imagine we can become friends and chat about old times. Maybe he will still need me even though I would walk away again. Could we talk about Katy, and would she feel better if her parents were in touch?

I wonder if the new owners living in Dad's house would let me visit the place where we buried Spike. Of course not. They wouldn't want to know a dog's ashes are buried in their garden. My mind is seeking something of the old imagined cosiness for memory's sake.

I put my designer sunglasses in my bag, touch up my lipstick and walk towards 33A, wondering if anyone's watching. I could have walked straight past my old house with the bamboo blinds and window in the roof. I didn't expect the outside to be painted bright white and a small tree planted in the front garden patch. I didn't expect to stand at a short distance and watch, as a slim woman leaves my house dressed in tight black Lycra, hair tied back and pushing a sports bike from the door to the road.

Gerry comes out, kisses her, then watches as her skinny body perches on the saddle and she disappears down the road. I turn away and, for another daft moment, still consider going to speak to him. The goodbye I made two years ago is underlined. I don't know why I came back. I no longer belong.

Katy hasn't mentioned her dad's new girlfriend. She appears to cope with us being apart, but I think she has emotionally buried the definitive move of us both settling down with other partners. Her young adult life is all consuming. We are both here for her.

I turn away. Gerry hasn't recognised me. I'm not the same person who left, and he isn't looking for the new me. I walk slowly and return to the seat, churning over old ground.

I started nervously with Amsterdam. Since then, I've been as far afield as Canada and the USA. In America, I went to LA and drove the Pacific Coast Highway alone. When I was in Santa Monica, I visited Stacey, Blake and baby Jack. I've grown to love the children and want to stay in touch. Stacey and Chester are now living separately, as Stacey wanted to be near her family and pursue her acting career. Chester couldn't get a job out there. Stacey was right about the money from Dad's house, it has helped support her and the children, and that's OK with me. Playing with little Jack and tucking him into bed gave me a sense of peace and satisfaction.

I'm disappointed that I didn't get the opportunity to modernise Dad's house before it was sold, but I wouldn't have had the time or the emotional energy. In the end, Stacey was helpful.

Work is always busy, with interviews for radio and TV, travel articles, and speaking tours with a photo exhibition. Although I have been on many trips, everyone always wants to know about the first one, and lots of women sympathise with me being unable to read maps. I have met women who want to travel on their own like I do, and others who have done better by far.

The East may be for the future. I think the women who have gone on these routes alone and of families who were a part of colonisation before communication technology, had hard lives. I am entertainment value and women identify with me; I am not a great woman, like others have been and are.

Monsieur Jacques has become a mini celebrity in France. *The reluctant hero who saved the English woman*, he is entertainment value in his own right. We have been on French radio together and, as much as I appreciated his helping hand, I was grateful it wasn't TV where we might have needed to sit closer and show some familiarity. His image is to remain a scruffy out-of-shape HGV driver. Photos and short videos of him are attracting attention on the growing phenomena of YouTube. He can be followed as he drives around Europe.

An odd thing about French farmers with pylons in their fields has happened; they claim to have a piece of my red skirt. There have been pieces of it for sale in various shades of pink and red on eBay at silly prices. Why would people want it? José has been offered a four-figure sum for his photo of me in my medium-size knickers and red dress top crossing the field. I have told him he's welcome to sell it. There's no Gerry to offend any more. Alex is very supportive, but most of the time leaves me to make my own decisions.

A French company has made a popular travel documentary of my journey and wants to make a film. It is to be fiction based on fact and I'm nervous that everyone might think it's intended to be biographical. They want to sex it up. I'm not quite ready to sign them the rights but my agent says "Do it now." She could be right.

The subject of Gerry still holds the interest of audiences. They want to know what he's doing and was I right to leave him. "Was there any doubt?" is always my response.

"Where are you going next?"

"I don't know," is my genuine answer. I receive an envelope with the destination a day before I'm due to leave. There are times when I wish there was less pressure, but I wouldn't get paid the same money. Each challenge gives me a rush of adrenalin, but I never feel very confident.

We have entered the days of masks and hand washing, with bird flu spreading to one or two humans, and I wonder if it will affect what I do.

Eastleigh's new coffee shop is inviting, it smells of rich coffee beans and sweet cakes. I glimpse Joan Littleton going by, she has aged even more and is reliant on a walking frame.

The disturbing thing is her aura of being lost and lonely. I'm sure bingo would have helped her, and others like her, cope. I swirl in the topping of chocolate powder with a sugar stick then change to a spoon, listening as it chinks against the sides of the large cup.

Harry has been in touch a lot lately, since his diagnosis of lung cancer. He's doing OK but hasn't been to the allotment much. His friends have taken over the chickens and the tasks of planting and watering. He thinks his outlook is reasonable and has tried to stop smoking, but it's too late now. I must visit his allotment one day soon and hope he will be there. Every time I smell or see carnations, I think of him.

The coffee settles my thinking pattern as I plan to go to Dublin and then travel to the Giant's Causeway on public transport. I'm using a video camera, and a TV station is going to track my trip. Modern technology makes disappearing for more than a few hours impossible. Someone always wants to know where I am. "Health and Safety to protect your employers," is the given reason.

Once I had a personal tracking device and was told off when I paid an accomplice to fit it to a dog's collar. I now draw the line on such an intrusion, but accept I'll call or email daily. Nothing can be done when I take off alone. Going it alone is the only way to spice up my stories, especially with the people I meet. I'm so looking forward to Dublin, meeting Irish people and experiencing their pub culture. I'd love to be a part of spontaneous music and singing, not that I'm any good at it. I've heard whispers of an underground arts scene, I'd like to find out about it. It's going to be a big challenge on my own.

In three weeks' time, I have a holiday, and it's going to

be special. Alex and I have bought a boat and moored it on the Canal du Midi. This is our third visit to France this year, because we're getting married.

Alex took me to Paris on holiday last year. It was late evening; we were halfway up the Eiffel Tower, looking out across Paris and watching the panorama of lights. Alex held me to him in a way I had forgotten existed, and asked me to marry him. It has become my most romantic place on earth.

The wedding will be a quiet affair in France, there will be no press, and no family, only a few close friends. My dress is pale pink, knee-length and gently full. My hair will have fresh flowers, and I'll manage on heels that are too high. The fashion editor has helped me decide on my outfit. She listened to what I wanted as well as encouraging me to try different designs. I emailed some photos to Linda, as I knew she would enjoy helping me choose. I'm not sure her comments fitted with my ideas, but she made me laugh.

Alex has taught me all I know about photography, and this has helped enormously with my job. We live in a small house in Kensington, London, and Katy has her own room. Alex has his two daughters come to stay, but they live too far away to come often. His relationship with his ex-wife is good and getting better. I'd like to meet her one-day. He encourages me to think that falling out with Gerry isn't forever, and that it would be good if we were on speaking terms. He's right, but so far I have failed on that one. It would help if he got in touch with me. The need for a sincere apology doesn't go away.

I love our Kensington house. It has a mix of modern and antique furniture; the walls and curtains are the colours of dried grasses. Alex and I worked on recreating parts of Picasso's *Guernica* picture. We made a collage of cuttings and pictures of wars, just as I had intended. It's hung in our hallway. Somewhere in the picture are the names of George Bush, John Lennon and Tony Blair. Broken and rearranged pictures of the peace walk are in there, if you look. Also a torn-up picture of my first wedding, but only I know where it is.

The kitchen is new with black granite worktops and stainless steel appliances. The bathroom is tiled from floor to ceiling and has an extra-large white bath. We have a small courtyard garden with a wooden table and chairs set. A waterfall falls in to a small pond, and we have a few feet of lawn. This is our bit of heaven to come home to.

Art galleries in London are my greatest pastime. I go to them every chance I get. My knowledge and experiences of art are increasing. It gives me something I can do on my own and when Alex is home, we visit art galleries together.

I felt sorry for Enid and Trev getting mixed up in my marriage problems, especially at the party, but Enid has sorted things. She told me she understood how I felt but she must stand by her own, and that we could keep our communications to special occasions. She mentioned how nice it would have been if I had made a success of myself sooner, and it might have saved my marriage. Trev has annoyingly got prostate problems, and she hoped it wouldn't ruin their great sex life when they had not long got into it. If Trev is anything, he is tolerant.

Must get going... off to Dublin to see what crops up there. Public transport can be confusing, and that is part of the challenge. Which side of the train station I should be on is crucial, and making the right train connections. The great thing about my job is that I can make mistakes, but they are never planned. It's still my nature to get lost. As long as I get home some time within reason that's all that matters. Being on my own and relying only on myself can be hard.

The turquoise Fiat Cinquecento is now a car of value. It has its own garage and a dedicated mechanic who keeps it on the road. Every so often I use it for work. The car has its own fan club, especially among Fiat enthusiasts. Every corner, scratch and dent I know. I never drive it without missing Spike, but he wouldn't have had a quality of life and we made the right decision for him. There are soft toys of Spike, but I don't want one.

Alex and I have a new BMW, but I can't get attached to it. I appreciate the smooth ride and its reliability. I drive the Fiat Cinquecento for opening fetes or supermarkets. A cheer goes up as I drive in and children want to jump all over it. One day it may end up in a car museum.

When this job is over, I have to find my way to Canal du Midi. Alex is already in France, preparing for our wedding, in the gardens of a chateau. Afterwards we will honeymoon on our boat. Alex is my friend, lover and soon-to-be husband. I hope I don't get lost on the way.

Forty-plus is a fantastic age to be.

No more medium-size knickers. Sexy lingerie is something I love.

21

Snippets from Katy's Diary

Went to the AWAY office with Mum. Want a job there.

Dad wants me to meet Smarty-Pants. Don't want to. Nothing in common. Never ever will have.

Year since divorce. Feeling better about it. Won't get married.

Cousin Nicholas has become a good friend. We write long letters about feeling rejected. He hasn't had a step-dad. Tracey didn't want another husband after Chester.

Jay Reece says he loves me. Bullshit.

If I marry it will be to someone rich and famous, because my mum is sort of rich and quite a bit famous.

Anita is good at listening. She has been on a counselling course. Says she knows lots from experience. Says it goes with her work as a beautician, because people tell her their problems.

Today Anita told me to shut up and get a life. It would be good for me.

Mum says I must go to Uni, study history and politics because it will make me a better journalist. What does she know?

Mum's friend at work said if I don't want to go to Uni then start as a secretary on the local Eastleigh Standard. Uni is sounding good.

Dad says I MUST meet Smarty-Pants. I will, but I'm not going to speak to her. Bet she will try and be nice to me – creep, creep.

If everyone keeps on at me, I'm going to give everything up and go to Thailand.

Met Jay Reece's big brother – YUM.

Played with little Jack today. Love him to bits. Calls me Kay Kay. He's only visiting as he lives in America. I blew rainbow soap bubbles for him, they touched my childhood memories as they popped into dust.

After Mum left, I asked her who the baby in the picture was. She said, "You don't remember?" and I didn't. She told me about my baby brother and the operations she had. Then went away on one of her work trips. I cried non-stop for three days – sobbed and sobbed. I would have loved a brother. I suffered a belated bereavement, at least that's what Anita said. Lisa remembered what it was like when the baby died and said these things happen. Mum had cried a lot. The air in my brain was clearer after a good cry.

I asked Dad why he slept with Lisa. Says he doesn't know. What sort of answer is that?

Reunion of Japan trip next week, Kyoto I will never forget… amazing buildings, and Hiroshima – can't believe it. More than one baby died there.

Aunt Susie is the best. Says take life as it comes. Mum talks to her if the going gets tough, and they are in the same country. I can tell Aunt Susie things I wouldn't put in my diary, like feelings about Lisa.

Swimming tomorrow with Reece brothers and a load of mates. Need cash – see Mum.

I told Katy today that life isn't worth living without challenges; I talked to her about Picasso. As I was talking, she disappeared out the door.

BOOK CLUB NOTES

Life changes at forty for Natalie. She expects to remain in her comfort zone in a sleepy market town. She has a job as a bingo caller, a daughter preparing for college and an elderly father making his own life. She has been married to Gerry for eighteen years but he loves sport more than her.

Gerry has a cycling accident in France. Natalie and her little dog Spike go to collect him. Poor map-reading skills take her on a journey through France and Spain. She finds a new self, but has to return home.

Emotions run high as Natalie tries to make a difficult marriage work. At her fortieth birthday party comes a painful revelation. Now she is released into a new exciting life of love and marriage. Her new life style attracts media acclaim and celebrity status.

Natalie's journey brings her laughter, tears, and surprises.

DISCUSSIONS

Was Gerry a likeable character?

If Gerry and Natalie had talked more, could it have stopped the demise of their marriage?

Why was Gerry unfaithful?

Should Natalie have tried to keep her marriage going?

If Natalie had not gone on her journey what would her life have been like?

What reasons caused a lack of self-confidence for Natalie in the early part of the book?

To what extent did being unable to have more children make Natalie less valued in her own eyes?

How much did the divorce affect Katy?

Natalie describes this period of her life as turquoise; if you described a phase of your life by a colour what would it be?

Is travelling alone a good or a bad thing, and does it matter what age you are when you go?